INTRIGUE MY DESIRES
HARRIS & KAT PART I

STEELE INTERNATIONAL, INC. - JACKSON CORPORATION A BILLIONAIRES ROMANCE SERIES CROSSOVER BOOK 4

CHARMAINE LOUISE SHELTON

CONTENTS

FREE BOOK

FREE BOOK!

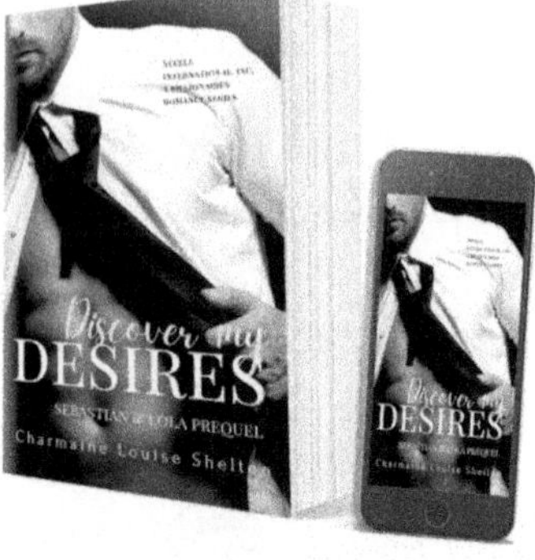

EXCLUSIVE FOR SUBSCRIBERS!

A Trilogy of Desires Roger & Leonie Parts I-III

A Trilogy of Desires Malcolm & Starr Parts I-III

Series Extras

Series Playlist

STEELE INTERNATIONAL, INC. - JACKSON CORPORATION
A BILLIONAIRES ROMANCE SERIES CROSSOVER

Tempt My Desires Lachlan & Haley Part I

Tease My Desires Lachlan & Haley Part II

Grant My Desires Lachlan & Haley Part III

Intrigue My Desires Harris & Kat Part I

Decode My Desires Harris & Kat Part II

Honor My Desires Harris & Kat Patt III

A Trilogy of Desires Lachlan & Haley Parts I-III

A Trilogy of Desires Harris & Kat Parts I-III

Series Extras

Series Playlist

ABOUT STEELE INTERNATIONAL, INC. - JACKSON CORPORATION A BILLIONAIRES ROMANCE SERIES CROSSOVER

Welcome to the titillating world of the multibillion-dollar global companies and the love affairs of the families that controls them.

STEELE International, Inc.- Jackson Corporation is a series of interconnecting Billionaire romance. Follow the Steele and Jackson families as they fly around the world chasing the women they love and their happily ever afters. Get ready for glitz, glamour, and steamy romance books. What's better than that? The Jet-set Lifestyle has never been hotter...

The Desires Series is not for the tea set; it's for the top-shelf vodka straight up in a pretty crystal glass coterie!

Don't miss any of the sizzling romance books in the STEELE International, Inc. - Jackson Corporation A Billionaires Romance Series Crossover:

Tempt My Desires Lachlan & Haley Part I

Tease My Desires Lachlan & Haley Part II

Grant My Desires Lachlan & Haley Part III

Intrigue My Desires Harris & Kat Part I

Decode My Desires Harris & Kat Part II

Honor My Desires Harris & Kat Patt III

A Trilogy of Desires Lachlan & Haley Parts I-III

A Trilogy of Desires Harris & Kat Parts I-III

Series Extras

Series Playlist

Visit CharmaineLouiseBooks.com for the complete list.

Intrigue My Desires Harris & Kat Part I

Welcome to the titillating world of the multibillion-dollar global companies and the love affairs of the families that control them.

Harris

I'm the last man standing in The STEELE Quaternity—my brothers and I dubbed such by the media as the most sought-after of the world's eligible billionaires. One by one they fell. Suckers.

Me? I hold onto my playboy card like a life preserver in a tsunami, as my fraternal twin sister teases me. Until the day I don't...

Kat

Those Jacksons think they're all that. Well, they're wrong. Dead wrong. And I'll use whatever and whoever I can to get what I want. Revenge. My red hair, pretty face, and curvy body get 'em every time. Including that Steele sucker.

Will Kat claim Harris' playboy card or will her true desire destroy the Jacksons and the Steeles?

Join Harris—her mouse—as he chases his Kat from Aberdeen and the Channel Islands to Thailand and more in their steamy, playboy falls for The One billionaire romance.

Anthem: "Nasty" Janet Jackson
https://www.youtube.com/watch?v=-s1fHtIVqiQ

Playlist:
https://www.youtube.com/playlist?list=
PLXwYvn0e218CfLUoSrHt0sWHJ2Thd8TIU

Visit CharmaineLouiseBooks.com

PROLOGUE

PROLOGUE

"Tilt your chin towards the corner over there. I want the light to cross the planes of your gorgeous face... A little more... Just... Right there! Now, hold still and allow me to capture your beauty."

My muse-cum-lover preens as my brush skims across the canvas before me. Her nipples pebble as though the soft sable tip caresses her flawless, porcelain skin. Sky blue eyes twinkle when she moves them to catch a glimpse of me at work.

I tsk at her, and a small smile plays at the corners of her Cupid's bow mouth.

We continue in silence for the next hour until I notice her shoulders shake from the exertion to maintain her position for an extended period of time. With a sigh, I finish one last stroke to the curvaceous hip on the canvas before I release her.

"Relax, My Beauty. We are done for now," I tell her as I

cover the canvas with a tarp. My preference to keep the unfinished work hidden mars her lovely face with a scowl. "No, you cannot see it yet."

"Oh... You're so mean to me!" She huffs and crosses her arms beneath her ample bosom. The move only serves to present them to me like a platter of tantalizing treats. "Well, I can't see. So, neither can you!"

She wraps the white silk sheet around her like a toga as she rises from the red velvet chaise gracefully. A glance over her shoulder as she sashays towards the ancient stone stairs drives me from my stool.

My long legs make short work of the distance between us.

My Beauty squeaks when I grip her hips and hoist her over my shoulder with ease. A firm smack to her rear makes her yelp and flail her arms and legs. Her tiny hands pummel my broad back, to no avail. Another round of smacks, and she drapes her torso over my shoulder in complete submission.

"Good, girl," I murmur as I carry her to the bed at the center of my studio.

She bounces on the feather mattress when I toss her to the middle. The silk sheet slips open to reveal her naked beauty in all its mesmerizing glory. The thatch of dark hair at the apex of her thighs glistens with her arousal. She notices my lust-filled stare and covers her mound as her porcelain cheeks flush a contrasting crimson hue.

Quick as lightning, I grab her wrists and pull them from her treasure trove to place them above her head. One hand pins them to the mattress while the other parts her thighs. A single thick, calloused digit breaches her slick folds.

Her back arches from the bed as a moan escapes her lips.

Rhythmic thrusts that graze the textured patch and stroke her inner walls have her writhing beneath me. A second digit has her panting. A tweak to her swollen bud, and she screams my name.

My mouth crashes over hers as I plank above her. Our tongues dance, and I swallow her moans greedily to capture every piece of her—beauty and pleasure. A shudder runs through me when her fingernails rake along my bare back.

Her dainty fingers reach between us, eager to unleash my turgid member.

Both of us groan at the carnal contact as her hand fists my erection. Her gentle tugs do not suffice to quench my lust.

With a primal growl, I take control and slam deep within her slippery core. Her warmth engulfs me from tip to base. My eyes roll to the back of my head.

My hips snap of their own accord as I drive her into the mattress. She meets each thrust with one of her own as her core flutters along my length.

The sounds of our carnal passion resound off the stone walls of my studio to soar towards the ceiling high above us. Through the open windows, the sea crashes to the shore in time with my thrusts. Her cries match the seagulls in their quest for food.

The base of my spine tingles. Three final snaps of my hips, and I roar my release. It ignites another climax for My Beauty. She keens her pleasure as she bows from the bed. I collapse atop her, and she winds her arms and legs about me.

I roll to my side, still intimately connected to my lover. She cuddles against my chest as my fingers draw circles around the two dips above her round derriere.

With the release of my creative and carnal passions, my mind returns to the request—rather demand—my father sent to me. I am to meet him along with my younger brother in the city tomorrow.

Undoubtedly, it's another of his threats. I will attend. But nothing he says will change my mind. Nothing.

I shake my head to rid it of the sense of impending doom. With a sigh, I roll My Beauty onto her back to lose myself within her welcoming embrace once again.

"Hello, Father, brother."

I nod at each of them when I enter my father's office.

My brother greets me with a sorrowful smile.

"Glad you can join us," my father responds gruffly. His dissatisfied scowl takes me in from head to toe, not at all pleased with my attire of a smock shirt, trousers., and paint-stained brogues. "You could not find an appropriate suit? Never mind. Sit."

Once I'm seated beside my brother, our father settles

behind his massive wooden desk. My artist's eye takes in the ornate carvings appreciatively. A master craftsman's finest work.

"Have you come to your senses and will take your proper place as the next to run our family's company?"

My father's question draws me from my musings.

I glance over at him.

We stare at one another for a heartbeat.

I look away first.

He sighs.

"With all due respect, Father. We have had this conversation many times before. I intend to follow my passion. I do not care to follow in your footsteps," I respond as I bring my gaze back to his angry one.

My brother cringes beside me. He knows the roof is about to blow off the building. Again.

Surprisingly, our father remains silent. He studies my face for any sign of a change of heart.

I remain steadfast and hold his gaze.

He rises to tower over me.

"From this day forward, I disown you and no one will speak your name ever again. Your presence erased from this family's history completely. As I speak, your *studio* is being destroyed and your harlot removed. Leave this city with what you have at this moment. Do not let the sunset find you here. Never return. Contact none of us again. Ever. Do you understand?"

His pronouncement sends a chill through my very soul.

The sense of doom comes to fruition.

I scan his face, hoping to find a crack in his countenance. Nothing. I turn to my brother, and he glances away from my imploring gaze. My eyes shift back to my father. He stands indomitable and raises his hand to point at the door.

"Leave now, or I will have you escorted from the premises," he commands.

I never guessed my father would go so far as to banish me. To obliterate me from our family. Ruin my dreams.

I open my mouth to implore him. But as he rounds the desk with an expression of such detestation, I flinch. Then suck in a breath when he grips the back of my shirt and lifts me from the leather chair.

Forcefully, he pushes me towards the door.

I stumble before I catch myself.

One last glance over my shoulder reveals his imposing figure glaring at me and my brother's stiff back as he stares straight ahead. No remorse. No sympathy.

"Goodbye, Father, brother."

The past few weeks have gone a little something like this:

Me:

"Hey, bro, the Knicks play the Warriors tonight, and there's still room in our box at the Garden. Steph's been on fire scoring thirty-point games and dropping 3s left and right. Let's make a night of it."

Sebastian:

"Ah, damn. Sounds like a good time. But sorry, bro. Lola and I have date night tonight since Mom and Dad are in town and want to babysit Slade, Sabrina, and Stella."

Me:

"I scored the last tickets to ride in the supersonic stealth jet XR-T2 before they decommission it. In two days, me and you will soar through the stratosphere under the radar, bro! You know you can't resist a thrill."

Malcolm:

"Two days? Fuck me. Can you change the date? Starr and I are taking Elios, Selina, Dione, and Iris to Aspen with Peace and Sun."

Me:

"Hey, bro. I'm in town Friday through Monday. How about we meet up at Jackson Smoke&Scotch Paris? Lucien has a pairings event Saturday night with Lachlan's new Jackson Scotch blend. He says it's one of his best ever."

Roger:

"No can do. Leonie and I jet to Villa dei Fiori with Rodolphe, Gaspard, and Daphne on Thursday after work for a week of R&R with Guy and Josy."

Me:

"Remember those triplets we hooked up with at LEVELS New York? Well, they left a message for us with the concierge. They're back from Buenos Aires tomorrow and want to see us again. You game for that hot action, or what, cuz?"

Laurent:

"Shhh! Hold on a minute... Now's not a good time to talk. But no, I'm not game, anyway. Gotta go, cuz."

Yeah, I'm the last man standing in The STEELE Quaternity—my older brothers Sebastian, Malcolm, Roger, and I dubbed such by the media as the most sought-after of the world's eligible billionaires. Handsome; six plus feet; ebony hair; shades of gray eyes; powerful Alpha Doms and males. One by one, they fell. Suckers.

Me? At thirty-two, I hold on to my playboy card like a life preserver in a tsunami, as my fraternal twin sister Haley teases me.

But what strikes me as odd is my cousin and partner in playadom Laurent Jackson. What the hell was he shushing me for and blowing me off? Like me, he's the youngest male of his family and an eternal playboy. Along with Lachlan and Lucien, he makes up the Jackson Trio of more of the world's eligible billionaires. Handsome; six plus feet; sable brown hair; shades of green eyes; powerful Alpha Doms and males.

Well, excluding Lach now that he's married to Haley—he's her fairytale Earl of Aboyne teenage crush and Sebastian's best friend, talk about forbidden love. Even their oldest sibling, Lydie, isn't single anymore. Cla-clank!

The Steeles and the Jacksons. An unbreakable bond forged by our mothers—Michelle aka Shelley a native New Yorker and Lucinda aka Lucie a New Orleans transplant, respectively—being best friends since their days in Manhattan as a shopgirl in a STEELE International, Inc. retail store and a bartender at a Jackson Corporation pub.

Then they met our fathers Morgan Steele and Connor Jackson, Marquess of Huntly. Titans in their industries with the New York City based luxury real estate development and management company and the Aberdeen, Scotland-based fine dining, distilleries, and vineyards corporation, respectively. Both multigenerational, multi-billion-dollar businesses with offices and properties all over the globe that attract royalty and the über-wealthy. Our closeness extends to our businesses as we partner in multiple ventures. Jackson's world-renown and award-winning eateries and products pair well within STEELE's casinos, hotels, resorts, and residential and retail properties.

Each of my siblings works at STEELE: Sebastian, CEO, president of the Retail Properties Division, and Chairman of the Board; Malcolm, president of the Entertainment Properties Division and First Vice President of the Board; Roger, president of the Residential Properties Division and Second Vice President of the Board; Haley the hacker and me the techie, co-founders of the subsidiary STEELE Technology and Cyber Security and members of the Board.

The same with our cousins working at Jackson: Lydie, COO and Vice President of the Board; Lachlan, CEO, President of Liquor, and Chairman of the Board; Lucien, President of Jackson Corporation Restaurants/Bars/Lounges and Second Vice President of the Board; Laurent, Director of Jackson Corporation Cigars Division and member of the Board.

Both families are close even without sharing DNA. Hence our cousin relationship and Aunt Lucie and Uncle Connor. We travel together and spend the holidays as a combined clan. Besides Baz and Lach being best friends, Malcolm and Lucien and Laurent and I are best buds and hang out the most. Being the youngest in the bunch, Haley, Laurent, and I spend a lot of time together. Lydie sees Baz as a confidante, and Roger floats amongst us all. Our relationships work well.

As I reflect on the last few weeks, I'm not mad at my brothers and my cousin for ditching hanging out with me in favor of their little family activities and for who the hell knows what. I wish them all the best. Good luck with all of that!

The best part of my siblings' pairings are my adorable AF nieces and nephews. I love those little buggers madly. Not saying that I want a child of my own any time soon, though. Uh, no.

Do their happily ever afters make me lonely and depressed?

Let me think about it for a millisecond…

Hell, nah!!!

I'll keep my playboy card happily thank you very much. No need to let that bad boy go. At. All.

Especially with a sinfully sexy toffee drop headed my way. The sway of her grip-worthy hips moves to the throbbing pulse of the sensual beat playing in the dance club at LEVELS London. The sight of the tantalizing beauty keeps any sad thoughts at bay.

Like the never ruffled lone wolf I am, I appraise her over the rim of my Waterford Crystal snifter with no outward emotion. My appreciative dove gray eyes take in every inch of her curves showcased in a gold beaded mini dress. Long, toned legs end in fuck-me stilettos.

She tosses a mane of chestnut curls over her shoulder as her obsidian eyes sparkle in the lights. A come-hither smile plays on her lush lips.

Our eyes lock.

I take a sip of my Jackson Special Blend Scotch, then twirl the amber liquid in the glass. My ten-inch cock twitches with interest in the trousers of my bespoke suit as she nears. A smirk lifts a corner of my full lips.

Yeah. Who needs to tie themselves down for eternity with one woman when you can indulge in a plethora of lovelies? Particularly since they're readily available at any of the LEVELS clubs.

I have Lucien and Malcolm to thank for my hunting grounds.

While completing his hospitality and culinary training at the prestigious Le Cordon Bleu in Paris, Lucien thought of a BDSM/dance club. He figured the club would fill the void for safe, uninhibited sexual activities amongst the world's wealthiest and most influential people. They convinced Sebastian a global, luxury, members-only entertainment venue focused on hedonism would add to STEELE's bottom line. Baz, the net-net guy, saw the potential and gave them the green light for the flagship in New York's Meatpacking District.

For consistency and members' comfort, locations share the same layout:

Main entry foyer has two sides with two greeter stations for access to Dine & Dance levels and BDSM levels, an All-Access member can choose from any of the seven levels: 7th Sky Lounge that offers a bar, restaurant by day dance club by night, coverable pool that's open for the summer, and a glass-retractable roof; 6th and 5th multilevel dance club with two bars and a lounge for food and drinks; 4th Level 4 Restaurant and bar open for breakfast, lunch, and dinner; 3rd has twelve private suites for members to continue their pleasure apart from the BDSM levels; 2nd Peepshow for BDSM with seating alcoves, main stage, performance rooms, and a bar that serves non-alcoholic mocktails; below ground the Cellar BDSM dungeon with mocktails bar. The Dine/Dance members only have access to the party levels—Sky Lounge, Dance Club, and Level 4 Restaurant.

London is the third after Paris of the exclusive clubs. Its site is a former bank set in the City of London, also known as The City and Financial District. They use the original vault for private parties. Locked behind its massive, thick steel door, who knows what all goes on inside. This LEVELS is an ode to the debauchery of money and the wealthy who wield it as power over others. How appropriate the Sky Lounge provides an unobstructed view of the Tower of London—the beast's lair.

Their venture with a high profit margin proved it's bigger than "a titty bar" as Baz originally called LEVELS. Malcolm and Lucien opened additional locations in Beverly Hills, Verbier, and Aberdeen. Even the LEVELS Laucala Island—a five-star resort in Fiji—sold out when it opened. An idea Lucien—*The Sexy Chef*—literally cooked up is worth millions and does more than add to STEELE's bottom line. It gives all of us a place to play.

And play I will tonight…

On my tantalizing toffee treat's wrist rests a green enamel bracelet signifying she's available to play. Perfect.

To avoid unwanted interactions amongst club participants, the system requires partnered subs to wear collars given to them by their Dom; partnered Doms wear gold bracelets; available subs wear red; available Doms wear white; voyeurs wear black; partnered couples wear silver; those available to play wear green.

I leave the Dom shit to Baz, Malcolm, Lachlan, and Lucien. Sure, I'm an Alpha male who enjoys giving a good spanking and bondage, even role playing. But I don't want a submissive. I want a woman who gives as good as I do. A feisty little thing, one who will challenge me. And that's more than enough to satisfy my carnal needs. Just for the night, that is.

Despite being the youngest Steele man and the jokester of our family, I fuck fast and hard but with finesse, bringing my partner to heights of exquisite pleasure. Years of honing my skills with girls around my age and with their mothers formed me into a skilled inamorato and a connoisseur of the female body and needs.

Let's see if Toffee will be the lucky one tonight.

"Hello, handsome. You seem to enjoy your drink… and the view. Might I join you?"

My smirk widens at her opening line. Her ultra-posh Queen's English accent in a raspy Demi Moore tone gives her extra points. Not bad.

I nod and lean back to ask the bartender for a glass of Champagne. Toffee appears to be the sophisticated type not partial to cutesy umbrella cocktails. The gleam in her eyes brightens at my request. Bingo. Am I playa, or what?

I stand and help her onto my vacated stool, then hand the flute to her.

She drags the tip of her tongue across her plump lower lip before she raises the glass to taste the sweet nectar. A smile blossoms on her heart-shaped face. She sighs as the essence slides over her palate.

My cock jumps at the thought of it being on her tongue and pouring my jizz down her throat. By far better than the Dom Pérignon.

"Does it meet your expectations?" I ask in a husky baritone as I bend down to murmur in her ear. Purposefully, my warm breath wafts across the delicate shell, and she trembles.

"Yes, it does, thank you," Toffee whispers throatily.

The outer curve of her ample tit brushes against my biceps. Her heat seeps beneath the wool of my suit jacket. When she rubs like a cat, I growl low in my chest. She purrs as her eyes flash.

"Do you toy with me, Toffee?" I ask as I trail the tip of my index finger along the bare skin of her inner arm. The touch to the sensitive erogenous zone makes her tremble again.

"N-N-No," she stammers, then throws her head back when I tweak her nipple poking against the front of her mini dress.

I take advantage of the exposed slender column and brush my lips from her collarbone to her ear.

"Then be very careful, or you will arouse the beast too

soon. Before we properly prepared you to handle it," I growl. "Dance with me."

She agrees breathily and places the Champagne on the bar.

I hold her hips as she slides from the stool. The petite thing barely reaches my chest when I settle her on her feet. She grips my arms to steady herself.

Taking her elbow, I lead her past the others to a spot on the dance floor. The opening chords of Grace Jones' "Libertango" make Toffee lift her arms overhead with her wrists crossed and shimmy her hips in a slow, seductive swirl. She mouths the words as I watch, mesmerized.

When she pivots on those fuck-me stilettos, I press my front flush to her back. My palms rest on her hips, and I guide her movements to my sensuous beat. Her fingers twine in the long hair atop my head, then stroke the shorter sides, dragging her fingernails against my scalp.

The bite of pain makes my already achingly hard cock thump against her lower back. It demands more from this vixen.

As she drops to a squat, she undulates against me and trails her fingers down my custom dress shirt to grip the waistband of my trousers. The back of her head presses into my cock. She tilts her head back to glance at me with hooded eyes, impressed with my length and girth. When she licks and bites her lower lip, I grip under her arms and hoist her up.

"Now, you will learn your lesson, Naughty Girl," I growl in her ear.

She mewls.

Without hesitation, I take her hand and stalk off the dance floor, headed for the elevator. The private suite I reserved awaits my latest tryst.

Toffee waltzes inside of the suite. The golden beads swish with each step, drawing my hungry gaze to her round ass. My palm itches to spank it for riling the beast after my warning. But first…

"What are your limits, Naughty Girl?" I ask.

Slowly, she spins around, grips the hem of her mini dress, and pulls it over her head. Her bare mons appears, followed by her bouncing double Ds. The puckered brown nipples make my mouth water.

"None," she states as the beaded material tinkles to the hardwood floor.

I smirk.

"Safeword?" I ask.

She drops to her hands and knees and crawls towards me—ass high, head low, tits sway—as she purrs, "Sticky pudding. Nice and warm."

Fuck. Me.

A trickle of pre-cum drips from my cockhead.

"Hand signal?"

She rises to her knees before me and snaps her fingers.

In the blink of an eye, she has my pants and black silk boxer briefs at my feet and my turgid dick in her fist. Her tongue flattens along the veiny bottom as her mouth engulfs my full length down her throat.

Did I say, Fuck me?

My thighs quiver as my head lolls back, mouth slack, and eyes closed. I'm lost in the sensations of her sucking me deep, swirling her tongue, and humming in carnal delight.

I inhale through my nose for a calming breath to regain control, then grip the sides of her head. My heated gaze meets hers, and I smirk. My pelvis pulls back for only my tip in her mouth, then my hips snap forward.

She gags as I hit the back of her throat. Tears pool in her eyes as I hold her nose to my groin. My cock widens her throat. A tear slips from each eye, and I pull her off to my tip for a breath. I repeat the movements a few more times to acclimate her to my girth. When her breathing evens out, I take it as my cue and fuck her face.

Toffee catches my rhythm and places her palms on my muscular thighs for balance. Soon the suite fills with the rhythmic slapping of my balls to my thighs and slurping. The sounds mingle with my grunts and groans of pleasure.

Erotic fire licks at the base of my spine and zips to my heavy balls. With a guttural roar, I unleash the beast's full force and fuck her face ruthlessly. She gasps around my massive girth and squeezes my thighs. But she doesn't use her hand signal to stop me.

My toes curl as I rise to the balls of my feet. A torrent of cum blasts from my throbbing cock straight down her throat to land in her belly. Her swollen lips kiss my groin as my hips rock to ride out my release.

"Such a good girl," I pant.

She hums and purses her lips as she preens from pleasing me.

"Up you go," I say as I lift her to wobbly legs. Then turn her towards the red leather spanking bench and smack her ass. "Drape yourself over the bench. Do not assume I forgot your punishment, Naughty Girl."

She yelps and hurries across the room.

I toe off my Gucci loafers, step out of my trousers and briefs, then stalk after her as I shed the rest of my clothes. I take a moment to appreciate her bodacious ass before I slip her wrists and ankles into the suede-lined cuffs.

She shudders when I trail a fingertip from her inner ankle up her thigh and along her puffy, soaked seam. To reward her for a most delightful blowjob, I plunge two digits into her pussy and curl them to stroke her G-spot. Her inner walls grip them greedily. But I withdraw before her orgasm surfaces.

She huffs in dismay and wiggles her ass.

My palm connects with her left ass cheek. I set a swift pattern of left, right, sits bones, left, right, upper thighs until she sags on the spanking bench. A smack to her pussy coats my fingers with her juices. I lick them clean and growl in satisfaction. She whimpers.

I sheath my cock with a condom from the shelf then position myself between her spread legs as I fist my erection. In one brutal thrust, I breach her slippery folds and sink into her sticky pudding. Nice and warm.

She keens as I finally allow her to cum. Her muscles grip me like a vice, and I grunt from the force. A spank to her right ass cheek has her loosening her grip. My hips piston as I pinch her engorged clit. She screams and cums again. Her arms and legs jerk at the restraints. But the cuffs hold fast. Another climax has her begging me to cum. But no safeword.

I continue to fuck her fast and hard until my balls threaten to explode.

"Cum with me," I command as I tighten my grip on her hipbone and tug at her clit.

She jerks and screams as another orgasm overtakes her wrecked pussy.

My groin slams against her red and heated ass as I throw my head back and roar my release. It reverberates around us and triggers another orgasm in her. She wails and collapses against the soft leather, replete.

Once I recover from the mind-blowing sex, I slide out of her pussy gently, pat her ass, and release her from the cuffs. I carry her limp form to the king-size bed and lay her on her belly, then stride to the en suite bathroom for a warm wet cloth and soothing gel. I toss the full condom and return to her side. Aftercare complete, I tuck her beneath the silk sheets.

I exhausted the poor thing, and she curls onto her side without opening her eyes. I wait a few minutes to ensure she's all right before I take a shower. Fully clothed, I leave a note to thank her for a spectacular time and to enjoy breakfast. I am a gentleman, after all.

One who hits it and quits it.

HARRIS

$\mathcal{A}$ LEVELS London chauffeur maneuvers the Black Badge Rolls-Royce Cullinan through the still-busy streets towards Knightsbridge. While in town for a STEELE Technology and Cyber Security summit and a tech conference at ExCel London, I'm staying with Haley. She and Lachlan have a penthouse flat in One Hyde Park—the world's most expensive apartment building and only the best for the Countess of Aboyne. I snicker at the thought, since my twin is as easygoing as I am, despite our limitless wealth.

We're super close, so she wouldn't hear of me staying at STEELE Mayfair or at any of our other hotels in London. Since pregnancy with Lilias, Leith, and Lewis, she's become motherly towards me. She fusses over what I do and how I'm still single. I indulge her new instincts and don't argue, despite not having any interest in settling down.

Her move across the Pond to Aberdeen didn't hamper our connection with me remaining in New York City. In fact, it's grown stronger. Not being a floor apart in The STEELE Tower or sharing offices makes us stay in contact more frequently, whether via video conference, FaceTime, or text messages.

Over two years ago, we split our offices and client list based on our locations, with Haley expanding our satellite office in STEELE London with some of her existing staff and new ones. The process went smoothly and even gained us new clients abroad.

Twice a year we have summits with our teams to gather as a whole for brainstorming, updates, and a chance to bond. Usually, the summits take place at one of STEELE's resorts over four days. Some team members extend their stay to a vacation afterwards. This time, we'll host it at STEELE London, since the biggest tech convention of the year begins the day after our summit ends.

I blink from my musings as the back door of the SUV opens. So lost in thought, I didn't realize we arrived at One Hyde Park. I thank the chauffeur and slide from the buttery leather, then nod at the doorman. The concierges greet me as I stride through the opulent lobby to Haley and Lachlan's private elevator.

Once outside of the penthouse flat's double doors, I type in the passcode to unlock them—the system one of many I designed. I get a glimpse of Hyde Park through the bespoke glass fireplace that separates the entry foyer from the double-height reception room with floor-to-ceiling windows. The stunning panoramic view includes the lights of London's buildings as they glow beyond the park's expanse of trees.

I take a moment to appreciate the view before I head to the kitchen for a late-night snack. As I enter the massive chef's delight, I spy Haley standing in a spotlight at the waterfall-edge marble island. A spoonful of her favorite butter pecan ice cream halfway to her mouth and the quart on the countertop.

With a smirk, I swipe my palm over the overhead light switch. The kitchen floods with light, and Haley squeaks. Her dove gray eyes—so like mine—narrow at me.

"Harris!" She hisses as she jabs her empty spoon at me. "You almost gave me a heart attack! Ugh!"

I chuckle as I stride across the stone floor and take a spoon from the utensils drawer next to the custom, hand-made French La Cornue range. I shake my head at the sight of the impressive appliance since my twin hates to cook and, despite taking lessons, still sucks at it. Brainiac but no chef.

"Sorry, Hal," I say, dipping my spoon into the quart. "Why are you in the dark, anyway? Not to mention up so late."

She huffs and swats my spoon away to dig hers into the tasty treat.

"Blame the hormones and the demands of twins," she replies as she pats her babies bump. "Round two coming up!"

Only months after the birth of their triplets, she and

Lach expect a set of twins. Virile fucker. But she's happy, so I'm ecstatic.

I grin and swipe some more of her ice cream.

Haley cocks her head at me.

"Where are you coming from, Casanova?" She smirks.

I pivot on my heel and prowl towards the refrigerator for a more substantial snack. With my head stuck inside, I mumble a response.

"Sorry, Harris, I didn't quite catch your answer," Haley snickers. "Care to repeat it?"

I turn back towards her with a platter of baked lasagna —clearly from one of Lucien's restaurants. I set it on the island and walk around her to the dishes cabinet. Before I can lift a square of the pasta to my plate, Haley jabs me in the side.

"Hellooo, Harris… Where were you?" She persists.

I face her, and she tilts her head back to eyeball me. Not that she's petite; she's five feet, eight inches and only five inches shorter than me. Formerly shy, she's now a fierce woman. But I know how to get her good.

"Banging the back out of a nice piece of ass at LEVELS London," I deadpan.

Haley's mouth drops open as her face flushes crimson.

I knew a crass response would shock her speechless.

With a snicker, I stride to the microwave hidden in a drawer. Then yelp when an object dings me in the back of my head. She can't cook, but she has a damn good aim.

"You filthy mouthed sexist—"

"Whoa, there, Ms. Prim and Proper. You asked for it," I

reply as I pick her spoon off the floor. "Anything else I can answer for you?"

She rolls her eyes and gets another spoon. Then glares at me as I wait for my pasta to heat. The ding breaks our silence.

"Sit with me while I eat," I say as I bump her with my hip on my way to the banquette. Then add with a smirk, "Spend some quality time with your older brother."

"You know what, Harris…" She says brandishing her spoon again. "You're lucky I love you!"

"You better!" I retort and point to the bench opposite me. "Now, sit your preggie butt down. I'm sure standing for long isn't good for your ankles, Mom."

Haley rolls her eyes again as she settles across from me. Her nose twitches as she catches the delicious aroma of the lasagna. She grins and scoops some off my plate, then shoves it in her mouth. She closes her eyes on a contented sigh.

"So fucking good! Give me this and you get some more," she demands as she slides my plate in front of her.

I throw my head back and laugh.

"Don't mess with a preggie lady and food, twin!" She exclaims gleefully.

After I heat some more, I rejoin her at the banquette. We eat in silence until I sense her appraising stare. Glancing up, I raise my eyebrow at her questioningly.

Haley shrugs and lowers her eyes to her plate.

"Spit it out, twin," I demand.

"Baz told me it disappointed you he couldn't go to the

Knicks and Warriors basketball game with you. Then Malcolm mentioned the jet and Roger said he couldn't hang out with you either," she starts then pauses to gauge my reaction.

I blank my expression.

She bites the corner of her lower lip before she continues with a sigh.

"We're all married and have children. I don't like that you're alone, Harris," she says, then lifts her hand to stop me from speaking. "I know you'll say you're not interested in a relationship. But *I* know you, twin. You're covering up your loneliness with bravado. Don't even try to hide it from me. I love you, Harris, and want you happy like all of us," she finishes.

Her dove gray eyes shine with unshed tears. But she holds my stare, determined to make me understand.

I get it. I just don't agree.

Sure, they're all boo'd up with kids. But I'm not so sure that's for me—at least not at this very moment.

I close my eyes, take a deep breath for a count of six, hold it for six, and exhale for the same time before I respond. My yogi sister-in-law Starr taught the cleansing breath technique to me, and damn if it doesn't soothe my soul.

"Haley, I understand what you're saying. I do. But I am not at the point in my life where I want to settle down. I'm happy for you guys. Truly. But it's not in the cards for me. At least not right now. Okay?" I respond as I clasp her hand.

She swipes at her eyes with the heel of her other hand and nods.

"I don't want you to be alone with all of us paired up. I only want you happy, Harris," she says wistfully.

"I know, Hal. And I thank you," I respond quietly.

I know she'll say it's the hormones making her teary. But I know it's not. She speaks from her heart. We've always done everything together. Now she's married with kids, and I'm still single over a year later.

Well, such is life.

"Hey! What's going on here?"

We jolt at Lachlan's booming voice.

He strides over to the banquette and drops down next to Haley. He wraps an arm around her shoulders and pulls her to him before he plants a kiss on her temple. Then he turns his emerald green eyes to me.

"Well, if it isn't Little Lord Fauntleroy... How may we help you, milord?" I quip.

He chuckles as he shakes his head.

"Late night, Harris?" He asks.

I roll my eyes and take a bite of my lasagna.

"Oh, leave him be, My Lord. Not all of us are on lock-down, you know," Haley retorts cheekily, with a mischievous wink at me.

Lach growls. Clearly not amused.

I grin around my fork and return my twin's wink.

No matter what, we always have each other's backs.

* * *

"Hı, Harris. I loved your presentation. You're just so incredibly smart!"

I glance down at the unfamiliar female who caught me after my session at the tech conference. I smile and thank her, then move on. Her hand on my forearm stops me. A glance over my shoulder and cock my eyebrow.

She giggles but doesn't let go. Instead, she loops her arm around mine and steps beside me.

"I'd really love to hear more about your thoughts. Perhaps we can have a drink later, or…" she says as she squeezes my biceps with her other hand. Then she licks her lips and adds, "I'm game for whatever you have in mind."

Good grief.

I've had enough of the women who stalk after me in hopes of a night in my bed or my ring on their finger. Often they'll attend my presentations—like this one—pretending to be techies just to get access to me.

One pretended to be a journalist for *Wired* and pulled out all the stops with a call to my offices to schedule the interview, then tried to jump my bones in the press suite. Upon investigation, she was the editor's girlfriend and wanted more than he could offer her. She wanted the multibillionaire he wrote about. Ridiculous as it seems, shit like that happens. All the time.

But not today.

"Miss, remove your hands, or I will call security to escort you from the premises," I reply tersely as I pin her with a sharp look.

A flush creeps up from beneath her low-cut silk blouse

to her hairline. She steps back, flabbergasted, stung by my curt tone.

I pivot on my heel and stride in the opposite direction without a backwards glance.

My mobile vibrates in my trousers pocket. I smile when I see it's a call from Haley.

"Hey, Hal. How'd your presentation go?" I ask.

"Awesome! Let's meet for lunch before the afternoon sessions begin," she responds. "We have three potential clients I want to tell you about!"

We end the call, and I increase my pace to reach the restaurant. Haley's excitement has me pumped. This is what drives me—accomplishments in our work. Nothing compares to the rush of success.

Well… A blinding, toe-curling, legs-give-out climax that empties my balls completely still tops my list. Naturally.

I laugh out loud. Haley would really pummel me if I told her that one!

The rest of the day goes as planned, and her driver takes us back to Knightsbridge.

I opted for babysitting duties while Haley and Lachlan have a date night. So I change into a long-sleeved t-shirt and sweats so I can romp around with my niece and nephews. They crawl around like nobody's business, and I need to keep up with them.

We spend the night in their nursery suite's lounge playing with toys, a tickle fest, and bottle feeding all on our own. Although I call Nanny Gail when it's time for diaper changes. Ain't no way this boy's dealing with stinky nappies! Nope.

By the time Haley and Lachlan return, I'm worn the fuck out and crawl to my guest suite, strip, and dive under the covers. Who knows how much later, I jolt upright with a pounding heartbeat and a sweaty face. Scanning around the bedroom, I realize it was only a nightmare. For a frightful minute there, five babies toddled with arms outstretched towards me, calling me Dada.

My entire body shudders at the thought, and I swipe my hand over my heated face.

One last peek around the room ensures all's safe before I pull the comforter over my head.

A calming breath, and I'm out like a light.

KAT

"Okay, lads, you can share the ball. Here, let me show you a game you can play together. It's really fun…"

I stand aside and watch them play. A wistful smile pulls at my lips as I think back to being their age. Unfortunately for my siblings and me, we didn't have a beautiful and wonderfully equipped children's center to spend our youth in Glasgow. We were too busy busting our butts selling newspapers and scraps, babysitting, running errands. Hell, we did anything to make some money so we could eat and pay the rent for our three-room flat.

Sure our parents—Ramsay and Allison—were around. Our mum cleaned for rich families. But our father, he was a dreamer. Always creating some invention or the other that would make him gobs of money. Until he died at a young age from a heart attack.

I toss my waist-length Titian hair over my shoulder as I

glance up to the sky, lost in memories. Titian for one, I scoff. An ex-boyfriend said my hair reminded him of the Renaissance artist's paintings of red-haired women. Whereas I always thought of my locks as a brownish-orange color. But I went along with him since he was more worldly than me, and the fancy description stuck.

Of course, Payton—my older brother by three years to my twenty-seven—teases me relentlessly about it along with other things. *Bah! You're a plain-old ginger, lass! Don't get it twisted with that uppity wanker you're with.* It's worse since I'm the only redhead while everyone else has brown hair.

My relationship with my other siblings—Michael, who's three years younger, and Charlotte, who's twenty-one—is better. Michael is a bit of a dreamer, like our father, and escapes our dreary lives through his sketches of Glasgow's architecture. Charlotte is the quietest of us and prefers to keep her head in the books. She looks up to me and wants to get out through a higher education, too.

I love each of them dearly and will do all in my power to make their lives easier.

After our father died, I realized the only way to escape poverty was to use my brain. My drive to succeed pushed me to study hard not just books, but the ways of the rich. I didn't want to get into a school and stick out. Rather, I wanted to blend in seamlessly. I studied French and the Classics, read the top fashion magazines and business periodicals at the library, and polished my accent. My goal:

become a suitable candidate for the finest university I could gain acceptance.

Ultimately, I won a full academic scholarship to the University of Edinburgh. I strove for not only the most prestigious institution in Scotland, but one of the best in the world. I, Katrina Roberts, entered its hallowed halls and continued to excel.

Less than one hour from the dingy flat to the beauty of the university—a whole new world awaited me. One in which I thrived. Always good with figures and strategy, I earned an MA Business Management degree and graduated with honors at the top of my class.

None of my family attended because of their obligations. But I prefer to keep my Glasgow life separate—less muddying of the waters. Besides, Payton would find a way to embarrass me. No, thank you.

"Ms. Roberts!"

"Ms. Roberts!"

Cries from the boys drag me back from the past.

I shake my head to clear it and smile at them as they come back into focus.

"Yes, lads?" I ask.

Their urgency spurred by who won since they tied makes me laugh out loud. Wow, if only my siblings and I had such simple concerns as tykes!

I offer them a solution that appeases both just as the bell rings for lunch break. They thank me, and I tousle their hair with a grin.

"Wow! What a busy morning, huh?"

I glance around to find my close friend—Isla Ritchie.

Looping my arm through hers, we turn towards the building and the cafeteria within it.

"I know, right! My highlight was refereeing the World Cup," I respond with a giggle as my emerald green eyes dance behind tortoise-shell frame glasses. "And I lived to see another day. Whew."

Isla giggles and shakes her head. Then tells me about her morning sessions.

We met at Aberdeen's Children's Center, where we volunteer on Wednesday evenings and all day on Saturdays. Around the same age, we became fast friends. While Isla is happily married, I'm single.

Sure, I've had a few dalliances over the years. But for the most part, work and studies then work again dominate my time. And when I need to scratch an itch, I reach for my trusty BOB—Battery Operated Boyfriend. Not quite a red-blooded male, or the sensation one can give to me. But it provides relief without complications. Unless I use up the batteries as known to happen…

Once we have our trays with sandwiches and soup, Isla and I settle at a table near the expanse of windows. I glance briefly at the beautifully landscaped playground and shake my head again. So nice.

"Ugh! I'm eating like a cow. But I can't help myself. At least I get to blame the baby," Isla says as she pops a Walkers Salt & Vinegar crisp in her mouth. She closes her eyes and hums in delight.

"Your hubby will love you no matter what state you're in, Isla," I tell her with a giggle.

I'm so happy for my friend. She and Gregor have been trying for a while now to get pregnant. So I say eat whatever makes her smile after months of sadness. She deserves it.

"So, how's it going with your boss? Is he still a prat, or what?" Isla asks with a frown marring her pretty face.

I sigh and roll my eyes.

"Yeah. But it's a great opportunity. So unless something more impressive comes along, I'll stick it out," I respond with a shrug.

After graduation, I turned down offers for management trainee positions in favor of an administrative assistant position at an international company's C-suites. Since then, I've had a few. I figure the best way to learn about business is straight from the source—the higher ups who actually run it.

Many a person takes a job as an AA to a ranking officer, gets to learn the ins and outs of the entire company, and lands a prime position either at the same place or at a comparable one. That is, if one has the smarts to do so, and I most definitely have what it takes, thanks to my upbringing and my doggedness.

"Well, I'll keep my ears open for an opportunity at Jackson Corporation or somewhere else. No sense in working at a place that's unpleasant," Isla says, then winks. "Until then, *smiogaid suas, nighean!*"

I lift my chin and grin at my friend as I repeat the Scottish Gaelic phrase for *chin up, girl*—my lifelong mantra.

Our conversation turns to plans for the weekend, and soon it's time for the afternoon sessions. We part in the corridor leading to the study rooms where we'll tutor the older children.

By the end of the day, I'm ready for a soak in my tub, a glass of wine, and a round with BOB. No better way to ease stress!

"Now, don't be nervous, Kat. Mr. Jackson is not like your current boss. Mr. Jackson demands the best from every employee. But he's fair and makes sure we have the guidance and training we need to achieve our goals. I've learned so much from him over the years. He counts Gladys and me as integral parts of his team and praises us for being smart and dedicated to our jobs. Plus, working directly for Mr. Jackson has major perks!"

Isla grins at me as she squeezes my arm with one hand and cradles her baby bump with the other.

She's heavily pregnant. So she and Gregor decided it's best for her to take an early leave, followed by maternity time off after she gives birth.

True to her word from a few months back, Isla recommended me to Lachlan Jackson—CEO, President of Liquor, and Chairman of the Board of Jackson Corporation—as her temporary replacement. She believes once I get my foot in the door, he'll see my potential for a permanent position by the time she returns as his administrative assistant.

Isla also thinks my chances of securing the role are high since Mr. Jackson met with quite a few potential replacements for her position. But not one reached his expectations. Prior to my interview with him, Isla had me meet with Gladys Sinclair—his personal assistant. I did my research on the company and impressed her enough that she recommended he meet with me after Human Resources did their background checks. Isla tells me he agreed, since my resume and references prove I'm worthy of an interview.

Now, my stomach churns as we leave the private lift area for his suite of offices on the executive floor of Jackson Town House. It's the landmark property on Union Street built by the company's founders of the famous Aberdeen granite. Jackson Town House is the second largest granite building in the world.

My gaze wanders as I take in my surroundings. The executive floor has offices for their legal, finance, operations, and technology departments, along with various conference rooms. Their other divisions have designated floors below. I scan the employees who move about busy at their tasks. The hum of their conversations and activities mixes with the soft classical music piped in through the surround sound system.

The decor highlights the Old World feel of Jackson Town House. A palette of caramel and Bordeaux hues with gold accents reminiscent of our Scotch and wines blend with the dark mahogany woods and leather furniture, crystal light fixtures, and original artwork. The reception area has a spacious desk. Three attractive receptionists with headsets in their ears and custom-tailored caramel-colored dress suits and skin-tone heels that serve as uniforms sit behind it. I smile and nod at them as Isla and I pass—my heels silent on the luxurious Aubusson rugs.

My emerald green eyes widen as we approach portraits of past generations who founded and helped continue the legacy of Jackson Corporation. First with who I recognize as the founder and the creator of the finest single malt Scotch Whiskey. He set Jackson Corporation on the path to the most renowned liquor company in the world. After him, successors of each generation have portraits ending with one of Lachlan Jackson.

I can't help but admire his breathtaking movie-star appearance. He resembles the classic American actor Cary Grant with his rugged masculinity and gorgeous looks. Blazing green eyes stare back at me from the canvas. Thick, sable brown hair slicked back from his chiseled cheekbones and strong jawline with a cleft chin add to his heartthrob persona.

"I know, he's a gorgeous man! And happily married," Isla whispers as she tugs my arm. "Come on, we don't want you late."

Heat suffuses my alabaster skin a crimson shade. Damn! I didn't realize I stopped and gawked at Mr. Jackson's portrait. Get it together, Katrina Roberts!

"Er… Right… Sorry… Let's go," I mumble, embarrassed by the blatant act.

We hurry our steps until we reach Mr. Jackson's outer office. I take note of a reception area, conference room, and a desk for Isla and one where Gladys sits. She lifts her gaze from her laptop screen and smiles at me. She's in her mid-forties and the type of woman I admire for her intelligence and cultured presence.

"Hello, Kat. You look lovely. Good luck. Although I'm certain you will do well!" She says with a thumbs up.

"Thank you!" I respond with a nervous smile.

I smooth down the front of my navy blue suit's A-line skirt, then swipe my palm over my hair to ensure no strands crept from the chignon. I learned the importance of investment pieces and purchased a few well-tailored, sensible suits, silk blouses, and heels. My biggest purchase —the Mulberry City Briefcase in hunter green for money —I hold tightly in my left hand.

"Isla, call through via the intercom. He's waiting for the both of you," Gladys adds with a nod towards the imposing double doors to Mr. Jackson's office.

Isla walks to her desk and presses the call button.

"Mr. Jackson? Are you ready to meet with us?" She asks.

He responds in the affirmative, and she smiles at me encouragingly before she opens the doors.

Mr. Jackson stands beside an equally gorgeous young woman not much older than me seated on a leather sofa in the seating area. Three adorable babies—a girl and two boys—sit on her lap and next to her as he helps her to settle.

He strides over to his beautifully carved mahogany wood desk as he gestures for Isla and me to sit in the guest chairs opposite.

As we take our seats, I glance at his wife and children with a smile and nod as I wave my fingers at one of the boys, who watches us intently.

"Oh, don't mind us. Do carry on with your meeting," his wife says with a genial smile.

I nod again and bring my attention back to Mr. Jackson.

"Mr. Jackson, this is Katrina Roberts, my friend who I recommend as my replacement. Katrina, this is Mr. Lachlan Jackson, CEO of Jackson Corporation," Isla says.

I reach across his desk to hold out my hand as I rise slightly from my seat.

"Thank you for the opportunity to interview with you, Mr. Jackson," I say as I grip his sizable hand firmly and look him straight in the eye.

"You're welcome Ms. Roberts—"

"Oh, please call me Kat," I interject with an amiable smile. My green eyes twinkle like emeralds behind tortoise-shell frame glasses.

He nods.

"Do you need me any further, Mr. Jackson?" Isla asks as she rests her hand on her baby bump.

He scans her face as though assessing her wellbeing before he responds.

"No, that is all for today. Call for one of the company

cars to take you home. They can pick you up in the morning, so you can leave yours in the garage overnight," he tells her.

Isla expresses her thanks and turns to tell Mrs. Jackson good night before she leaves his office. He watches her with a concerned expression as she makes her way across the office and through the doors.

She wasn't joking when she told me he cares for his employees and about the major perks. A ride home and back the next morning in a chauffeur-driven company car? Wow.

He turns his emerald green gaze back to me.

"So, Kat, tell me about yourself and why you believe your skill set makes you suitable for the role of my administrative assistant," he says.

Okay, Katrina Roberts, *smiogaid suas, nighean*!

I take a deep breath and sit up straighter in the comfortable leather seat. Then I proceed to answer in detail. My goal: get the job.

An hour later, Mr. Jackson calls an end to the interview and escorts me to the doors of his office.

Gladys looks over, and he asks her to see me to the lobby.

With a smile, I extend my hand, and he shakes it.

"Thank you, Mr. Jackson. I do hope I satisfy your requirements and hope to hear from you soon," I say with another firm grip. Then shift my emerald green gaze to his right and smiles. "Nice to see you, Mrs. Jackson. Your triplets are adorable."

"Thank you, Kat," she responds with a brilliant smile that illuminates her dove gray eyes.

Another nod to Mr. Jackson, and he shuts the door behind me.

I sag in relief and place a hand over my heart.

Gladys laughs as she rises from her chair.

"That's a good sigh or a bad one?" She asks.

I join her in laughter and respond, "Both! Good because I think I did well and bad because he didn't offer the position at the end. I couldn't get a read on him."

Gladys pats my arm and shakes her head.

"Mr. Jackson keeps things close to his chest. He wouldn't have kept you for an hour if he weren't somewhat interested. So don't worry," she assures me.

Once we're in the well-appointed lobby, I thank Gladys and wish her a good evening. Standing outside, I turn to face the magnificent Jackson Town House. Then lift my gaze to the sky and nod. I did my best. Now, let's wait and see.

* * *

"Ms. Roberts!"

I glance down at the cute little blonde-haired lass and smile.

"Yes?" I ask.

"Can you read the story again? Pretty please!!!" She responds as she clasps her tiny hands together and widens her baby blue eyes.

I can't help but to chuckle at her and to agree with her request.

It's raining this evening, so my volunteer work keeps me indoors. I'm just thankful to have a distraction from worrying about the job at Jackson Corporation. It's been a few days and no word. Isla doesn't even have an update for me.

With a sigh, I re-read the fairytale, enacting the characters the way the children enjoy. Just as I finish, my mobile vibrates. The screen reveals an unknown number, but I answer anyway—fingers crossed.

"Hello?"

"Ms. Katrina Roberts?" The woman asks. When I confirm, she continues. "This is the Human Resources department for Jackson Corporation. Mr. Lachlan Jackson would like to extend an offer to you as his temporary administrative assistant…"

I barely contain my whoop of delight as I hop to my feet and rush from the library at Aberdeen Children's Center. When she finishes, I accept the offer and agree to come in during my lunch hour the next day. We end the call, and I do a jig. Then I send a text message to Isla to thank her and to tell her I'll call once I return home.

The rest of the evening goes by in a blur, my mind on tomorrow. I'll resign after I sign the offer letter. Goodbye to the old prat! Hello to a fresh path!

KAT

"Kat, kindly come into my office. Thank you."

My heart stutters in my chest at Mr. Jackson's unexpected request. Various scenarios race through my mind: someone detected my unauthorized access to the server; security spotted the listening devices I planted around the offices; tiny cameras found. Bloody hell.

I school my face before I rise from my desk. A surreptitious glance at Gladys doesn't reveal any hint of what I can expect. She's typing on her keyboard while she schedules Mr. Jackson's upcoming trip to South Africa's Coastal Region for visits to their wineries.

Pull yourself together, Kat Roberts! You're too good for them to catch you.

Besides, I've only set up surveillance for now. No need to rush despite Chet's demands for intel like yesterday.

This is my play. I will follow my schedule—not to mention my gut that's guided me all these years successfully.

Chester Stewart, aka Chet, the forty-year-old vice president of Stewart Scotch. His family's company is Jackson Corporation's top competitor. Add on a centuries-old bitter rivalry over some silly noble title the king gave to the Jackson family instead of to the Stewarts, and you've got the perfect partner for me. One that has the resources to supply the costly equipment and connections I need. Plus the millions to pay me.

In researching the Stewarts, I opted to approach Chet instead of Bram—his younger brother by two years and also a vice president. Their father Magnus serves as the CEO and Chairman of the Board. However, it's well known the brothers vie for the lead positions. Their father encourages the competition and will only announce his successor when one of the brothers "proves their worth." And Chet wants the role. Badly.

My thoughts wander back to my first encounter with him as he left his la-di-da men's social club—The Royal Northern & University Club Aberdeen—one evening.

"Chet Stewart, I can help you destroy the Jacksons."

He gawks at me for a moment, surprised by my forthright pronouncement, before he blanks his face. His denim blue eyes do a scan from my Titian head, pausing on my full breasts and curvy hips down to my heels. An appreciative gleam shines in his irises as he zones in on my pretty face. Tilting his head to the side, he responds.

"That's a bold statement, little lass. But I'm a busy man with

no time for your game," Chet sneers as he moves past me. Purposefully, his arm brushes the side of my breast.

The arrogant prat.

I pivot and follow him to his Bentley sedan idling at the curb. As he slides in, I slip in behind him.

He starts, then scowls at me.

"Everything all right, sir?" His driver asks as he leans into the door he still holds open.

I arch my eyebrow at Chet and repeat my statement as I cross my long, toned legs.

His eyes track my movement, then lift to search my face. Satisfied with what he sees, Chet nods and tells his chauffeur to drive until instructed otherwise.

The soft thud of the door sends a shudder down my spine. However, I straighten it, determined to prove myself and to set my plan for revenge in motion.

"Yes, Mr. Jackson. I'll be right in, sir," I respond through the intercom in an unruffled tone.

Then I smooth my suit skirt and brush my hand over my hair. I straighten my shoulders and lift my chin, confident my expert hacking skills didn't fail me nor my gut mislead me.

Okay, Katrina Roberts, *smiogaid suas, nighean*!

"Have a seat, Kat," Mr. Jackson says as he nods towards the guest chairs across from his desk.

He watches me approach with an unreadable expression on his handsome face. Once I'm settled on the chair, he leans back in his seat and runs a hand through his silky brown hair.

"You have acclimated well to the company and to your tasks as my administrative assistant in the few months you have worked for me," he begins.

Then he sits forward and folds his hands on the desk's surface. His emerald green eyes seem to stare into my soul.

I have to force my gaze to remain on his face impassively and my body not to fidget under his scrutiny. Again my mind whirls, wondering if he knows something after all.

"—the position on a permanent basis."

I snap back to attention at his words. However, I missed the first part and curse myself silently for allowing my nerves to distract me. With a shake of my head to clear it, I ask Mr. Jackson to repeat himself.

A slight frown appears between his eyebrows but disappears quickly.

"Isla contacted me a short while ago. She and her husband decided she needs to remain home with their newborn and not return to Jackson Corporation after her maternity leave ends. I offer you the position on a permanent basis," he responds. He pauses to gauge my reaction before he continues.

"Also, remember I will take my paternity leave in two months, and you will report to Ms. Jackson. She will split her time between here and New York City. Her administrative assistant will help, too."

Instead of jumping up and double fist pumping in the air, I take a breath and smile.

"Thank you, Mr. Jackson. I appreciate the opportunity

and promise to do my absolute best," I respond. While in my mind, I tack on *to ruin your bloody family.*

"Oh, Isla! I'm so happy for you and Gregor! Not to mention delighted to have the position permanently. But only because you're not returning, of course!"

I exclaim with a grin as I curl up on my couch with a glass of wine later that evening.

The time couldn't go by fast enough for me to get out of Jackson Town House to make my calls. The first one goes to Isla.

Oh, Isla…

Little did she know I befriended her as a means to infiltrate Jackson Corporation.

As one of the few employees in the CEO's inner circle and with the most access, I chose her since we're closest in age and share a commonality of being from less fortunate families. The Aberdeen Children's Center served its purpose. I volunteered since she spends so much time there and would never expect I was after her job.

When she confided her difficulties in getting pregnant, I asked Chet if he had any connections with a reputable fertility doctor. He came through with an appointment with a renown OB-GYN fertility expert and paid the hefty fee. Isla only had a minimal amount to cover. I shared the details—sans payment arrangements—with her. Then poof, she's preggie. And owes me.

Isla fell for the stories about my bosses. Chet arranged

my most recent job with managers who would supply recommendations, and in the case of the last one, go along with the prat scenario. The man has many who owe him favors, and he's as manipulative as me.

Now with Lachlan going on paternity leave, I'll move to the next phase of my plan. However, they call his sister *The Shark*—not that her brother is a slouch. So, I'll have to be extra careful with her. At least she'll only be in Aberdeen part time.

Sadly, Isla is right. He's a decent guy and treats his staff well.

I shake my head and admonish myself. *Smiogaid suas, nighean!*

"You deserve it, Kat! Especially after the prat. But if you need help with anything, just let me know. I'm here for you."

Isla's words add to the tiny, tiny nugget of second thoughts. But not enough to change my mind. No.

I make an excuse to end our call. I cannot allow even a modicum of emotion to influence my decision.

With a nod, I pick up one of my many burner phones.

"What have you got for me?"

I roll my eyes and bite back a groan.

This guy here…

"Isla resigned. I have the position permanently and will have something for you shortly," I respond in a clipped manner.

After Chet tried to feel up my leg in the back of the Bentley, he learned the hard way not to fuck with me. We keep things strictly business and our conversations to the minimum.

"It better be soon and worth my time."

I pull the mobile from my ear to stare at the screen.

He hung up.

The bloody prat.

"Hey, preggie twin. You look fantastic, Hot Mama. How're you feeling?"

I flew on Lachlan's Sikorsky S-92 Executive Helicopter to Aberdeen after a week in London at STEELE Technology & Cyber Security offices. With Haley due to give birth next month, we're in the process of reviewing projects and assigning staff to prepare for her maternity leave.

Just as before, with the birth of The Trips, we expect our work to go as planned uninterrupted by her absence. I'll split the month with two weeks at our offices in New York City, followed by two weeks in London.

Knowing Haley, she'll make herself available for video conference meetings within a couple of weeks of giving birth. Sure, she'll have a second nanny. But I'll insist she stay focused on her little family. No need to rush back to business like she did the last time.

Even with our expanding portfolio, I'm confident STCS will continue to prosper.

Haley gives me a wry smile and pats her sizable babies bump.

"Oh, just fine with two cantaloupes battling for space in my belly…" She responds with an arched eyebrow. "But thanks for the compliment."

I chuckle and shake my head.

"Five and counting, huh?" I ask.

She whacks me with the back of her hand and growls.

"No *and counting*, Harris Steele! You better cut it out!" She responds with a glare. "Do not tease your twin like that. And boy, I cannot wait until the shoe is on the other foot! You know karma is a—"

"You-know-what." I interject, nodding my head towards Lilias, Leith, and Lewis, who play on the floor in front of us with Bonnie and Bella—their Golden Retrievers.

WHACK!

"Don't tell me to watch my words! I know, Harris Steele!" She snarls as she cuffs me again.

Mouth agape, I rub my arm and stare at my twin.

The scowl falls from her face, and she opens her arms for a hug.

Warily, I lean over and pat her back.

"Sorry, Har. It's the hormones, and my back bothers me… My legs are all crampy… My ankles swelled up to cricket balls. I'm an absolute mess," she says, then hiccups.

I squeeze her to my chest and rub the back of her ebony haired head.

"It's okay, Hal. I get it. But there's no way you're *an absolute mess*. Heck, you can't be because we look alike, and I'm a handsome devil," I say.

That gets her giggling, and I smile.

I give her another squeeze, then pull back to scan her face.

"Good?" I ask.

She sniffs and nods, dove gray eyes glimmer from the tears.

"All good," Haley responds.

I reach for my laptop and nod for her to pick up hers. We spend the next couple of hours going over work. As I expect, she jumps right in and forgets about her bit of sadness. Like me, Haley loves what she does and thrives on it. We live up to the nickname our brothers gave to us—the Dynamic Duo.

After we're done, I go to my guest suite in Haley and Lachlan's Aberdeen penthouse to change for my lunch with him. As much as I tease Lach, I enjoy hanging out with my cuz-turned-brother-in-law. Not to mention he's the liquor guy!

I go back to Haley's home office and tell her and The Trips I'll see them after lunch when we'll go to the park. Bonnie and Bella yip in excitement since they recognize the word *park*. I grin and scratch them behind their ears. Their feathery tales thump on the floor.

HEY, bro, I'm sitting in the lobby.

A moment passes, then the three dots appear indicating Lachlan is typing a response appear on the screen of my mobile.

On my way down.

I scroll through my email while I wait.

"Mr. Steele? Mr. Harris Steele?"

A soft Scottish lilt says my name like I'm Bond. James Bond.

And like a Bond Girl, this one is stacked. Her prim librarian facade of low heels, stockings, a conservative suit with an A-line skirt and a waist-length jacket, pussy bow blouse, and tortoise-shell glasses fails to hide her bodacious body. Thick, glossy red hair pulled back in a no-nonsense bun. Talk about a scene at LEVELS London. Hot damn!

As my gaze takes in her long legs, grip-worthy hips, ample tits, and lush mouth, her natural beauty takes my breath away. Emerald green eyes stare back at me, unaffected—dare I say bored—by my heated gaze.

I put on my most dazzling, panty dropping smile and mimic her Scottish accent in my deep baritone timbre.

"Aye, bonnie lass. And who might ye be?"

I think I see a flash of something in the depths of those intriguing emerald orbs. But it's gone in, well, a flash.

She squares her shoulders and peers down her nose at me.

Her attempt to show confidence only serves to push her delectable tits out.

I smirk.

Her eyes narrow slightly. Then her face blanks again.

Lady Gaga's "Poker Face," anyone?

"Kat, Mr. Jackson's administrative assistant," she responds.

Oh, fuck me. Why does this one have to work for Lachlan? Damn.

The realization wipes the flirtation from my mind in an instant.

"Mr. Jackson asked me to escort you up to his offices as a call detained him," Kat continues. "Kindly follow me, Mr. Steele."

Without waiting for me to acknowledge her statement, Little Kat pivots and stalks towards the executive floor's elevator.

Okay, Little Kat may be Lachlan's admin. But the sway of her hips and her round ass call to me like a siren's song. I follow like she's the Pied Piper.

The alluring scent of her perfume fills my nostrils as we stand side by side in the elevator. I guesstimate her height at five feet, eight inches in her two-inch heels since I tower over her by five.

Surreptitiously, I ogle her in my periphery. Wild thoughts of yanking the pins from her bun to free that red mane, hiking her skirt up, and hoisting her long leg around my hip as I drive my hungry ten-inch cock balls deep inside of her wet, willing pussy fill my head.

The ping of the elevator doors opening interrupts my sexy fantasy.

As I follow Little Kat, I adjust my burgeoning length. And avoid staring at her sexy strut.

She knocks on Lachlan's doors and opens them.

"You may enter, Mr. Steele," she says as she steps back.

"Thank you, Kat," I say with a nod. The taste of her name sweetens my mouth.

I step inside, and she closes the doors behind me.

My hand drags down my face as I blow out a long breath.

Fuck. Me.

When I open my eyes, Lachlan stares at me with his head cocked as he continues to speak on the telephone. I shake my head and point to his en suite bathroom. He nods but watches me with a furrowed brow.

Once inside, I fully adjust my cock, then stare in the mirror.

"Did that Little Kat crawl under my skin? Fuck… Am I doomed like my brothers by one glance?" I say aloud to my reflection. Then I grin. "Hell nah! Not this playa, baby!"

I chuckle as I shake my head to dislodge *that* unsavory thought, rinse my face with cool water, and stride from the bathroom.

Lachlan lifts his gaze from his laptop when I re-renter his office. He lifts an eyebrow questioningly. Then goes back to his call when I wave him off.

I plop down on the leather sofa and grab a magazine to distract myself from the memory of Little Kat's allure. With each flip of the glossy pages, my mind falls back to her glossy red hair. I want to run my fingers through it like they slide across the pages. It's her gorgeous face with its smooth complexion and luminous green eyes that stare back at me from the photos. The scent of her floral perfume still swirls in my nose like a fresh bouquet of roses.

"Earth to Harris!"

I jolt and slam the magazine closed. A guilty flush of crimson climbs up my face as though Lachlan caught me with my nose to the centerfold in *Playboy*. I glance up to find him standing on the other side of the coffee table, frowning at me.

"You didn't hear a word I said. Did you?" He asks as he shakes his head. "And I take it you weren't really reading that magazine, either. Were you?"

I open my mouth for a retort, but glance back at the magazine's title. Oh, fuck me… It's some parenting gibberish. Cold busted like a mug.

To save face, I shrug it off and rise from the sofa.

"I do have nieces and nephews, you know. It never hurts to learn more about taking care of them," I respond, buttoning my Tom Ford suit jacket. "Do you have a problem with that, Little Lord Fauntleroy?"

He snorts and turns towards the double doors of his office.

"Whatever you say, Uncle Harris," Lachlan chuckles.

I follow him out to the reception area and smile at Gladys. But I avoid eye contact with the redhead siren. However, she doesn't get the memo…

"Good day to you, Mr. Steele," she pipes up pleasantly.

Not to be rude, I glance over my shoulder. Her eyes glitter like the gemstones they resemble, while her face remains a cool mask. I nod and mumble a response, sure that my voice would crack like a pubescent boy if I verbalized an answer.

The corners of her lush mouth quirk up briefly before she lowers her head to her laptop.

I turn back and bump into Lachlan, who smirks at me.

We walk to the elevator in silence, only broken by his staff greeting him as we pass. Once inside, he cocks his head at me. After no words from him, I shrug with both hands palms up.

He chuckles. But the doors ping open. He signals for me to go first and follows.

We enter Jackson Restaurant through its lobby entrance. Lucien turned the generations-old eatery into a three Michelin star restaurant that features his versions of traditional Scottish fare. The tantalizing aromas make my stomach growl, reminding me I haven't eaten yet.

The hostess smiles politely at Lachlan but widens it when her eyes land on me. I note she's a pretty brunette with topaz eyes and a slim figure. But no reaction whatsoever.

Well, damn.

I shake my head, confused by my lack of interest.

She leads us to a center table in the bustling dining room filled with the lunch crowd. Several people acknowledge Lachlan's presence—including some women. He ignores their hungry looks as he shakes hands with some others. The women flick their gazes to me, and I frown. They know Lach is married. His and Haley's wedding was the talk of the UK and worldwide. Thirsty broads, I harrumph.

After we order the day's specials—Lucien's fancy versions of Cock-a-Leekie Soup and Scotch Pie. I take a sip of Jackson Cabernet Sauvignon and settle back in my chair.

"So, what's on your mind?" Lachlan asks with a smirk. "You seemed flustered when you entered my office and when we left. Oh, and before you give me some bollocks story, I would guess it has something to do with Kat."

I choke on my next sip of wine.

He grins like the Cheshire Cat and lifts his Waterford Crystal glass in salute.

"Cold busted, Harris," he chuckles.

I decide the honest route the best course to take. Besides, I have nothing to hide.

"Aren't you Sherlock Holmes, Lachlan old chap?" I smirk as I appraise him over the rim of my wineglass.

The fucker throws his head back and laughs uproariously.

"Hell, I can admit she's an attractive woman. So what? She's your administrative assistant. Therefore, she's hands off," I respond coolly.

Although in the back of my mind, I hope he's not bothered if I am interested. Not saying I'm walking down the aisle or anything like that. Nah! But a good—rather a great

—shag sounds about right. Besides, Little Kat may not be interested. Yeah right!

Lachlan makes a wry face and snorts.

"Don't pull that unaffected attitude with me, Harris Steele. I've known you your whole life, bro. She has you in all sorts of ways. And no, she's not hands off. You're not a Jackson, so it's not inappropriate if you pursue her. However, she's a good AA and I don't need your personal shit fucking up her work. And she's a grown woman who can decide on her own," Lachlan says.

At first, I roll my eyes at him using my full name. Obviously, he's picked up on Haley's habit. But when he gives the all-clear, I grin wolfishly and damn near howl.

He chuckles. Then he threatens my balls if I make Little Kat run for the hills screaming and leave him stranded without an administrative assistant. When I tell him she would scream but not for the reasons he thinks, it's his turn to choke on his wine.

I take a sip from my glass and smirk when it goes down as smooth as silk.

Just as I imagine Little Kat will soon.

"Kat, I have a last-minute call. Kindly escort my brother-in-law Harris Steele up from the lobby. He's over six feet tall with jet black hair and gray eyes. Resembles my wife. Thank you."

I acknowledge Mr. Jackson's request and stride towards the elevator.

Harris Steele.

As per my research, he's the last single brother of their family, never pictured with the same woman twice, a brainiac. And bloody hell... More handsome and captivating in person. Even from across the lobby, he exudes the primal sex appeal of an Alpha male who's accustomed to yes and only yes. No way I'd miss that strapping lad.

I have the sudden urge to run my fingers through the longer strands of the glossy ebony hair atop his head. My other palm cups the back of his head, skimming over the shorter sides. I tug as he buries his stunningly handsome face between my quivering thighs. The slight scruff on his cheeks abrades my sensitive skin as he makes a meal of my throbbing pussy—

"Oh! Excuse me, lass! I didn't realize you were stopping so abruptly. Are you all right there?"

A bump from behind jolts me from my erotic reverie.

My hand flies to my chest as I gasp.

I glance around to ensure Harris Steele didn't notice before I nod at the older gentleman. Then smile to reassure him as his dusky blue eyes scan my face. Once he moves on, I straighten my spine and admonish myself for drooling over a relative of the enemy.

But as I near Harris Steele, my steps slow. It won't hurt to observe him while he's distracted by his mobile. Always good to know your enemy in all states. At least that's the reason I claim, not because he's a magnet, and I'm a piece of, well, steel.

His full lips curl up into a smile at something on the screen of his mobile. A laugh rumbles in his chest as he runs his fingers through that hair. And my fingers flex in jealously. My pussy clenches when he draws the corner of his lush mouth between his perfectly straight pearly teeth. I want my lower lips in that mouth. More jealousy strikes, sending a shudder down my spine.

I blink and shake my head.

Pull yourself together, Kat Roberts!

"Mr. Steele? Mr. Harris Steele?" I ask as I quicken my pace to stand before him, seated with his muscular thighs spread wide on a leather sofa. His expensive suit enhances his mouthwatering physique.

Again, I can't stop myself from admiring his masculine beauty.

Below thick eyebrows, dove gray eyes brighten to molten platinum as his gaze glides over me from my legs to my face.

It takes a Herculean effort for me to school my expression while my thighs press together, my lower belly flutters, and my nipples pebble. But I do. I stare back at him with what I hope is a look of boredom, despite his lust-filled gaze.

My resolve falters when Harris' face lights up with a million-dollar—no, scratch that—a multibillion-dollar smile.

"Aye, bonnie lass. And who might ye be?" He asks with a flawless Scottish accent in a deep baritone timbre.

Forget molten platinum. Melted chocolate drips all over my naked, heated skin as the sensuality of his words engulfs me. A crack forms in my bored visage. Bloody hell, Harris Steele is good!

Stop it, Kat Roberts! Focus.

Once again, I square my shoulders and peer down the bridge of my nose at him. Unfortunately, the movement lifts my full breasts higher.

A smirk replaces his megawatt smile as he enjoys the new view.

I narrow my eyes, then school my face. I refuse to allow him to get to me—more than he already has…

"Kat, Mr. Jackson's administrative assistant," I respond.

Harris' eyes widen, and it's his turn to pull himself together.

My belly flutters again at the expression of disappointment in his dove gray orbs. Well, I guess I'm not the only one who senses an attraction between us. I shake my head. Enough!

"Mr. Jackson asked me to escort you up to his offices as a call detained him," I continue, proud I pulled it off in my most professional voice. "Kindly follow me, Mr. Steele."

Without waiting for his response, I pivot and walk towards the executive floor's elevator. I dare not glance over my shoulder at him.

A delicious warmth wraps around me as I sense his gaze on my ass while he follows. An extra oomph sways my hips to give this player something to play with. Not saying I want him to play with me, per se.

I do my very best to ignore his covert glances as the lift rises. But the compellingly sensual scent of his cologne—floral, earthy, and vanilla—permeates the air to heighten my unexpected arousal. My lips part to breathe through my mouth as an avoidance. Now, I taste him on my tongue. Hmm, what must his cock taste like? My mouth waters. Bloody hell!

Harris towers over me as I risk a side glance up at him. A slight furrow forms between his eyebrows as he closes his eyes and shakes his head. It gives me a moment to take in his face unseen.

Simply gorgeous.

The lift doors open, along with his eyes.

I avert my gaze and hurry ahead of him. Not soon enough, we arrive at Mr. Jackson's doors. I take a deep breath before I knock and open them.

"You may enter, Mr. Steele," I say as I step back.

"Thank you, Kat," he says with a nod before he steps inside.

With a sigh of relief, I close the doors behind him. My body sags from the sexual tension and the loss of Harris Steele.

"Are you all right, Kat?"

Gladys' question makes me raise my head and re-open my eyes.

I plaster a smile on my face and turn.

"Oh, yes. Just catching my breath. I didn't want Mr. Jackson to wait too long, so I hurried to fetch Mr. Steele," I respond as I head to my desk. "Did I miss a call or anything?"

As Gladys assures me all is well and tells me she appreciates my enthusiasm to please Mr. Jackson, I think the best way to avoid detection is to detract. I don't need her to question my behavior in any way. Remain under the radar, Kat Roberts.

And keep your legs closed!

Moments later, Harris follows Mr. Jackson out to the reception area and smiles at Gladys. He avoids eye contact with me.

Jealousy flares within me.

"Good day to you, Mr. Steele," I say in my most bonny

voice. My Scottish lilt rolls off my tongue as a reminder of his mimicry from earlier. However, I maintain a detached expression. No need for him to think I want him.

He glances over his shoulder, nods, and mutters an incoherent response.

My mouth quirks up briefly before I lower my gaze to my laptop. I note how in his haste he bumps into Mr. Jackson, who smirks.

As they walk away, my mind whirls with possibilities.

Well, perhaps I should rethink my strategy.

The single Steele and twin of Mrs. Jackson could prove a boon to assist in the ruination of the Jacksons and perhaps the Steeles too.

I'll use whatever and whoever I can to get what I want. Revenge. My red hair, pretty face, and curvy body get 'em every time.

Including that Steele sucker.

"And how's my Hot Mama twin and my newest nephews this bonny morn?"

Haley's smile could light the darkest corner of the most remote Scottish moor during the winter months.

A week ago, she gave birth to the Honourable Stirling Jackson—a city known as the Gateway to the Highlands—and the Honorable Struan Jackson, the Scottish word for stream. She and Lachlan named their twin boys in honor of the Steele name and Lachlan's love of the water and sailing.

We think it's because their eyes bear the Steele trait of gray hues while their ebony waves match ours. As our Mom declared, The Trips look like their Daddy, and The Twins look like their Mama. I say both sets are absolute perfection, just like my twin.

"Oh, Harris! We're fantastic. A wee bit tired, but great nonetheless," Haley says with a weary grin.

I bend down and press my lips to the top of her head. She leans into me and sighs.

"You look fantastic, too," I say as I stand and grin at her. "I told Little Lord Fauntleroy I would escort you and the little lads to brunch. Shall we?"

I bow and raise my hand to her.

Haley giggles and takes it, then curtsies.

"Why thank you, dear brother. You are so kind," she replies.

I gather Stirling and Struan into my arms while Haley loops her hand around my biceps. As we walk to the elevator, she tells me about their latest achievements. Struan lifted his head while on his tummy. Stirling acknowledged Haley wiggling her fingers at him from a foot away. I crack they're smarter than their *Da*, then chuckle when she whacks me.

"Guess who's here!"

"Oh, sweetheart, you're flushed!"

"Bonjour, chérie!"

As always, the entire Steele and Jackson clans, along with the Beaulieus and Knights, flew in for the birth, and over the next few weeks, some will remain, and others will return. To allow Haley to bask in motherhood, I plan to work from STEELE London and stay Friday evening through Monday morning here at Aboyne Castle. My babysitting duties will kick up to the next level with the addition of The Twins. However, their two nannies will be of the utmost help, naturally. No poo and wee nappies for Uncle Harris to change!

"So, week one down. How do you and Lachlan feel with five tykes?" Baz asks with a smirk.

"Yeah, the newly crowned Big Papa. Tell us all about it," Malcolm adds with a chuckle.

Lachlan grins and runs a hand through his hand.

"Not as debonair now," I say with a chuckle at the disheveled *Da*.

He laughs, and everyone joins in.

"No, but I couldn't be happier. You should try it soon, Harris," Lachlan responds. Then adds with a smirk, "You may find yourself a bonny lass while you're here."

"Yeah, like that New York Lotto commercial. *Hey, you never know!*" Roger chimes in.

Laurent shakes his head and grumbles, "Yeah, tell me something I don't know..."

Outwardly, I roll my eyes. But I have to admit to myself since I first saw Little Kat last month, I can't get her out of my head. She stunned me then and left an impression so deep, I haven't entertained another woman. I've left LEVELS New York unfulfilled.

So, yeah, I don't mind in the least working out of London and staying in Aberdeenshire. Both give me access to the redhead siren, who taunts me in my dreams. Not to mention the fact her less than enthusiastic reaction to me poses a challenge. It's rare a woman doesn't throw herself at me, or at the very least, displays a spark of interest.

Lachlan may be on to something more than he realizes.

* * *

"Ah, hello, Ms. Roberts. What keeps you late at the office?"

She yelps and spins around. Her tortoise-shell frame glasses slip down the bridge of her nose. A flush creeps across her cheeks as she presses a palm to her ample tits.

I raise an eyebrow questioningly.

"Oh, Mr. Steele. I—I didn't hear you. Excuse me," she says breathlessly.

The rise and fall of her chest distracts me.

She angles her body to showcase her curves fully. With a shy smile, she stares up at me from beneath her thick fringe of eyelashes.

"I was so caught up in my filing, I must have lost track of the time. What is the hour, Mr. Steele?" She responds. Her emerald green irises glint in the light.

I swallow around the sudden lump in my throat, then slide my suit jacket sleeve back to glance at my Audemars Piguet The Royal Oak Complication watch. Clearing my throat, I tell her it's half past seven.

Little Kat gasps and widens her eyes. Her breathing speeds up again and I find myself staring at the wall behind her to avoid ogling her heaving rack.

"Oh, my! Time sneaked up on me. I'll just finish up on Monday," she says, then pauses. "What brings you here, Mr. Steele? Might I help you with something?"

The inflection of her voice makes me wonder at a double meaning. I cock my head to the side and bring my eyes to hers.

"Well, since you asked so nicely, Mrs. Roberts, Mr. Jackson asked me to pick up something for him before I continue on to the castle," I respond. "I'll be sure to tell him how diligent you are in his absence."

Lachlan started his paternity leave and left Lydie in charge. Since she had a dinner meeting, I volunteered to bring files to him.

What a delightful surprise to find Little Kat.

"Thank you, but not necessary," she says with a smile as she leaves his office.

The scent of her perfume wafts through the air when she steps past me. Fascinated, I turn to watch as she struts to her desk. The loose-fitting skirt does nothing to hide the curves of her ass and hips as she bends over to retrieve her handbag and attaché from the bottom drawer.

"Mrs. Roberts," I call out.

She stands and faces me.

"Would you care to join me for a drink downstairs at Jackson Restaurant? I'll only be a moment," I ask, pinning her with an intense stare that leaves no room for argument.

Slowly, she blinks and brings her gaze back to mine. The tip of her little pink tongue pokes out to moisten her lush lips.

"Yes, that sounds lovely, Mr. Steele," Little Kat purrs.

My cock jumps. And expel the breath I didn't realize I was holding in.

"Mr. Steele is my father. Harris will do, Kat," I say thickly.

She nods and responds, "Harris, then. I just need to pop

into the ladies' room to freshen up, then will meet you by the lift. Good?"

"Indeed," I say. "Although you are *lovely*, Kat."

The scarlet flush reappears on her alabaster skin.

Briefly I muse if her round derriere will appear the same shade should I spank that ass.

She must sense my colorful thought since her cheeks deepen to crimson before she scampers away.

I chuckle wickedly and readjust my burgeoning erection, ready to poke a hole in my bespoke trousers.

Minutes later, I extend my elbow to her as we exit the elevator in the lobby. At this hour, the staff closed the lobby entrance for the restaurant. I lead Little Kat into the cool summer night to the main entrance.

While she was in the restroom, I called the host to reserve one of the high tables by a window in the bar. He shows us to our seats, and I help Little Kat into a tall leather and wrought-iron chair. She graces me with a beatific smile as she thanks me.

A server appears to take our order.

I'm surprised when she orders a neat Jackson Special Reserve Scotch. Impressed, I request one.

"Good choice, Mr.... Er... Harris," she says as her emerald eyes sparkle in the light of the candles on the table. "A man after my own heart."

I smirk and nod.

"A woman after mine," I counter as I give her a heated stare. "Now, what would you like to nosh? I wouldn't want you to think I'd get you drunk and take advantage of you."

Her tinkling laughter floats around us. The sound fills my heart with joy.

"Oh Harris, I would never think such a thing of a man like you. Despite you being a notorious billionaire playboy. Oh, no!" She scoffs gleefully.

Ouch, that stung.

So that's what Little Kat thinks of me? Hmmm. Not the best. But not the worse either, I suppose. But I need to change her perception of me in my way.

"Correction: multibillionaire, little lass. Is it so horrible I have no inkling to settle down? Does that make me a playboy? Really?" I question.

She pauses her answer as the server places our drinks in front of us and takes our food order. Once she steps away, Little Kat leans across the round table and pats my shoulder.

"Duly noted. I wouldn't say horrible. However, I would think it's unfulfilling to go from one woman to the next that never satisfies your heart and soul," she says. Then she sits back and adjusts the napkin on her lap. "But I do not judge you and your needs, Harris."

She glances up at me from beneath her thick eyelashes. Her eyes scan my face for a reaction.

It's a bit of a blow and not the response I expected. It certainly doesn't change her perception of me. At. All.

I bite my lower lip and nod.

"No worries. Perhaps I have not met the one woman who will satisfy me in every way?" I say, then pin her with an intense stare. "Or perhaps I have?"

I let the question hang in the surrounding air. A shift in the atmosphere heightens the sexual tension between us.

Little Kat likes her lips and swallows as her gaze drops to her lap again.

In a blink, she meets my stare with one of her own as she raises an elegantly arched eyebrow.

"By the end of this evening, we shall see," she rejoins.

Challenge accepted, Little Kat.

We spend the rest of our time asking about our families, favorite pastimes, and other getting to know you on a first date questions.

It strikes me in a not so unpleasant way that our time together indeed resembles a date and not a precursor to fucking. Not that I'd mind getting Little Kat writhing beneath me. The carnal sounds of her purrs and her moans amplified as I pound balls deep within her soaking wet pussy. My cock thumps in approval of the thought.

But like most first dates, tonight is not the time to shag my bonny lass.

However...

"Would you care to have dinner with me tomorrow evening, Kat?" I ask.

Once more, I stun her, and she blinks.

What seems like hours pass before she offers a shy smile and nods.

"That would be wonderful, Harris, thank you," she responds. A frown mars her beautiful face. "But aren't you headed to the castle now?"

I shrug and take the last sip of my Scotch.

"My plan will change if you're interested," I respond as I watch her over the rim of the Waterford Crystal snifter.

The liquid goes down as nicely as her response.

"Oh, I *am* interested, Harris," she purrs, then finishes her drink with a smile.

"Well, then, it's settled. Where shall I pick you up at eight?" I ask in a deep rumble.

She recites her address and phone number as I type them into my mobile.

After my driver and I drop Little Kat at home, he takes me back to STEELE Aberdeen. The door to my suite shuts, and I strip as I hasten to the shower. My aching cock can't wait another second for relief.

Warm water sluices over my tense muscles as I press my palms against the marble wall of the Roman shower. My head hangs with eyes closed as I drum up a vision of my Little Kat kneeling naked before me.

Her flaming red hair plastered to her head and down her back. Strands kiss the top of her ass. Long eyelashes spiked from the water cast shadows on her cheeks, pinkened by the steam. The enticing fragrance of her arousal and pheromones fill my nostrils as I take a deep inhalation. The scent imprinted on my brain.

My cock thickens and lengthens to jut proudly toward her lush lips, parted to allow its entry. I fist the base and stroke the velvet-covered steel shaft. A smirk spreads across my face as she watches my movements with emerald eyes darkened to malachite with carnal lust. I tap the mushroom tip against her mouth, and a drop of pre-cum falls to her bottom lip.

Her little tongue darts out to lick my essence into her mouth.

She hums and closes her eyes in bliss.

I groan.

"Open wide for me, Little Kat," I command. My voice gruff with desire.

Her eyes open, then narrow seductively as she does my bidding.

The wet warmth of her tongue wraps around my girth. She teases the vein on the underside with the flat of her tongue and hums in delight. A delicate hand cups my heavy balls and kneads them.

My hands slip into her tresses to cup the back of her head. Shifting my stance, I hold her head as I drive to the back of her throat with one snap of my hips. Her gag spurs me on.

"Open your throat for me, Little Kat. I want my bulge outlined in it," I growl.

She moans in response.

I slip deeper down her slim throat. It's a snug fit, but she works it with ease, accustomed to my demands.

"Make me cum, Little Kat," I command. "Swallow every single drop of what I give to you. Understand?"

She nods and hums as tears slip down her flushed cheeks. The slippery sounds of her taking every one of my ten inches echo around us. The rhythmic slapping of my balls to her chin reverberates off the marble. Her drool mixes with the water.

I throw my head back and bellow.

My release damn near knocks me to my knees. I slap the shower wall with one palm while the other jerks my cock viscously. Copious jets of cum shoot out of my angry purple cockhead to smatter against the marble. It drips to the floor.

"Every fucking drop, Little Kat," I growl.

The vision of her smiling up at me as the last of my jizz flows down her throat to fill her belly dances behind my closed eyelids.

I groan and press my sweaty forehead to the cool marble.

"Soon, Little Kat, my dreams will become our reality."

KAT

"Hi, Mum, I won't be able to come home this weekend after all... I know. I'm sorry. But I have an important dinner tonight... Work related—"

"What the bloody hell, Kat?! Ever since you got that hoity-toity job, you act like you're too good to spend time with your family! Now you have Mum all upset. Again!"

My mouth drops open at my older brother's rant. His accent thickens the more he goes on and on. Nothing new there.

Payton seethes since he lost another job and still lives at home with our mother's support. If he would do something with his bloody life like I have with mine, he wouldn't hate on me. Well, then again, he'd still find something to complain about and start a fight. As usual.

I'm sure he was counting on me bringing the cash I give to my mother each month. Without a doubt she gives him some, if not all, of it every. Single. Time. When I call her out on her charity to Payton with the money I earned, Mum uses the same excuses he does for his lack of work. The boss treated him poorly; his co-worker crashed the delivery van; the customer lied on him.

And here he is yelling at me for not coming home. Give me a bloody break!

But I haven't missed many of my monthly visits to Glasgow since I left home for school years ago. Do I enjoy being back in the little flat? Uh, no. I go because they're my family. The only one I have and the connection to them is important.

If only Payton would stop his madness.

"—Charlotte came home from university. You can't make it from work?! What? Your time is more valuable than any of ours?!"

"Zip it, Payton! If you'd get off *your* high horse, maybe you'd keep a *job* longer than four bloody days!" I snarl. "Now, give the phone back to Mum. Or. I. Will. Hang. Up."

Silence.

Heavy breathing.

A snarl.

"Who the bloody hell do you—"

"Enough, Payton Roberts… Kat, it's Mum. I just miss you, lass. But I understand. Come home when you can. We love you," my mother says.

I swallow around the tears that clog my throat.

"Sorry, Mum. I love you more than anything. It will be better soon. I promise. Talk to you next week," I whisper.

My fingertips swipe at the tears as they flow down my

flushed cheeks. I close my eyes and visualize how our lives will improve once I get the millions from Chet Stewart.

No more cleaning after rich families for my mother. I'll move her into a gorgeous flat and hire a maid to clean for her! Michael will study architecture in a formal university program. Charlotte won't have to work as a part-time server at a pub and as a tutor while she finishes her degree. Payton, well, he'll have to work and prove he will not squander money I'd give to him.

Me? I'll have the financial security I've always wanted and travel the world for a year. Unwind and do nothing but follow the sun. No worries.

A deep breath clears my head.

I open my Swiss bank app on my mobile and smile when I see the balance in my secret account. Chet was true to his word and deposited a lump sum of six figures when I delivered my last intel.

Jackson Corporation has a new launch for a Scotch blend the master distiller has worked on for the past sixty years. It's a limited-edition run in a custom hand-blown Lalique Crystal bottle with a storage box made of the most rare and most expensive African Blackwood. The price tag? A whopping one-million pounds.

Clearly, I couldn't get the recipe. But I was able to uncover the launch plans and other details Chet agreed were worth the hefty sum he paid to me. He didn't tell me how he plans to use the intel. Undoubtedly, he will use it to Stewart Scotch's advantage and sting Jackson Corporation.

Not my concern. Only the dollars matter, along with

the pleasure I derive from knowing he hurt that family makes a difference in my life.

I click the transfer confirmation button on the bank app to send the first of several deposits for the monthly money to my mother's account. To avoid a money trail, I set up increments that won't draw attention. Plus, the transactions go through quite a few channels after my account before they end up in hers. One can't be too careful.

With a sigh, I log out of the app and power off the mobile for my family and banking. I toss it onto the table. Later I'll put it back in the lockbox beneath the floorboards in the closet.

I pick up my everyday mobile and click the phone icon to call Isla. Oddly enough, what started as a ruse turned into a genuine friendship. I don't keep many friends— better to remain aloof. But find I enjoy spending time with Isla.

"Kat! How are you?" She asks after one ring.

A broad smile stretches across my face as I sit back on the sofa and tuck my legs beneath me to settle in for our chat.

"Good! How's everything with you? Tell me all about the babe's latest developments," I respond.

Isla gushes on about her new little family and the joys of motherhood. Her happiness is contagious. By the time we end our call, my disposition brightens, and the argument with Payton fades.

I head to the Aberdeen Children's Center for my

Saturday volunteer sessions. With the school year complete, fewer kids show on the weekend. But those who do still need us to spend time with them. Even more so since they must not have summer activities or time with their families to occupy them. Reminding me of myself at their ages. I love helping those kids even more.

By the time I return home, I need a shower after hours of kickball, potato sack races, hide and seek... Whatever they had in mind, we did it and then some. But it was just what I needed to keep my mind off dinner tonight with Harris Steele.

That man is a god.

Powerful, handsome, sexy AF.

But he's one with the enemy.

Yet the idea of him makes my nether region sing.

Ugh!

The steamy shower does nothing to wash that man out of my head. If anything, it makes me wonder what shower sex with him would be like. My back slams against the subway tile. Ankles crossed behind his firm ass. Screams pour from my gaping mouth as he pummels my pussy with his massive cock.

Fuck!

I slide my hand down the flat expanse of my belly. Fingers slip between my swollen lower lips. Moisture from my arousal coats them as they glide along my seam to pinch my engorged clit. The zing curls my toes. My other hand cups my heavy breast while my thumb and index finger tug the turgid nipple. A second finger joins the first as they fuck my tight, wet pussy in the way I imagine Harris Steele would with his dick.

A true wail bounces off the shower walls when my climax knocks me sideways.

I lean my shoulder against the tile. My pants puff the steam around my head as shudders wrack my limp body. I dial down the heat to cool off.

"You look lovely, Kat."

"Thank you, Harris," I respond as I glance down at my outfit.

Not sure of what to expect, I chose a wrap mini dress in lilac chiffon with tonal sequins and a plush velvet belt. The length accentuates my long, toned legs while the v-neck draws attention to my décolletage. The blouson sleeves and loose fit keep it classy. Paired with iridescent lilac slingbacks and a green clutch, the look can fit in any occasion.

I bring my eyes back to his and smile as I toss my hair over one shoulder and down my back. Not the style I wear for work. But this isn't work, is it? And if I want to hook this playboy, I need to bring it.

His heated stare confirms I did well with my selection.

"Come," he says.

We leave my flat with his hand on my lower back.

I note the possessive move and can't say it displeases me. At. All.

With a courteous dip of his head, the driver opens the back door of the Rolls-Royce sedan. I slip inside. My thighs slide along the supple leather seat. Violins from a classical music score flows from the high-quality sound system. An inhale fills my nose with the decadent scent of Harris' cologne. I close my eyes for a moment to revel in it.

"Are you all right?"

His deep baritone voice and the weight of his sizable hand on my bare thigh rouse me.

A slow smile spreads across my face.

"Yes," I respond.

"Good. I want you to enjoy yourself this evening," Harris murmurs as his dove gray eyes dilate. "I have plans for you."

A shiver makes my nipples poke against the fabric of my mini dress.

His eyes drop, and he licks his full lips.

I swallow thickly and nod.

Am I out of my depths with this one? Oh, do I hope so.

To steer the conversation to safer territory, I ask him about his choice of music. For the rest of the ride, our conversation stays away from riskier subjects. Yet the undercurrent of sexual tension hangs in the air.

The sedan pulls up in front of Moonfish Cafe on Correction Wynd—the popular one Michelin star restaurant. I've always wanted to eat here, but they have a notorious wait list for reservations. One needs to know someone to even sign on for a spot six months out. And here Harris invited me only last night. Of course, he'd get in with ease.

The valet opens the door, and Harris steps out. He reaches back inside to help me from the car.

I grin to myself when his eyes light on my thighs. With care, I keep them closed to avoid a snafu and slip from the seat. His powerful hand lifts me to my feet. I lean into him to catch another whiff of his masculine scent.

The maître d' glances up as we enter. She smiles in welcome at me. Then her dark brown eyes gleam when her gaze lands on Harris behind me.

"Mr. Steele, welcome to Moonfish Cafe, sir!" She gushes as her caramel cheeks flush. "Mr. McFarley told me to expect you. I'll show you to the sought-after table in the kitchen. You'll have the pleasure of watching the chef prepare your meal. Unless you require anything else, kindly follow me, sir."

She flutters her long eyelashes as she stares up at Harris.

I bite down on my molars to prevent a retort from escaping. Gratification comes when he squeezes my hip and tells her he's good.

As we pass through the restaurant, I notice other women ogle Harris. Some even seated with men of their own. The brazen hussies! Once again, he makes it all about me and disregards their blatant stares as he keeps his hand on my lower back. It doesn't hurt some men turn to gaze at me. Vindicated, I raise my head high and sashay behind the hostess.

"Steele! Good to see you again, mate."

A man with a full beard, wire-rimmed spectacles, and

shoulder-length hair approaches us as we enter the bustling kitchen. So captivated by the tantalizing aromas, I almost missed him.

"McFarley! I didn't expect to see you tonight. How's your beautiful Edith?" Harris asks as the two men bro hug.

They exchange pleasantries before Harris introduces me as his date.

Butterflies swirl in my belly, and I barely hear the owner of Moonfish Cafe tell us he has a tasting menu the chef designed for our dinner. The fact I'm on a date with one of the world's richest bachelors excites me more than I care to admit. It makes my focus on using Harris more complicated. However, pretending to be attracted to him will be super easy.

I start to admonish myself but decide to give in to the moment and bask in the benefits of being on the arm of a man like Harris Steele. And being the focus of his attention. As I am now with him staring into my eyes intently.

"Have you been here before, Kat?" He asks as he extends his hand across the table.

I place mine within his and shake my head.

"Never. It's impossible… Well, not for you apparently," I start with a giggle. "It's been on my list for a while. Thank you for bringing me here."

Harris rubs his thumb over my inner wrist.

The sensual touch causes goosebumps to scatter across my skin. I bite my lower lip and glance up at him through my eyelashes.

His eyes flash like lightning, then narrow in on my mouth.

Purposefully, I let my lip pop out from between my teeth and flick my tongue across it.

A growl rumbles deep in his chest.

"What you do to me, Siren," Harris says gruffly.

He brings my palm to his mouth and kisses it. His eyes never leave my face.

"Tell me," I say, suddenly bold from his attraction to me.

He lowers his eyelids, and the lashes—long and thick enough to make women jealous—fan across the tops of his cheeks. When he raises his gaze back to mine, his hooded eyes reveal more than words could ever convey.

The chef appears, and Harris lets go of my hand.

The loss of contact makes me sigh.

While the chef explains the dishes and accompanying wines, Harris locks his eyes on me with a carnal stare. He's more interested in devouring me than any item the chef offers. Harris nods his head and licks his lips. Nothing and no one disrupts his stare.

The attention unsettles me in a good way. My pussy clenches, and I have to shift in my chair, concerned my thong may not provide enough coverage to prevent a damp spot. I avert my gaze to the chef.

Not to be denied, Harris uses the top of his shoe to snag my calf. He lifts my leg until his hand catches it. Deft fingers knead the muscles.

I bite back a groan of pleasure.

When he slips my slingback off and runs his knuckles

along my instep, a gasp escapes my mouth. I bring my wineglass to my lips as cover. He smirks wolfishly.

The chef leaves us.

"Ready for a delicious meal, Siren?" Harris asks in a sinfully deep timbre. "Or shall we skip to dessert?"

I choke on my sip of wine.

Real cool, Kat Roberts…

He rises in a flash and uses his napkin to dab at the liquid on my chest.

My nipples pebble to the point of pain.

"Careful, Siren. We want you at full capacity," he says as he crouches at eye level.

I swallow.

"I'm fine, thank you," I whisper.

"Indeed you are, Siren," he murmurs.

I watch as he returns to his seat.

Our server brings another linen napkin to him and offers a glass of seltzer for me to clean the wine from my mini dress.

Another server sets our first course before us.

I glance across to Harris for a clue.

If he lifts his fork, I will too. But if he wants dessert, I am all for it.

Disappointment washes over me when he places the napkin in his lap and reaches for his knife and fork.

Darn…

Throughout the meal, erotic energy pulsates between us. To heighten the attraction, I moan around a forkful of Thai Prawns with Miso Brown Rice. His nostrils flare.

"Come," Harris says as he pushes his chair back from the table.

I arch an eyebrow.

He extends his hand.

I take it and rise.

He pulls me onto his lap, uncaring of those around us as they move about the kitchen. I no longer care about them when the massive bulge of his erection presses against the curve of my hip. He purrs in my ear.

"I want to feel the vibration of your moans as I feed you, Siren," he states.

My head jerks, and my mouth gapes.

He takes advantage of my surprise and pops a morsel of his steak into my mouth. The juices dribble from his fingertips to my lip. He leans forward and licks the drops off. With a groan, he nips my lower lip.

"Even more succulent," he purrs.

Surprise turns to shock, and my mouth remains agape.

Harris chuckles wickedly. His fingertips come below my chin and press up to close my mouth. As I chew, his thumb brushes my lips while his eyes bore into mine.

"Good, girl," he says in a smokey voice.

I mewl.

Harris continues to feed me from both of our plates until I'm too full. Then he finishes what I left and brings his fingers to my mouth for me to lick them clean. All the while, I sit on his lap.

The servers clear our plates, and the chef returns to present the dessert.

Too enthralled with each other to hear the details, Harris and I listen barely. His hand rests beneath the hem of my mini dress with his fingertips grazing my inner thigh. When the chef finishes, Harris spoons some of the dessert into my mouth. The erotic feeding continues between sips of Jackson Scotch.

"Satisfied, Siren?" Harris asks when we finish.

"Yes, thank you," I reply, my voice low and throaty.

"Excellent," he says. "Let us get you home."

Once again, my mouth falls open.

Home? What the bloody hell?

He wound my body tighter than a gnat's chuff!

Harris chuckles, and I realize I spoke aloud.

I drop my head to his shoulder and groan in embarrassment.

"Thank you for a lovely evening," he murmurs with his lips pressed to my hair. "Will you have dinner with me next Friday? I promise I will make it worth your while, Siren."

Despite the disappointment of not having him pound my pussy with the monster against my hip, a thrill runs through me at his proposal. Even though a week seems so far away… I understand he works in London, so I'll deal.

I raise my head and smile.

"I had a lovely evening too and look forward to your promise, Harris Steele," I respond.

HARRIS

"Now, do tell me what restaurant requires us to board a helicopter, Harris?"

I grin like the Cheshire Cat at Little Kat as she approaches me atop STEELE Aberdeen.

Her eyebrow quirks up as she cocks her head to the side. Emerald eyes glint with excitement.

"The kind that takes longer to get to than a drive in the car," I reply. Then I take her elbow to guide her to the open door of Lachlan's Sikorsky S-92 Executive Helicopter. "Hop aboard, Siren."

She returns my grin with a dazzling one of her own as she climbs the steps.

I hated ending our first date without her writhing beneath me. But I wanted to gauge her reaction to my advances. If she rebuked them, then we wouldn't go any further. Except I know for a fact I wouldn't give up so easily.

This woman intrigues me like no other.

Not only does she stay on my mind, a sense of loss when we're apart overtakes me. I shake my head as I recall Baz telling me when I fall, I'll fall hard, just like he did for Lola after one glance. At the time, I scoffed at his declaration. Now, I wonder.

The dinner last week was a good barometer. She blossomed from a demure librarian to a sexy AF Siren. That dress was a hot number. She even ditched the eyeglasses. A complete 180. Her body so responsive, she warmed beneath my touch and ate from my hand like a baby bird. By the end of our night, I struggled to leave her at the flat's doorstep.

This time—little does My Siren know it's not just for dinner, but for the entire weekend—will push it to the limits. No holds or positions barred. If we end up wanting more of each other after this tryst, we're golden.

One thing I learned from my brothers and from my twin, the heart always knows when it comes to love.

Love?

Well, maybe I won't go that far just yet. But it is one step—the first of many, many more—away from my playboy card for sure. I've never felt so inclined with any other woman. So I'll give it a chance to unfold.

To repeat Roger: *Hey, you never know...*

"The pilot is ready for lift off when you are, Mr. Steele."

The flight attendant's comment brings me back to the cabin.

I glance at Kat beside me in a leather captain's chair.

She smiles, and I turn to the flight attendant with an affirmative nod. He leaves us and closes the privacy door that separates the crew from the passengers.

"Where are we headed?" Kat asks as she glances out the window at Aberdeen below.

"It's a surprise," I reply, waggling my eyebrows. "So sit back and enjoy the stunning view. I certainly intend to do so."

Her alabaster cheeks blush.

I brush my thumb over one. She has the softest silky skin.

She closes her eyes and leans into my touch with a sigh.

"Okay, you got me," My Siren whispers.

Little does she know.

"Holy cow! Are you serious with me right now? This is much more than a car ride, Harris!"

If I thought Kat's emerald eyes bugged out when the helicopter landed beside my Gulfstream G650ER private jet at Aberdeen International Airport, they damn near fall out at Jersey Airport.

Since I couldn't reveal my intention to fly her away for the weekend, I had to opt for a destination that would not require her to present a passport. Not officially a part of the UK, the Bailiwick of Jersey is one of the Channel Islands known as a Crown Dependency. Situated in the English Channel between the UK and France, Jersey offers the perfect weekend retreat.

Plus, it has STEELE Jersey, a five-star restored manor house built in the fourteenth century. A boutique property comprising only twenty rooms and suites set on twenty pristine acres with gardens, swimming pool, tennis court, and spa. Guests can charter its luxury yacht to cruise the English Channel. STEELE Jersey provides an ideal intimate—dare I say—romantic escape.

One can never say Harris Steele doesn't know how to charm a woman.

Except this woman scowls at me.

"I assumed we were going far, but to another country?!" Kat screeches as she jabs a finger at the airport signage.

"Well, you know the old adage about when you *assume*. And what a bonny ass I see," I reply with a smirk.

She spins and shoots emerald daggers at me. Her arms fold beneath her tits, and they jiggle under her silk pussy bow blouse when she stomps her foot.

How cute.

Since she arrived straight from the office, she's back in her librarian garb.

I'll soon divest her of the suit. That is, after a bit of role play.

"Is it really so bad to spend the weekend with me, Kat?" I ask with an arched eyebrow.

A flurry of emotions blankets her face. Her eyes dart from me to the jet and back. Teeth worry her lower lip.

I wait. The decision is hers.

She nods her head.

"Words, Kat. I will have your words," I say.

Her eyes widen at my command.

"Y—Y—Yes, Sir," she stammers.

Now I nod my head.

"Not Sir, Kat. I'm an Alpha male but not a Dom. And you, lass, are no sub," I correct her. "Let's get going. I am starved…"

Her cheeks turn crimson, and she agrees, verbally. Good girl.

I take her hand and lead her to the awaiting platinum Rolls-Royce Wraith convertible with white leather interior.

She slips inside when I open the passenger door. Then grabs my hand as I step away.

"Thank you, Harris. It's a wonderful surprise," Kat says softly.

I lean over and slant my mouth over hers. My tongue flicks inside as she gasps. It sweeps around to gather her flavor—buttery and malty flavors of Scotch—before her tongue dances with mine.

We groan in unison.

My hand cups the back of her head to angle it for a deeper kiss. Electricity shoots through our connection. The pent-up passion flares hot.

"Taste so sweet," I murmur against her plump lips.

She mewls and laps at my mouth like a kitten.

Kitty Kat.

I may not be a Dom. But I wouldn't mind my diamond collar around her graceful neck.

My Kitty Kat. Mine!

I nip her lip and rise.

Blown pupils stare up at me as she sucks the bite.

A feral growl falls from my mouth.

The ride to STEELE Jersey can't end fast enough. The entire time, my erect ten inches tents my trousers. I keep Kat's hand on my thigh with her pinky finger resting against the base of my pole. She doesn't squirm.

So far, so good.

The general manager meets us in the lobby to escort us to the Lord's Suite. Situated on the manor's grounds, it's a private stone cottage with two bedrooms with en suite bathrooms and closets of new clothes for us, a lounge, and a kitchen. Panoramic views of the gardens and of the English Channel lie beyond the mullioned windows. The cottage will serve as our own little world. A hideaway within the retreat.

"Oh, Harris! So gorgeous," My Kitty Kat exclaims.

I cock an eyebrow and retort, "Why thank ye, lass. I am a bonny lad."

She giggles and swats my arm as she shakes her head.

"I mean the cottage, silly!" She says, then winks. "However, Harris Steele, I agree you are a bonny lad."

The general manager chuckles.

I forgot he was still here. A quick thank you, and he's gone.

Alone. At last.

I prowl towards My Kitty Kat. The wolf and the cat face off. I growl as I pull her into my arms and cover her mouth with mine.

She melds her soft, curvy body against my hard,

muscular frame. A purr vibrates from between her kiss-swollen lips when I suck on her tongue.

"Tell me. What do you want, Kitty Kat?" I growl.

"You, Harris. Only you," she breathes.

I sweep her from her feet and carry her to the primary bedroom. My heart pounds with each step. Without a doubt, she must feel its rapid beat against her pillowy tits.

Beside the king-size bed, I let her slide down my body until she lands on her feet. My hands glide along her flanks to rest at her hips. Once again, I devour her mouth. Her hungry moans spur me on. My fingers dig into the soft flesh.

"I want you. I crave you, Kitty Kat," I utter in a hoarse whisper, barely audible.

She shudders. Her tits jiggle against my chest.

"Please," she cries.

Deftly, I disrobe her and toss the offensive garments to the side. No time for role play tonight. I want to bury myself balls deep within My Siren. Librarian be damned.

Bared before me, My Siren takes my breath away.

Luscious DD-cup tits tipped with rosy pink distended nipples make my mouth water. The flat expanse of her belly leads to a smooth mound. Pussy lips drip with her juices as her engorged clit peeks from between them. Grip-worthy hips add to her hourglass figure. Long, toned legs beg to wrap around my hips and lock at the slim ankles. Even the fire-engine red polish on her toenails calls to me.

Her siren song plays in my ears.

MINE!

I take her mouth in a savage kiss to conquer her once and for all. The searing kiss ends, and I nip, lick, and suck my way down her throat. She swallows, and the sensation sparks against my lips. My head dips to one plump nipple. I engulf it. Then suck. Hard.

She groans from the pain-tinged pleasure and bows her back. Pushing her tit deeper into my hungry mouth.

I want to fuck her until I can't walk. Until I'm blinded by my orgasm, and I pass out.

My Siren must sense my need and tears at my suit jacket. The buttons of my custom dress shirt scatter to the hardwood floor as she rends the front in two. It hangs open, only held together by the cuff links at the sleeves. Her tiny fingers tug at my belt and zipper until my rock-hard cock bounces free to thump against my eight-pack abs.

Pre-cum dribbles from its purple tip.

"Oh my God, you're huge!" She pants. "I—I don't know if you'll fit. I—I haven't had sex in a while—"

My mouth descends on hers to stop her babbling. I possess every inch of her mouth until she sighs and leans against me heavily.

I lift her up and toss her onto the bed where she bounces amongst the countless fluffy pillows. With my eyes on hers, I toe off my Oxfords, remove my cufflinks, and rip the rest of my shirt off. My trousers follow it to the floor.

One knee plants on the bed as I reach over and grasp her ankles.

"Spread your legs for me, My Siren," I demand.

They fall open to reveal her engorged clit and the glistening pink petals of her pussy. Her juices coat her inner thighs.

I descend on her bounty.

My tongue, teeth, and fingers coax three orgasms from My Siren before I deem her ready to take my length and girth. I want her sore from my fucking. But not in pain.

I kiss my way up her body until our mouths meet again. I make My Siren taste her pussy juices still fresh in my mouth as I drive my tongue between her slack lips.

She moans and sucks the musky flavor.

My hips settle between her thighs, and my forearms frame her gorgeous face flushed from her erotic pleasure. I cradle her head against my palms. Otherwise, my first thrust will send her flying towards the headboard. I. Want. Her. Bad.

My tip notches to her core.

"Open up and let me in, My Siren," I command.

She trembles but relaxes beneath me.

I surge forward with a snap of my hips.

One thrust impales her on my condom-covered dick.

She wails at the massive invasion.

My hips still to allow her pussy to adjust to my size. I cover her face and mouth with hungry kisses to urge her body to accept me.

The soft yielding of her core intoxicates me.

I shift position to lower my hands beneath her round

ass. Each one grasps a butt cheek to hold her steady for the impending fucking.

"Look at me, My Siren," I growl. "I want to see your eyes as you cum all over my cock. Do not look away for a second."

She whimpers. But her hooded eyes focus on mine.

My hips draw back until only my cockhead breaches inside her pussy. Then I ram my dick forward to the very end of her core. The sensation of possessing My Siren fully makes my eyes roll back in my head.

A long. low groan falls from my slack mouth.

"Fuuuck… You feel so good. So… tight… So wet," I rasp.

"Oh God, Harris… Oooh…" she wails and stiffens.

The first flutter of her pussy along my length signals her fourth orgasm. Her inner walls clamp down on my cock in a vise-like grip.

I grunt and begin to piston my hungry cock in and out of her creamy core. Time stands still as my dick stretches and fills her tight pussy. I open my eyes to stare down at her as my fingers dig into her lush ass to hold her just so.

"I can feel how you respond to me, My Siren. So willing and so soaking wet," I grunt between thrusts.

She shudders and cries out in wild abandon as another orgasm rips through her quivering pussy.

"YEEESSS!" I roar as I pummel her again and again, chasing an epic release.

My knees dig into the mattress to gain purchase. One hand lifts to grip the back of her neck and lift her torso to my chest. Her flaming red hair falls around us like a curtain as she holds on to my shoulders. My pelvis punches up.

Deeper.

Deeper.

Deeper.

"Unh… Unh… Unh…" I grunt.

A zing races down my spine. My heavy balls draw up.

When my release is upon me, I throw my head back and roar.

"MINE!!!"

HARRIS

"**G**ood morning, Kat."

She moans as I cup her swollen mons and press my front against her back.

I know she's sore. Over the course of the night, I fucked her again, fed her, then woke her up to fuck her twice more. As expected, she barred no positions. My Kitty Kat has a well-used pussy.

My fingers play with her clit. The sensitive bud still responds to my touch as it blossoms. I stroke it gently with my thumb while my index finger caresses her puffy seam.

Despite my hard rides, My Kitty Kat arches her back and plunges her fingers into my hair. She tugs, and I groan. Her head turns to seek my mouth.

I oblige her unspoken request with a slow-burning kiss. Her moans get swallowed up as I stroke her tongue with mine. I play with her some more but won't take her again. Not yet.

"Come. Time for a nice warm soak," I say as I press a kiss to the side of her neck.

She tilts her head to give me better access, and I give her more kisses before I smack her ass and rise from the bed.

I chuckle at the sight of the tangled sheets, then at the comforter with most of the pillows on the toppled to the floor. I make a mental note to call for housekeeping for fresh linens. We need our nest ready for the next bout of mind-blowing sex.

"Mmmm… That sounds lovely. I hope they have some essential oils," Kat says as she stretches her arms overhead and arches her back.

My eyes jump to her DDs. The puckered nipples call to me. I lick my lips but shake my head. Not now.

I toss her over my shoulder and carry her into the en suite bathroom.

She giggles and slaps at my ass. Her tiny fists bounce off the firm muscles. I flex them to give her a show. She can thank their power for the multiple orgasms she screamed from all night long.

Bending my knees, I place her atop a vanity, then turn to the oversized antique copper tub. A shelf has an assortment of oils and salts. Perfect.

"What do you prefer? Lavender, ylang ylang, bergamot, lemon?" I ask.

Kat hops down and stands beside me. Her head reaches my shoulder barely.

"Let's mix lemon with bergamot. I need a pick-me-up

after that sex marathon!" She exclaims with a laugh and nudges my side.

I kiss the top of her head and chuckle.

While the tub fills, we brush our teeth, and she combs her hair into a topknot. My fingers never stopped running through them. Talk about bedhead.

She purrs like a satisfied kitten as I bathe her. Then I loosen her hair to wash and condition the long fiery tresses. Afterwards, she insists upon washing me—not that I complain.

We tear into breakfast like starved animals. Only the sounds of her moans fill the cottage. And bring my cock roaring back to life. When our platters of sausage links, bacon, and pastries sit empty alongside the carafe of freshly squeezed orange juice, I sit back and smile at Kat.

"I appreciate a woman with a hearty appetite," I say.

Her gaze turns to the window, and she slips the napkin off her lap.

Fuck! Did I embarrass her? She doesn't strike me as the type of woman who gets upset with whatever she does.

"Hey," I say as I reach across the table for her hand. "I didn't mean to offend you, Kat. You have a banging body, babe."

For a moment, my hand hangs in the air. When she glances at it and puts her hand in mine, the breath I didn't realize I was holding escapes with a sigh of relief.

"No, you didn't offend me, Harris," she says as she squeezes my hand. "From a child, I've always eaten whatever I was given. Nothing wasted…"

Kat trails off and rises from her seat.

I tug her hand to bring her attention back to me.

"You haven't told me much about your family. I'd like to know more. Do you have siblings? What about your parents?" I ask.

She's shared her school years, work, and volunteering with Isla. But nothing about her family. I didn't want to pry since I know from my Mom and Aunt Lucie family isn't always close. Now, with Kat mentioning her mother, I'd like to learn that side of her life.

She ducks her head, and her hair slides over her face, effectively blocking it from my view.

I push my chair back and pull her onto my lap. My fingertips brush her tresses behind her ears, and I cup her chin. At eye level, she can't hide from me.

She squirms but stops when I cock an eyebrow and growl.

With a sigh, Kat stares out at the English Channel.

I wait.

"I prefer not to speak about my family, Harris. A drunk killed my father and mother in a car accident. It's just me. Okay?" She says as her lower lip wobbles and tears glaze her eyes.

This is worse than the food gaffe. No wonder she doesn't talk about her life before university. My Kitty Kat is all alone.

I band my arms around her, pulling Kat flush to my chest. My lips kiss the tears away. But I can do more to ease her sorrow.

I cup her ass and rise to carry her back to the bedroom. Not for a sex marathon, rather for gentle lovemaking.

* * *

"How phenomenal, Harris!"

As the wind whips Kat's hair, she clings to the railing on the port side of the yacht as it cuts through the waves. Salty sprays fly back and sparkle like diamonds in the summer sun. The receding coastline of Guernsey forms the backdrop of Kat's elated visage.

It's our last day, and I want to make it extra special. After two days holed up in our little world, I chartered STEELE Jersey's yacht to take us island hopping in the Channel. We motored by the uninhabited islands of Jersey and head to the Bailiwick of Guernsey and its outlying islands of Herm, Jethou, and Lihou.

The chef prepared local favorites and fresh seafood, including the delicacy ormer. A selection of wines accompanied each dish for perfect pairings. Crème brûlée and an assortment of fruit for dessert rounded out the delicious meal.

"I don't want to leave. Ever!" Kat exclaims.

Her tinkling laughter makes my heart swell.

So much better than her moment of sadness when she spoke of her family.

I shudder at the thought of losing mine. It must be hard as fuck for her all alone. Holidays, birthdays, celebrations of accomplishments. They didn't even get to see her graduate university. Damn.

The situation reminds me of Lola and her parents. I make a note to tell my sister when Kat meets my family.

Meet my family? Um.

"Would you care for some tea and scones, Mr. Steele?"

The steward's question breaks through my thoughts.

I drag my gaze from Kat to the crew member.

The woman preens with her enhanced tits pushed out beneath her fitted polo shirt as she flashes me with a dazzling white smile.

"Or something else to your liking, Sir," she purrs as her fingertips skate along the hemline of her thigh-grazing skirt.

"I—"

"We are fine. You may go below deck. Now."

My head jerks to my left.

Emerald daggers shoot out at the steward. She flinches at Kat's biting command before she scurries away without another glance at me.

Hmmm… My Kitty Kat's claws came out. Meow!

She flicks her gaze at me. Eyes narrow to gauge my reaction to the steward's advances. When I grin, Kat purses her lips and folds her arms beneath her tits—way better and natural.

"Find something amusing, Mr. Steele?" She snarls.

I tug her onto my lap and kiss her silly.

The only response necessary.

. . .

DURING OUR RETURN FLIGHT, Kat slumbers with her head against my shoulder. She didn't want to sleep in the bedroom since we're airborne for a little over an hour.

I can't blame her since we gave the cottage an explosive going away party. My cock throbs at the memory.

To prevent a full-blown—no pun intended—dick, I open my laptop to work on some code. No better way to stave off an erection than data structures, syntax, variables, blah, blah, blah. Soon I'm immersed in my second favorite pastime.

The running joke is how Haley and I speak English, French, and code. Yup, the Dynamic Duo through and through.

I chuckle to myself and get back to my business.

As the lights come up to prepare for landing, I notice in the reflection of my screen Kat's eyes open as she stares at my work. For a moment, it strikes me as odd she didn't move or speak up when she woke. Only sat in silence. I'm not sure for how long.

But I shrug it off when she lifts her head and stretches her arms. The move bares the creamy skin of her belly as the midriff top rises above the waistband of her skin-tight jeans. I run my index finger along the patch of skin, and she giggles.

Her arms drape around my shoulders as she slants her mouth over mine for a searing kiss. Soft moans stir my cock again.

Sadly, the pilot announces the time to buckle up for

landing. Otherwise, My Siren and I would have made the Mile High Club.

"Oh, well, Mr. Steele," she purrs as she sits back and inserts the tongue into the buckle.

I'd like to insert my tongue into her tight sheath.

Once we step out of my jet at Aberdeen International Airport and spy the Rolls-Royce sedan with the driver beside it and STEELE London's Sikorsky waiting for us, reality sets in.

Our weekend rendezvous ends.

Kat will ride home, and I'll board the helicopter for London.

We haven't discussed when we'll see each other again.

I glance down at her, and she's biting her lower lip, eyebrows pinched. I cup her chin to bring her gaze to mine.

"Hey, I hope you had fun," I say as the pad of my thumb frees her lip. "I did. Thank you for giving me a chance."

She sucks my thumb into her mouth.

I groan from the wet warmth.

She pops it out and peeps up at me from beneath the thick fringe of her eyelashes.

"Thank you, Harris, for the best weekend of my life," she whispers. "I'd give you another chance if you let me."

Hell. Yeah.

I lean over and capture her mouth with mine. All the passion we shared over the weekend comes out in a blistering kiss.

We groan, and she rises on her toes to grab fistfuls of

my hair. The erotic pain shoots straight to my semi. In seconds, it's fully erect.

I pull her into my embrace and bend my knees to align our pelvises. Mine grinds into hers to prove just how much I'd give her another chance.

When we come up for a breath, panting heavily, I press my forehead to hers and breathe her air.

"I have to go to Thailand for business Thursday and Friday. Will you join me after work? I'll send my jet back for you," I say.

My Siren squeals and tightens her grip on my hair as she bounces on the balls of her feet.

"Ouch!" I yowl.

Kisses pepper my face as she strokes my head.

"I take that as a yes?" I chuckle between kisses.

"Absolutely!" She squeals.

I give My Siren another kiss, then walk her to the Rolls-Royce.

She hugs me tightly with her face pressed against my chest. A parting kiss, and she slips onto the back seat.

I close the door and wave as the sedan drives off.

As Baz said, the harder I'll fall.

KAT

"Kat, I want you to know your work pleases me. Despite Mr. Jackson being out on paternity leave for a month, you maintain your duties, and accept more responsibility from me. I relayed my sentiments to him, and he agrees you've become an asset to Jackson Corporation quickly. We upped your clearance level to give you access to information I may need posthaste..."

I sit stunned before Lydie Jackson.

When she called me into her offices, I feared the worse. Especially with the Head of Security seated in the guest chair. My steps faltered as I entered. I assumed the worse.

The Shark breaches the surface for the kill.

Duuuunnnn duun... duuunnnnnnnn dun dun plays in my head.

Inwardly, I sigh in relief as I plaster a smile on my face and thank her. Then my grin spreads as I realize the intel now available at my fingertips. However, I must place my steps carefully. No way do I want blowback.

Strategies formulate in my mind. I can use the excuse of familiarizing myself with the information as I glean viable intel for Chet. Done in stages to prevent unwanted attention. Perhaps over a month or two works best.

Hell yeah, Kat Roberts!

"My administrative assistant has the day off tomorrow. I want you to sit in on my meeting with Lars Gustave, our Head of Technology. My admin added the event to your calendar," Lydie says.

This just gets better and better.

I accept the invite and my updated security pass. As I leave Lydie's offices, my buoyant step carries me back to my desk.

With Gladys in only three times a week until Mr. Jackson's return—she's still paid in full, talk about perks—our area stays quiet. Perfect for me to check out my new access without interruption or a questioning glance.

I reboot my laptop to allow the settings to change. Once loaded, my fingertips fly across the screen. This first glance serves to provide an overall view of what I can access. And it's a lot. A whole lot. Clearly, not at a super-high level. But enough to offer Chet intel in exchange for big bucks.

An alert sounds for a staff birthday party. A quick glance at my clock reveals lunchtime. I perused for over two hours! Reluctantly, I log out.

My attendance at the party and at other social gatherings—baby showers, wedding engagements—keeps my ruse strong. Who would suspect the quiet librarian-type who gives hand-knitted blankets as the culprit?

I stand and push my glasses—not a prop—up the bridge of my nose. Then pick up the bag with the knit scarf gift from my closet. A glance around confirms all is in order before I leave Mr. Jackson's offices suite for the conference room downstairs.

"HOW WAS your first day back after the weekend? Able to sit okay? Or do you still feel my cock deep inside of you, Siren? The sting of my palm on that round ass?"

Even over the line, Harris makes my face heat with his naughty words.

Sure, I've had sex before. But not one guy compares to Harris' virility. The man is definitely an unstoppable, insatiable god. The way he makes my body thrum and draws out orgasm after spine-tingling orgasm speaks to his skills. Fingers, hands, lips, tongue, and above all, his ginormous dick.

Oh, my!

My eyes flutter closed as my empty pussy clenches.

What Harris Steele does to me… Exquisite.

"—tell me you're thinking about me. Right. Now."

I missed the first part of his words, so busy reliving our weekend fuckfest. My heart races.

"Most certainly. And yes, you left quite an impression on my ravaged pussy and on my sore ass. Not to mention my throat," I respond. Another flash of heat sweeps over my body at the memories.

Harris chuckles wickedly.

"Nice to hear," he responds, then he continues in a deep baritone. "Do you want me inside of you now, Siren?"

I squirm on my sofa and nod.

"Absolutely," I purr.

My nipples pebble and heat floods my core. I squeeze my pussy walls for a modicum of relief.

"Ah, ah, ah," Harris says.

Like a misbehaved lass caught by the teacher, I sit up straight and widen my thighs.

"I want you hot and needy for me this weekend. Do not touch my pussy. Do not use the spray from a shower head. Do not seek any form of relief. And most definitely, do. Not. Cum. Understood?" He states.

And he says he's not a Dom…

Yet like a sub, I comply.

"Yes," I whisper.

"Good girl," Harris says. "Now, I have the logistics for you…"

I can barely listen to his instructions since he made me so hot for him.

All I want is to jump in bed with my trusty BOB— Battery Operated Boyfriend. Not that the toy can replace the mushroom head and the thick, long, veiny shaft of Harris' beautiful cock. Even his sac of heavy balls is a work of art. Better than Michelangelo's David for sure—and a helluva lot bigger. Again, a total god. Adonis. Apollo. A deity of pure masculine beauty.

"—the sky turned green."

I jerk my head back and frown. Whaaat???

Harris snickers.

"You are not listening to a word that comes out of my mouth, Kitty Kat," he admonishes. "What's on your mind, little lass?"

I smile at his flawless execution of a Scottish lilt. I exaggerate mine.

"You, Harris Steele. You taunt and you tease me. What's a wee lass to do?" I respond, ending in a giggle.

Silence.

I shift in my seat and stare at the mobile screen, wondering if I lost the call. No, he's still there.

"Har—"

FaceTime rings on my mobile. I accept the video call. Harris' face fills the screen.

Did I say gorgeous? Damn.

"Go to your bedroom. Strip. Lie down in the center of your bed. Legs spread wide. Prop the mobile between them," he commands.

I blink.

"Now," he adds with an arched eyebrow.

I hasten to do his bidding. My pulse quickens, and my body tingles. In position, I await his next command as I hold my breath in anticipation. His demanding tone has my pussy juices dripping to the sheets beneath my ass. The mobile rests against the bunched-up duvet.

My pussy and my puckered hole on full display for his wolfish, dove gray turned obsidian eyes. A shudder wracks my body.

"Good girl," he purrs. "So beautiful. Pink and wet. Show me what you want to do as you think about me fucking that greedy little pussy raw."

My mouth falls open.

"Do not turn shy now, Siren," he rumbles. "Show me. Or you will not cum until Friday. If at all…"

My eyes widen. But I settle back on my forearms and close my eyes.

"No. Eyes on me the entire time," Harris commands.

They fly open and stare straight into his hooded feral gaze. I moisten my lower lip with the tip of my tongue.

He groans.

I pile pillows behind me to keep my head propped up and my gaze on his. Then resettle into position. Ready to give Harris a proper show.

One hand reaches up to cup my heavy breast. Fingers knead the mound and tug at the turgid nipple. I cry out. The other hand glides up my belly to tease the untouched nipple. The palm strokes the sensitive bud. Thumb and forefinger pinch it to bring it to a point.

My hips lift from the bed as his pussy contracts from the erotic zing.

Both hands lift to my mouth, and I suck on the fingers. Suitably moistened, they pinch and twist my peaked nipples to mimic Harris' mouth and teeth. I throw my head back and moan lustily.

He growls, and I return my hooded gaze to his.

Once again, I moisten my fingers. This time, they slide in and out to the knuckle. I twirl my tongue around them and pull the wet digits out of my mouth with a pop.

Harris groans and tucks his full bottom lip between his teeth.

I purr seductively with half-closed eyes.

The fingers slither down my flat belly to the bare mound. They cup my sex and come away dripping. I bring them to my mouth and suck. Hard.

"Fuuuuckk," Harris breathes out as he shakes his head.

The fingers slip back to his pussy and pinch the labia. I groan as they part and skim across his engorged clit. My hips buck again. The heels of my feet dig into the mattress as I widen my legs. First one, then another finger slides inside of his pussy, knuckle after knuckle. Fully seated, they stroke his inner walls and tease the sensitive G-spot.

Unable to keep my eyes open, I thrash my head from side to side and cry out in wild abandon as a climax sneaks up on me. His pussy pulsates around the buried fingers, clamping down on them like a vise.

"Do. Not. Stop!"

Harris' command comes with the sound of skin on skin as his hand jacks off his cock. Heavy breathing and grunts sound through my mobile speakers.

"Oh, Harris!" I wail as fingers plow into his clenching pussy.

Another climax rips through me when the other fingers

pinch his clit. My back bows from the bed. Sweat dampens my flushed skin. I keen.

My thighs quiver, and my feet slide against the sheets, unable to hold my limp form. My chest heaves with each pant from my agape mouth.

"KAAAT!!!"

Harris' roar breaks through my orgasm-induced coma.

With hazy vision, I lift my head from the pillows and glance at the mobile. Not in sight. I drag myself up and rifle through the strewn sheets and duvet until my fingers grasp the device. Harris' half-mast eyes stare back at me from his flushed face. We gaze at one another, unable to use our motor skills just yet. Still caught in the erotic rapture.

He's the first to speak.

"No more orgasms for you until Friday. Good night, Kitty Kat," Harris murmurs.

An incoherent mumble falls from my mouth as I roll over into a fetal position. Exhausted, sleep takes me as soon as my eyelids close. The pleasant thought of seeing Harris wraps me in a blissful cocoon.

My only wish to reawaken aboard his jet on Friday and not face any of my life's concerns. Like my meeting with Chet.

* * *

"I DO NOT HAVE loads of bloody time. You called this in-person meeting. Get on with what you have for me. And it better be good."

As Chet barks, I envision his face melting. His eyes droop and slide along his cheeks while his lips drop off his face and the hole of his mouth fills with the gooey substance until he chokes.

The bloody obnoxious, self-possessed prat!

For a moment, I consider storming away. To hell with him!

But revenge simmers in my soul for the Jacksons to fall to their knees.

Then a flash of guilt passes through me since Lachlan and Lydie treat me well. And I've fallen for Harris more than I care to admit. Tomorrow can't come fast enough.

I take a deep breath to clear those thoughts. The only one that matters: take care of my family with the money Chet gives to me. That thought must remain forefront in my mind. Period.

With a sarcastic smile stamped on my face, I hand the flash drive to Chet. It contains information on Jackson Corporation's upcoming launches. The most intel I could uncover without drawing suspicion.

He cocks his eyebrow as he stares at the memory stick.

"Well, what's on it?" He asks with a sneer.

I hold back an eye roll and tell him.

His beady eyes gleam as he snatches the drive from my fingers. He mutters how he'll wire six figures to my Swiss bank account if his *people* confirm the intel worthy.

Now, I roll my eyes and respond snarkily, "It's bloody well worth it, and you know it!"

His eyes widen, then narrow.

"Fine. I will complete the transfer in the morning," Chet grouses. Then he rolls up the window of his Bentley sedan.

I watch as it pulls into traffic.

"Prat!" I whisper shout before I stick out my tongue.

I head to the bus stop for the ride home. My mind drifts to Thailand and to the Adonis who waits for me. Again guilt rears its head. I know Harris is as attracted to me as I am to him.

Well, I can have fun before I disappear for good. I deserve it.

"Nice bag, Kat. Where are you off to for the long weekend?"

"Yeah, you look like you can't contain yourself!"

Two assistants from the finance department approach as I wait for the executive floor lift.

They're friendly enough. But I'd rather not disclose my weekend getaway with Harris. Too many women fall all over him, even when he's with me. If I broadcast being with him, it's bound to reach the tabloids. I've seen plenty of photos of Harris linked to a bevy of beauties and tales of his conquests splattered across the Internet.

No, thank you.

I smile and shake my head.

"Thanks. But nowhere special. Plans to attend a friend's birthday party in Newtonhill," I say, then deflect. "What about you?"

We ride down to the lobby and head for the doors.

Harris' Rolls-Royce sits at the curb with the driver beside it. He tips his hat and opens the back door for me.

"Wait a minute, Kat."

"Nothing special, you say?"

I grin and waggle my fingers over my shoulder. Then slide into the back after the driver takes my bag. The door closes with a soft thud. I gaze at the pair from behind the window's darkened glass.

Their mouths hang agape as the sedan pulls off.

My grin widens bigger than the Cheshire Cat's smile as my mobile rings with a FaceTime call from Harris.

"I see you're in the car," he says.

My gaze lifts to the privacy screen. I guess the driver told him.

"No, he didn't tell me. I have my ways," he smirks.

I giggle and shake my head.

"A man of mystery. I like," I say.

We talk until I get on the elevator at STEELE Aberdeen for the ride up to the roof where Lachlan's helicopter awaits to take me to Aberdeen International Airport. My mobile rings once we're airborne with another FaceTime call from Harris. Aboard the jet, we continue to talk until well after midnight in Thailand.

Afterwards, I enjoy a delicious five-course meal on Bernardaud China and water and wine in Baccarat Crystal glasses. The white linen tablecloth and napkin with silver cutlery finish the posh dinner. I thank the flight attendant for a snifter of Jackson Reserve Scotch before I move to the living room area and stretch out on a white leather sofa to watch movies.

When my eyes droop, I head to the bedroom and change into the red silk negligee and robe laid out on the bed. I notice it's Lola's Coterie—his sister-in-law's luxury lingerie and evening wear company. They're elegant and to die for. I take a selfie, blowing a kiss and text it to Harris. When he awakes, he'll have a reminder of what's coming.

No sooner than my head touches the down-filled pillow encased by platinum gray silk, my eyes drift closed. The soothing scent of lavender wafts through the air. Once again, dreams of a life with Harris lull me into a peaceful slumber.

THE GULF OF THAILAND'S sparkling aquamarine water tipped with white caps stretches out beneath the helicopter as we fly towards Maenam Beach on Koh Samui. Coconut trees sway in the breeze. Their abundant fronds cast shadows on the powdery white sand. The idyllic spot clear of locals and tourists.

As we near, I spy one figure with a hand shading his eyes. He stands bare chested in white board shorts. Tan skin over taut, lean muscles glistens in the sunlight. He raises a hand in a wave. A grin spreads across his handsome face.

Harris Steele.

Sex on the beach. Yum.

I'm out the door as soon as the flight attendant opens it. Harris jogs towards me, and I leap into his arms, wrapping my legs around his narrow hips. My sundress rides up my thighs.

He growls as he cups my ass and slants his mouth over mine for a toe-curling kiss.

My needy pussy clenches from the heat of his body. Sans panties, I grind my core against his washboard abs like… Well, like a cat in heat. I swallow his growls as we devour each other's mouths.

How I've missed this man. *My* man.

Leaving the butler to gather my bag, Harris turns around and strides back through the stone path between the foliage. Its density hides the helipad from the gardens of the magnificent beachfront villa. Fragrant scents of jasmine and hibiscus fill the balmy air. I'm nearly dizzy with delight.

"Missed you, Kitty Kat," Harris murmurs against my lips. "A lot."

I nip his lower lip, and he groans.

"I missed you more, Harris Steele," I purr. "How will you make up the time to me?"

He chuckles darkly as his eyes flash silver.

My Wolf prowls.

"Oh, Siren, you are not at all ready for what I am about to give to you," he responds with hooded eyes. "My tight, little pussy will need ample prep time until it gushes and begs to be fucked long and hard."

I shiver and mewl.

Carnal images dance in my head. Every single one involves a strapping Alpha male fucking me senseless in each of my willing holes.

"Keep looking at me like that, and I will fuck you against the next coconut tree, Siren. Staff be damned," he growls.

He strides up a set of stairs, and I glance over my shoulder.

My jaw drops.

Up close, the luxurious villa leaves me breathless.

In keeping with the local style, it has five thatched-roof, open-air, whitewashed pavilions. The center structure includes an oversized salon, dining room, chef's kitchen, and full bathroom. On either side, two pavilions connect to the main one via stone pathways. The four structures house enormous suites with sitting rooms and indoor/outdoor bathrooms.

Lush green grass and more flowering plants surround an infinity pool with white chaise lounges and umbrellas beside it. A stone terrace has an outdoor kitchen, a sitting area with white sofas and a firepit, and a dining area with a long elliptical wooden table and chairs. The table reminds me of a supersized surfboard.

The stunning beach spreads out before the villa. An invitation to dive into the calm aquamarine waters.

Simply paradise.

"So beautiful," I whisper in awe.

"So beautiful," Harris repeats.

I turn my gaze back to him.

He stares at me with lust-filled eyes, obsidian with his carnal need.

"I mean the villa and beach, silly," I giggle.

"I mean you, Siren," he rejoins, eyes pinned on mine.

My hands cup his face.

"Well… I'm hot and needy just like you wanted. So what will you do about it?" I purr as I lap at his full lips, hungry for his taste.

The thick shaft of his cock thumps against my pussy. I couldn't ask for a better response.

I tighten my grip on his shoulders and bounce up and down along his cock. My heels dig into his firm ass for leverage.

"I want you now, Mr. Steele," I rasp.

He smacks my ass, and I shudder to a stop.

"You get when I give, naughty lass," he growls. "Lucky for you, I am ready now."

With that, he shifts me in his arms to toss me over his shoulder. Three smacks to my exposed rear end make me screech and grab his waist. Another flurry, and I cry out as my pussy contracts. Juices make my inner thighs slippery.

Harris runs a thick finger along my seam to collect the proof of my arousal. A sucking sound follows.

My cheeks redden—as crimson as my alabaster ass—with the knowledge he's cleaning my juices from his finger. At the same time, the action turns me on even more. I whimper in need.

"Oh, I got you, naughty lass. Do not worry," he croons, stroking my ass.

He strides into a bedroom suite pavilion closest to the beach.

A gentle breeze sways the white gauzy curtains tied back with stands of fragrant yellow flowers. A king-size bed covered in white sits in the middle of the suite opposite the open fourth wall. Carved wood nightstands with white shade, blown glass lamps flank the bed. To the left of it, an arched opening leads to a bathroom with a closet. The other side serves as the sitting area with white sofas and more carved wood tables with lamps and more flowers. Sand colored tile covers the floor.

Before I can comment on the tranquil space, I fly through the air and bounce on the bed. A yelp bursts from my mouth. My arms and legs flail, then splay out.

Harris pounces.

His hands make quick work of my sundress. I lost my flip flops along the way. He puts my crooked eyeglasses on the nightstand, then kneels between my thighs as he pulls the string on his board shorts. His massive cock springs free.

Absolutely ready.

Pre-cum gathers at the bulbous tip. Veins stand out in bas-relief along the hard shaft. Heavy balls sway as he rolls a condom over his dick, then lowers to his elbows.

Arms loop under my thighs for firm hands to hold the tops. Fingertips skim my inner thighs, enticingly close to my sopping core.

I wiggle to bring the digits closer to my most-needy

place, only to yelp when Harris nips the sensitive skin of an inner thigh.

"Behave. Or you will not cum, naughty lass," he snarls. "Last warning."

I swallow and nod. Then catch myself and verbalize my understanding.

Harris smirks.

When the tip of his tongue prods my engorged clit, a low and guttural moan escapes me. At last, relief…

Just as starved for me as I am for him, Harris gorges on the bountiful fount of my pussy. He hums his appreciation as he laps up my cream. The vibrations flow through me, increasing my pleasure.

I lose count of the orgasms he wrings from my core. My mind blown.

"Now you are as ready as I am, Siren. A soft and yielding pussy ripe for fucking," he purrs, then kisses my lower lips.

Harris continues a trail of kisses to my mons, up my quivering belly with a pause to lave a beaded nipple. His suckling steady. As he passes the valley between my breasts, he sucks skin into his mouth and worries it—sure to leave a mark. He murmurs *mine* before he moves to the other nipple.

I mewl and arch my back. Fingers dive into his ebony hair to cradle him to my breast. His mouth feels so good.

Kisses pressed to the side of my neck lead to my lips. Our tongues tangle until he nips mine with a low growl of passionate dominance. I respond with a soft cry of acceptance.

Harris' hand snakes between our damp bodies to fist his rock-hard dick and press it against my slick seam. A snap of his hips seats him fully within my core. His tip grazes my cervix.

I cry out from the burn of his massive cock as it stretches and fills my tight pussy. Greedily, it sucks him deeper, fluttering along his turgid length.

He murmurs filthy words against the delicate shell of my ear as he thrusts and circles his hips before he drags his cock out to the mushroom head. The pace constant. The rhythm as old as time.

A blinding orgasm shoots down to curl my toes and up to bow my back. I gasp and wail because of the unexpected rush.

Harris grips my hips and flips me to my forearms and knees—ass high, head low. With a feral bark, he pounds into my pussy. Hips snap my punished ass. Balls slap my swollen clit.

My fingernails shred the sheets as he impales me over and over on his long, thick cock like a rag doll. Screams and grunts echo around us as another climax rips through me and he chases his release.

More dirty words fly from Harris' mouth as his cock grows impossibly larger and harder. He stills and throws his head back with a conquering roar. His cock pulsates deep inside of my wrecked pussy. His sweat drips onto my back. Nearly replete, his thrusts switch to a languorous pace as he spills every drop into the condom.

I whimper from the loss when he withdraws.

His hands guide me flat onto the bed with my head on my folded arms. A kiss to my lower back and the mattress shifts. I hear him pad to the bathroom and return a moment later.

A damp cloth cleans the sticky cream from my thighs and my butt cheeks. I purr in a state of sheer euphoria and wiggle my hips.

Harris chuckles. His warm breath tickles my ear.

"Be careful what you ask for, Siren," he warns with a sharp smack to my ass.

I smile as my eyes drift closed.

Yeah, a life with Harris Steele sounds and feels good.

Another missed weekend? What's going on with you? Who has you ditching your fam? Fess up to your twin, Harris Steele...

I chuckle at the text message from Haley. She's on point with her guess. Always in tune, we can never hide anything from the other. Talk about Wonder Twins powers activate.

I had meetings in Thailand and stayed for the long weekend. I'll see you when I get back. Give my niece and nephews zerbets on their tummies. Love ya, H

Three dots appear as Haley types her response.

Mmmhhhmmm... Love you, too.

Ah, Haley. She's going to give me hell when she finds out I've been seeing Kat. One woman for more than one encounter? I snort. Obviously Lachlan didn't break the Bro Code and spilled the beans to Haley. I would have heard from her by now. Good man.

Not that I want to hide Kat or our fledgling relationship. No. However, I want to give it some time. See how it goes. I'll tell Haley since we don't keep secrets from each other. Especially since I forced her to cave in about Lachlan. And I'll tell him too, since Kat is his admin. Only fair.

As for the rest of our family?

Well, STEELE Foundation's annual fundraising gala happens in a few weeks. If all is still well between Kat and me, I'll fly her over to my family's beachfront compound—Steele Southampton Village. That'll put us at two months together. A good amount of time before I introduce her to everyone.

Satisfied with my decision, I rise from the sunbed and dive into the shimmering waves. I glide under the water until I reach Kat and put her thighs on my shoulders before I surface. She screeches as she shoots out of the water.

"Harris!" She yells as her fingers grip my hair for purchase.

I laugh and nip her inner thigh. My hands hold her legs as I dog paddle to keep us afloat.

"You nearly gave me a heart attack!" Kat continues. "Don't drop me!"

"If you haven't noticed, lass, I'm a brawny lad," I say. "But it's time for you to get... WET!"

Kat squawks as I drop back below the surface until we're submerged. Beneath the water, she wiggles from my grasp and spins around to face me.

I grin and reach for her waist.

My little mermaid lass doesn't want to be caught. She turns and swims for the shore. Topless with her round ass covered by a tiny string bikini and long, toned legs, she enthralls me. I swear I hear her Siren's call. And don't hesitate to follow it.

As we swim back, I swipe at her legs. Kat growls and carries on. When her feet touch the sandy bottom, she pivots and arcs her arm through the water to douse me as I stand.

"Take that, Harris Steele!" She shouts.

A water fight ensues until I grab and toss her over my shoulder. She squirms but settles down when I swat that ass. I lower her to the sunbed and straddle her hips.

"You proved too irresistible, Kitty Kat," I tease as I tickle her. "I can't keep my hands off of you."

She squeals and wiggles until breathless.

I lean down and suck a puckered nipple into my mouth. Warm salty water and Kitty Kit's natural taste slide across my tongue. I pinch and roll her other nipple to a peak. As I lick my way to it, my fingers slide down her belly and beneath her bikini. I finger fuck her to a quick climax then sit back on my haunches to clean my fingers.

"Better?" I ask between licks.

She stretches like her namesake and purrs in contentment.

I smirk and rub sunblock on her alabaster skin, then lie down beside her. When she rolls over and rests her head on my chest, I kiss the top of it. With the warm sun on my body and my woman in my arms, I smile and close my eyes. Bliss.

* * *

"That's it! Go, Kat, go!"

I cup my hands around my mouth and shout more words of encouragement as she rides a wave for the first time.

Seconds later, the surfboard zips from beneath her feet, and she falls into the water with a spectacular splash. With the ease of an experienced surfer, I jump up and catch the next wave to help her. Kat surprises me and pops out of the water, laughing and wiping her face. She swims to her board and slips out of the water to straddle it.

I grin and wolf whistle at her upturned rear, clad in a black bikini bottom. Unfortunately, a long-sleeved rashguard covers her luscious tits. But her nipples press against the shirt.

Kat laughs.

"Not bad, huh?" She asks with a wink. "Now I know why surfers love it so much. I could do this all day. Fersure, dude!"

I raise my hand with thumb and pinky up and middle fingers curled as I wave it back and forth.

"Right on, dudette!" I respond, grinning. "Let's go again."

We drop on our boards and paddle back out to the surf line. As we approach, other guys congratulate Kat on her ride. I bristle at their attention to my woman and throw glares at them. They nod their heads in understanding and resume their watch for the perfect wave.

"Caveman."

I glance back at Kat, and she rolls her eyes.

"They were only being nice, Harris," she admonishes me.

"Well then, call me Captain Caveman because I do not give a fuck," I say. Then raise my eyebrow and fold my arms across my chest. "Unless you need them to be nice, Kat."

She huffs and pouts.

I cock my head.

"Of course not, Harris! Give me a break," she responds. "And by the way… Did I get my knickers in a bunch when every woman on the beach and everywhere else, for that matter, ogle you?"

I drop my arms.

"Exactly. Now excuse me while I catch a wave," she says and paddles off.

I watch her go. She makes good on her word and rides a wave almost all the way to the shore before she falls off her board. A couple of surfers help her, and I bite back a growl.

This woman gets under my skin like no other.

I swipe my hand over my face and take the next wave. As I stride to our blankets, I ignore the women who sidle up to me. Yeah, I can see what Kat means. Not that I'm a conceited prick, but women flocking to me happens so often it doesn't faze me. It comes with the Steele name, my billions, and of course my handsome mug.

"What's so funny?"

I stop chuckling at the sound of Kat's voice.

"You're right, I'm a possessive bloke, bonny lass. So get used to it. I'll make a deal with you. We're exclusive," I say as I drop beside her. "Deal?"

She blinks, then scans my face for any sign of deceit. Finding none, a brilliant smile spreads across her gorgeous face, making her emerald green eyes glitter behind her glasses back on after surfing. She throws her arms around my neck and presses her lips to mine.

"Deal!" She says between ardent kisses.

* * *

"This is incredible. It feels like a dream."

Kat tilts her head back to gaze at the rocky cliffside as the longtail boat meanders along the channel between the natural walls. Water eroded the sandstone, leaving the cliffs with dramatic fissures and caves. Fauna covers the surfaces as plants and trees cling to the sides, growing in abundance. Their vibrant green hues reflect in the water below for a turquoise tone. The clear water glints in the dazzling sun and reveals its depths where colorful fish in every shade of the rainbow swim.

I smile at her excitement as I sit back and watch her reactions to the natural beauty of Thailand.

As I plan for every trip we take to end on a bang, I

arranged the cruise and dinner on a secluded beach. I want My Kitty Kat to leave with a smile on her face and the desire to see me again makes her needy. I want to show her and give her things she's never had before me. What no other man can do for her. Make her addicted to me and not just to Harris Steele, the multibillionaire.

And so far, so good.

"Oh, Harris! I've seen nothing like this. Amazing," she whispers in reverence. "Will you take our picture?"

Mission accomplished.

I grin.

"Of course, babe," I respond as I hold my hand out to her.

She moves from the front of the longtail boat to where I sit along its side. When she settles on my lap, I take her mobile and extend my arm for the shot. I wait until a vibrant patch of the cliffside appears behind us and press the button. I kiss her cheek and take another as she giggles. Then a third with her kissing me back.

"Thank you so much for another incredible time, Harris," My Kitty Kat purrs against my lips.

I rest my forehead to hers and breathe in her air for a moment before I respond.

"You are more than welcome, Kitty Kat," I murmur. "But you have more to see."

Right on cue, the channel widens and the longtail boat glides towards the beach.

"Look," I say as I clasp her chin between my thumb and forefinger to shift her gaze.

She gasps.

The gentle breeze blows the white gauzy canopy with its four posts covered in ropes of yellow ratchaphruek Thailand's national flower and colorful hibiscus and jasmine. It floats above a table set for two with a floral bouquet at its center. Chairs have more gauzy material draped over them with a bow in the back and a wreath of flowers. The billowy topper resembles the clouds above and the table appears as one of the many islands of the country.

Bamboo torches around the perimeter and white tapers on the table will provide lighting once the sun sets below the line of the cliffs.

Phase two will be make love beneath the stars. We'll move to the sunbed covered in white, sumptuous bedding beneath a second gauzy canopy. A bonfire to the side and more bamboo torches situated nearby, ready to be lit. Next to the sunbed, Dom Pérignon Champagne and two Baccarat Crystal flutes chill in a bucket nestled in the sand.

A romantic ending to our rendezvous. If I must say so myself...

I CARRY A STILL SPEECHLESS Kat through the shallows to the beach. Her gaze darts from the table to the servers and the sunbed.

As we near the setting, the tropical scent of the flowers mingles with the aromas from the tantalizing dishes on the white linen tabletop.

I nuzzle My Kitty Kat's neck and inhale the alluring scent of her perfume. Combined with her natural musk, it surpasses any of the tropical flowers and foods that surround us.

"Oh, Harris," she breathes at last as I set her on a chair. She cups my face and continues. "I don't know what to say. You treat me so well—"

Her words catch in her throat. She glances away with tears shimmering in her eyes as her hands drop to her lap.

I crouch beside her and lift them to my lips. I place a kiss on the tip of each finger and on her palms.

Her eyes remain averted as she shakes her head.

The situation overcomes My Kitty Kat, I muse. However, I will not allow her to sit quietly.

"Kat, you fill my heart like no other woman. I never expected to fall for you at first sight. But I did, and you please me beyond my wildest dreams. True, we have only known each other for a short period. However, time means nothing when your heart tells you otherwise. I only want to please you, too. Enjoy our time together. Each and every second, sweetheart, because I know I do," I say.

The words pour from my heart unchecked. Yet I do not regret them. The truth holds power I will no longer deny. I can't say it's love since I've never experienced love of a woman aside from my mother and my sister. But it's pretty damn close to what I imagine it to be.

The breath I didn't realize I was holding falls from my lips when My Kitty Kat returns her tear-filled eyes to gaze at me. Her chin wobbles as she sucks in a breath.

I stroke my thumb over her bottom lip before I cover it in an emotion-filled kiss. I pour my heart and soul into it. My body backs up my words as I claim Kat Roberts as mine.

She wraps her arms around my neck and sags into me. Completely giving in to our newfound commitment to one another. To us. Just as I did moments before.

"Spill it."

I chuckle at Haley's blunt demand. My twin's expression brokers no room for denial.

We're sitting on chaise lounges by the swimming pool at Aboyne Castle. Since it's a warm August day, the staff retracted the glass walls and ceiling of the pool house. It's one of several outer buildings on the castle's one hundred acres of manicured lawns and rolling lands.

Not far away, the impressive six-story castle sits. Made from Aberdeen granite, it features towers on one side of the center keep and battlements on the other. From the highest point, the Jackson heraldic flag ripples in the wind. A granite bridge spans the sparkling stream that flows before the castle.

Lachlan took Lilias, Leith, and Lewis to the stables for their daily visit. Even though they're only thirteen-months old, he wants to familiarize them with horses to prepare for riding lessons next year. As an avid polo player—along with Uncle Connor and his siblings—the equestrian lifestyle ranks high for him.

My siblings and I ride too, so I get it.

While Stirling and Struan asleep in their nursery with the nannies, my twin and I have time to ourselves.

And it's obvious she's not wasting any of it with preamble. Straight to the point for Haley.

"As long as you promise not to crow I-told-you-so, I'll fess up," I respond.

Haley rolls her eyes and blows as she shrugs her shoulders.

"Yeah right. If it's a woman, you might as well get ready to hear it, brother!" She snorts. "So get on with it already."

Always true to her word, I have no doubt Haley will rub it in. If the roles were reversed, I'd do the same. I smirk and give in.

"Yes, a woman. Specifically Kat Roberts, Lach—"

"Lachlan's admin?!" Haley shouts. When I nod, she continues. "For real? Does even he know? Since when? She's not using you, is she? Give me a break. Not another bloody gold digger…"

Haley goes on and on.

Understandable since she's witnessed a stalker sub with Malcolm, a money-grubber kidnapper with Roger, among other unsavory encounters. Add in some friends of hers who used Haley to get to her brothers and cousins—including Lachlan. *That* did not end well. So, yeah, Haley is super protective of us. Who can blame her?

Hell, I know when I introduce Kat, Baz will have his *guy* do an extensive background check on her. Even when I tell Baz not to bother, since she passed Lachlan's Human Resources review when they employed her at Jackson Corporation. As the eldest sibling, Baz takes his Big Brother duties seriously. He's our second father and has become more paternal since he's had children.

And God help Kat if she is up to no good—not that I believe so—then Malcolm *The Enforcer* will handle her. He's the one others come to for solutions. We don't ask what he does. We just know the situation ends in our favor.

On the other hand, our mother will be ecstatic. Her last baby involved in an actual relationship? The first woman to meet the family since my high school prom date? But being a mama bear, she won't tolerate a woman with ulterior motives.

Poor Kitty Kat.

I hold up my hands palms out to halt Haley's sound off.

She sits back against her chaise lounge and folds her arms across her chest. Eyebrows furrow and lips purse to the side as her dove gray eyes narrow.

"Fine. Go on," she huffs.

I sit up with my feet on the travertine pavers to face her. Of everyone, my twin's opinion matters the most. I need her to like Kat and for them to get along.

She'll also need to do well with Lola, Leonie, and Starr. From the start, my sisters-in-law blended into our family and became loved members to the point where I consider them sisters like Haley. I'm sure they'll embrace Kat.

"Hal, I understand how you feel and appreciate your concern. Trust me. However, Kat is different. She's not some chick aiming for a phat ring. Nor just a date for an event or a one-night stand. I actually like her and enjoy being with her," I say, then smile when Haley's expression softens. "The moment I laid eyes on her... I—I felt an attraction to Kat. To be honest, her banging body hidden beneath a demure suit helped—"

"Oh, Harris! Really?!" Haley cuts in and swats my knee. She mutters about men and which head they think with before I continue.

"But seriously, Hal. I get what Baz said about Lola. Hell, what Roger said about Leonie when he heard her laughter outside his office door. Or Malcolm when Starr bumped into him," I say. "Only you knew your true love all of your life. Now I think I may have found The One."

Haley's eyes fill with tears, and she sniffs. She sits next to me and wraps her arms around my neck.

I hold her while I say a silent prayer of thanks.

"Okay, so what did I miss?"

Lachlan's' booming voice sounds from behind us.

Haley and I turn to face him as he strides over in an open short-sleeved shirt, swim trunks, and flip flops. He grabs a colorful Missoni terrycloth towel from the pile and tosses it over his shoulder. The sun glints off his aviators as he grins.

My twin looks at me, not wanting to divulge my news —not even to her husband—without my consent.

I smile at her, grateful for the consideration.

Lachlan kisses the top of her head and claps me on the shoulder. As he drops onto another chaise lounge, he cocks his head expectantly.

"Kat and I agreed to be exclusive," I say.

Lachlan lowers his sunglasses and flicks his eyes between Haley and me.

"Don't cockblock, Lachlan Jackson!" Haley orders, as she folds her arms again and glares. "Kat may work for you. But her private life is none of your concern."

Lachlan and I guffaw at Haley's feistiness.

"Yes, ma'am," he says, then he turns to me. "I already told you I have no problem with you seeing Kat."

Haley gasps.

"Wait a minute. You knew before *I* did???" She asks wide eyed. When Lachlan nods, she narrows them. "And you didn't tell me??? Something about *my* brother?!"

I open my mouth to save Lachlan from her wrath. But he speaks first.

"Yes. And if he wanted you to learn about it first, he would have told you. It's not my place to mouth off about his business," Lachlan responds. Then he raises his eyebrow and adds, "Besides, you and I have had plenty of secrets kept from The Big Four."

Haley rolls her eyes at her nickname for her brothers and mention of the secrets with Lachlan they kept from us as they dated. But she relents with a sigh.

"Fine," she says reluctantly.

Lachlan blows a kiss to her, and she snatches it from the air to plant it on her lips as she giggles.

Any other time I would tell them *eewww, gross*. But now I get what it's like to feel strongly about someone and to share wussy moments with them. So instead, I grin and tell the lovey-dovey pair my plan to introduce Kat to the family over Labor Day weekend.

They agree it's a good idea, and Lachlan says she can take a few days off from work to make it a full holiday. Since I have to fly back to New York City before then, they'll let Kat join them on their jet for the flight over. They're staying for a while. So, I'll send her back on my jet, or Lucien can drop her off in Aberdeen before he returns to Paris.

With my news shared and well received, we dive into the pool and romp around. Haley challenges me to ride the giant inflatable ball, and I accept. The damn thing proves harder to wrangle than I imagined. As I flounder around, she slips from the pool and starts a video with her mobile.

"No way will I let everyone miss your shenanigans!" She laughs. "The last time Roger was here, he did it without a hitch!"

Her taunt of Roger's success gives me the gumption to ride that ball like a bronco, to Haley's delight. My twin laughs so hard she snorts and the mobile almost drops into the water. Lachlan bumps me off and takes over. She keeps recording until he falls off.

When we tell her it's her turn, she says it's time for lunch with The Trips and darts to the ladies' showers. Lachlan and I call her a chicken and climb from the pool to head for the men's changing room. Freshly changed, the three of us take the golf cart back to the castle. A far easier ride than the blasted ball…

"Malcolm texted back. He challenges you both when we get to Southampton Village," Haley tells us. "Yeah, Mr. Daredevil himself, always down for a thrill!"

I whip out my mobile and text back: *Challenge accepted. Come strong or be gone!*

Lola replies she's in, and Lydie adds she'll take bets.

Back at the castle, Lachlan calls for the nannies to bring The Trips to the terrace where the staff serves lunch. Since Stirling and Struan woke from their nap, they'll join us too.

As we settle at the table, the butler appears with Uncle Connor and Aunt Lucie.

"Surprise!" She exclaims.

"We were in the neighborhood," Uncle Connor adds.

"All the way from Jackson Castle?" Lachlan snorts. "Just admit you want to see your grands."

They laugh and nod.

Right on time, the nannies walk through the glass doors and Lilias squeals when she sees her grandparents. Leith and Lewis toddle forward, arms out. We scoop all three into our arms, and Haley and Lachlan take the twins.

Lunch waits while we catch up and play with the lass and lads. I tease Haley they sound more and more Scottish every day. Uncle Connor puffs his chest out and sharpens his emerald green eyes on me.

"Of course! They are Jacksons, you know!" He states emphatically.

We laugh at his pride in the Jackson family.

After his failed attempt at a marriage between Baz and Lydie, Uncle Connor pushed Lachlan for heirs. Now, Uncle Connor has five wee ones, and he couldn't be happier. Or more possessive…

"When are you flying to Southampton Village?" Haley asks.

"That's also why we stopped by. We want to know how long you're planning to stay," Aunt Lucie responds.

They chat on about logistics while Uncle Connor, Lachlan, and I talk sports—shinty, who realized?—and sailing.

Instead of flying back to London, I stay the night along with Uncle Connor and Aunt Lucie. I want as much time with the grands as they do.

After this month, I won't be in Scotland as much since I'll rotate back to our New York City offices. If things go well with Kat, we'll meet up for the weekends. More than likely I'll fly to Aberdeen since I can get to STEELE London for work quicker than she can get to Jackson Corporation from Manhattan. Or we'll pick a spot within a short flight time from Scotland. Either way, we'll manage for both of us. As couples do.

I chuckle at the thought. Me—the ultimate playboy—a willing part of a couple. Ha!

KAT

"Hi, Mum! I'm here! Where are you? Michael? Charlotte?"

I put the bags of groceries and Indian takeaway I picked up on my way from the bus station onto the kitchen counter. Then put the bouquet onto the table. While I wait for them to appear, I place the milk, cheeses, steaks, and other perishables in the refrigerator and freezer.

"Hey, Kat."

I glance over my shoulder to find Michael striding towards me with a grin. His emerald eyes sparkle as they meet mine before he pulls me in for a hug.

"Hey yourself!" I say, then rub his chin. "Nice beard."

His cheeks flush, and he ducks his head.

"Kat, honey?"

We turn to our Mum and Charlotte—who smiles in greeting beside her. I embrace them while Michael puts the rest of the groceries into the cupboards.

"Wine, too? Thanks, Kat!" He says, holding up two bottles of Cabernet Sauvignon.

"And flowers for you, Mum," I say as I hand them to her. "Your favorites."

She palms my cheek and smiles up at me.

"Such a good girl you are, Katrina. Thank you," she says. "Charlotte, will you hand me the vase, honey?"

While our Mum arranges the flowers in the chipped Waterford Crystal vase one of her employers planned to toss, Charlotte and I set out the food. Michael comes over with plates and forks, then goes back for glasses and a bottle of wine.

I don't bother to ask about Payton since it's Friday night.

Undoubtedly, he's at the pub around the corner getting drunk with whatever money he scraped together over the week. He'll come around soon enough when he realizes I'm here with money.

Even though I transfer funds into our Mum's bank account, I always bring some cash for her to have on hand. To avoid an argument at the start of our weekend, I'll just pretend I don't notice her giving it to him. At least not in front of her. However, I *will* tell him to his face he's a lazy louse!

I turn to Charlotte.

"How're your classes going this semester?" I ask.

She smiles and, like Michael, her eyes sparkle bright as the gem.

"Fantastic!" She says then gushes on about classes, study

groups, and a guy she's seeing.

I smile happy for my younger sister. She reminds me of my excitement for a new phase in my life, away from the not-so-stellar environment we shared. I also smile at her enthusiasm for her new relationship. Also like mine.

It did not thrill Harris we wouldn't spend time face-to-face this weekend. He'd asked me to join him in London. He said he wanted to share an experience with me. But gave in when I told him I had a Girls' Getaway planned months before.

The lie didn't sit well with me. However, I have no other choice. I can't very well let him know my parents didn't die and my nonexistent siblings exist. That would ruin everything. All that I've accomplished thus far. And that I cannot allow.

So, I refocus on Charlotte.

Michael teases her about being gaga over a bloke for the first time. She retorts how he's just as into her as she is into him. They banter back and forth while our Mum smiles on.

Despite the dark circles and the sag to her shoulders, her eyes still shine with love for her children. She's done so much for us on her own. Tolerated so much from employers—some of whom treat her poorly. It's not her fault she married into a family cursed with dreamers. She deserves a long, happy life free from financial constraints and the stress they cause.

And no matter what—or who—I will give it to her.

After dinner, I wash, Michael dries, and Charlotte stores the dishes as we did since we were children and I stood on a stool at the sink. And Payton did then what he does tonight, make himself scarce. Then we take the last of the wine and join our Mum in the living room where she plays music on the record player.

Michael bows and extends his hand to me for a dance.

I giggle and place mine in his, roughened from labor.

We twirl around the room mindful of the furniture while our Mum and Charlotte dance together beside us. When Michael insists we *listen to music from this century*, he pumps up the volume on his mobile for tunes from a playlist.

Charlotte attempts to show our Mum the latest dance moves, much to her delight. Michael and I clap and urge her on with words of encouragement. Not bad for a woman who turns fifty next year!

I go back to the kitchen for the second bottle of wine. When I return with it held aloft, everyone cheers. Our dance party gets more boisterous and continues until well after one in the morning.

Our Mum tells us goodnight and goes to her bedroom at the far end of the hall. Still giddy, I bump hips with Charlotte as we head to the room we shared. Michael pulls out the bed from the sofa since he prefers to sleep in the living room instead of in the bedroom with Payton. Who could blame the lad? Not I, said the Kat!

CRASH!

"What the bloody hell?! Dammit, Payton!!"

"Oh... f-f-f-uck offff... M-M-Michael..."

Charlotte and I jump up from the bed. But I stop her

from leaving the room. She protests. But I shake my head and whisper no sharply.

I rush down the hall towards the living room.

Michael stands in pajama bottoms, glaring down at Payton, who's sprawled out fully clothed on the sofa bed. The stench of cheap liquor burns my nostrils as I move closer.

"Watch out for the lamp!" Michael says as he points to the floor at my bare feet. "The dumb wanker knocked it and the table over before he fell onto my bed. And me."

He shakes his head in disgust.

"Hold on. I'll get the broom and dustpan," he adds as he spins on his heels and strides to the kitchen.

"You prat, Payton!" I whisper shout so as not to wake our Mum who's still asleep. "When will you bloody well grow up?!"

In silence, Michael returns and sweeps the shards of pottery and glass while I angle the dustpan to collect them. Both of us tired of our eldest sibling's abhorrent behavior.

"Help me roll him. He can sleep on the floor. You sleep in your bed," I tell Michael.

His mouth drops open as he stares at me, shocked by my words and vehement tone.

"Come on," I add.

He nods, and we manage to move Payton's dead weight to the space between the chair and the sofa. Michael turns Payton's head so his cheek rests on the hardwood floor to avoid him choking should he vomit in his sleep.

I fold my arms over my chest and shake my head in

disgust. I am beyond pissed right now. He's just ridiculous and needs to help our family, not make matters worse. Add to the equation, not subtract.

Michael takes the garbage bag with the remnants of the lamp, broom, and dustpan back to the kitchen. When he returns, he gives me a hug, and we part.

"What happened?" Charlotte asks as I climb back into bed with a heavy sigh.

"Your drunk brother Payton knocked over the table, broke the lamp, and passed out on Michael's bed. I'll order a new lamp as close to the other one as I can find," I respond. When she frowns and opens her mouth, I add, "Don't worry. Go to sleep. Since Mum is off tomorrow, let's go get mani/pedis. My treat. Cool?"

Charlotte shakes her head.

"I know what you're doing, Kat. It's not fair to you to make up for Payton. But... I appreciate and love you very much," she says, then hugs me before she snuggles back under the covers.

As I lie in bed, I ask for the strength to be the leader of our family. To take the burdens from our Mum's shoulders. To provide for my younger siblings. With that prayer in mind, my eyes drift close.

* * *

"WHICH COLOR DID YOU PICK, MUM?" I ask as she sits between Charlotte and me at the nail salon.

Our Mum glances at the bottom of the bottle with red polish inside. She squints her eyes and hands it to me.

"Vivacious Vixen… Risqué!" I laugh and hand it to the aesthetician, who smiles. "Even for your hands?"

Mum shakes her head.

"Oh no. Don't bother with color on my hands, miss. It'll just get worn off in a few hours," she responds as she looks at the aesthetician. Then looks at them and adds, "But she can tidy the nails up. The cuticles are a bit ragged, I suppose."

I flick my gaze to Charlotte, who bites her lower lip as though holding back a comment.

I know what she's thinking.

Our Mum doesn't wear gloves when she cleans. Never have and never will, she tells us. So naturally, the polish won't last when she dips her hands into hot bleach and water solutions. Years of harsh chemicals leave her hands rough and flaky, despite the special creams I send for her to use. But she's set in her ways, and we don't want to argue with her.

We say nothing in response. No benefit to upsetting our Mum.

"What did you choose, Charlotte?" I ask to change the subject.

"Retro Pink for my hands and Vavavavoom for my toes," she responds with a small smile. "And you?"

I raise the bottles and show them a blush pink for my hands and a fire-engine red for my toes. Like our Mum, my work dictates my hands. I don't want a flashy color. The nude pink pairs well with my conservative attire. But they don't need to know all those details.

We chat while the aestheticians finish our nails. It's so nice to unwind with my Mum and sister. Michael, Charlotte, and I didn't tell her how the lamp broke specifically, only that during the night it bumped from the table.

Of course, Payton was still asleep when she came out into the living room. Not that he'd remember, anyway. Michael managed to put him back on the refolded couch.

I found a replacement lamp and ordered it to arrive in a few days. At the end of the day, that's all that matters. It's not quite a match for the other lamp. But then again, nothing in the flat meant to go together. Our Mum made the individual pieces work.

"How about we go for lunch? We can call Michael to join us," I suggest, as we leave the salon.

"Kat, you really shouldn't spend your money on us like this," our Mum says.

"I agree with Mum, Kat. The mani/pedis were enough," Charlotte says with a shake of her head. The sunlight glints off the natural highlights of her shoulder-length brown hair.

I shake my redhead and respond, "Well, we have to eat. Don't we? It's not a waste if it's a necessity in life. Right?"

"Fine!" They say in unison.

We laugh, and I call Michael.

Eagerly, he agrees to join us at a chippy near the salon in twenty minutes. It's his day off too, and he's nearby sketching some buildings.

Our Mum, Charlotte, and I stroll towards the fish and chips restaurant. We take our time window shopping at the stores we pass along the way. It's a beautiful sunny day, and we take advantage of the August weather.

When we enter the chippy, the delicious scent of fish and chips permeates the air. I smile at the welcoming aroma as my tastebuds water. As much as I aim to blend in with the posh crowd, I still love the everyday person's meals. Fresh haddock with lots of chippy sauce will do me just right!

As we settle into a booth, Charlotte spies Michael glancing around at the entrance. She stands and waves him over to our table.

"Hey!" He greets us as he slides onto the bench next to our Mum and kisses her cheek. "Don't you lasses look refreshed? Show me the fingernails."

Our Mum giggles and holds out her hands. The fingernails gleam from the buffing in the sunlight filtering in from the window beside our booth.

Charlotte and I take turns showing our hands to him as we giggle. Michael nods his approval.

The server comes over, and we place our order. The food is as delicious as I expected. Golden brown, crisp, flaky fish and chips. The sauce adds the right amount of flavor. The pints of stout complement our meal.

"We showed our fingernails to you. Now, it's your turn," I tell Michael.

He chuckles and raises his hands.

I roll my eyes.

"Not your nails, silly. Show us your drawings," I say.

Michael picks his battered leather rucksack off the stone floor and pulls the sketchpad out. As always, his talent and attention to detail amaze us. Without him saying, we recognize the buildings he's put on paper. Amazing.

"Incredible as always, Michael," I say with a smile.

Charlotte raises her glass.

"Here's to a wonderful day of beautiful buildings and sexy mani/pedis!" She exclaims.

"Hear, hear!"

"Yes, honey!"

"Absolutely!"

Late Sunday night, I return home from Glasgow, reinvigorated and refocused.

The weekend was fun except for Payton's stunt. My only concern was Mum being short of breath and light-headedness on Saturday night. She attributed it to the wine the night before and to Saturday's activities.

So she, Charlotte, and I spent Sunday binge watching romance movies on Netflix in our pajamas. Michael went out with a lass he's seeing then came back in time to watch the latest Chris Hemsworth movie with us.

I call Mum to let her know I made it and then crash onto my bed.

Just as my first dream forms, I hear the distant ring of

my mobile. I jolt awake, fearing it's from my Mum. But realize it's my regular mobile.

"Hello?" I ask.

"Hi, Kitty Kat."

A grin spreads across my face as sleep falls away. It's Harris. His distinctive baritone voice sends a shiver through my body. And I miss him immediately.

"Hi," I purr.

He chuckles.

"How was your Girls' Getaway? Did you miss me?" He asks.

I roll over onto my side and hug the mobile to my chest. This man is just what I need after Payton's shenanigans. A reminder that someone can take care of me. Give me insurmountable pleasure. I sigh and place the mobile on the pillow next to my head.

"It was nice. But not as nice as our weekends together," I respond. "Did you miss me as much as I missed you?"

A groan slips from his mouth.

I moan in response to my lover's need for me.

"More than you can imagine, Kitty Kat," Harris rumbles.

My pussy clenches, and my nipples pebble. But I can't take my pleasure. It belongs to him. I whimper.

"Next weekend I'm sending a STEELE helicopter for you. It'll be you and me in London Friday night through Monday morning. I'll get you back in time for work," he growls. "Do not even try to say no, Siren."

I close my eyes and inhale deeply. This man knows how to make me want him more and more every. Single. Day.

"Did you hear me, Siren?" He demands in the silence.

My eyes pop open, and I sit up as though he can see me. The mobile held aloft.

"Oh, yes, Harris, I heard you and will be ready—dripping pussy and all," I respond.

He inhales sharply through his nose.

It excites me I can elicit such a lusty response from him.

Air slowly seeps from his mouth as he regains control.

"Good girl. You will need all the natural lubricant you can produce to get you through what I have in mind," he says in a voice laced with dark promises.

Another shiver drops me back to the mattress.

"I cannot wait," I respond breathlessly.

"Good. Now get some sleep and dream of me," he purrs. "Good night, Siren."

I sigh as I roll onto my side.

"Good night, Harris Steele," I whisper. "Dream of me, lover."

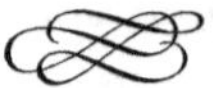

"Cheers to the perks of doing what you love for work and being able to do it anywhere in the world. Even on a superyacht in Monte Carlo on a summer evening!"

"And dressed in a tuxedo with a fine glass of Scotch in hand and a beauty on the arm!"

I chuckle and raise my Baccarat Crystal snifter at Lucien and Lauren's remarks.

We're aboard the STEELE Monte Carlo's four-hundred-foot yacht for a Jackson Hole party.

Six years ago, Lydie and Lucien approached Baz for STEELE International to partner with Jackson Corporation's new members-only, high-end, jet-set hot spots. The concept a combination of beach bar, restaurant, and dance club with the first location at our hotel and marina in Monte Carlo followed by our St. Barth's resort.

The name, as expected, is typical Lucien—Jackson Hole,

a play on a watering hole for drinking liquor and accessible body areas. Their brands of liquors and cigars would be the exclusives and Lucien would create the menus and signature cocktails. The three areas would be the bar, the restaurant, and the beachfront that offers cabanas, beds, and chaise lounges. Sexy hosts, bartenders, and servers plus dancers and live bands and deejays would round out the staff and entertainment. In essence, Jackson Hole's version of LEVELS on the beach minus the BDSM.

Over the course of five years, they rolled the spots out at key STEELE properties worldwide. As with LEVELS, people sign up for the new member's list that averages a five-month wait, and that's just for the application. The business of pleasure thrives.

Laurent called to tell me about the party, and I jumped on my jet for a chance to leave the variable weather—even in the summer—of London behind. And as Lucien said, being my own boss and with my business on my laptop, I can work anywhere. Who wouldn't opt for the sunny clime of the French Riviera?

Besides, it's been a while since I hung out with my partner in playadom Laurent. Although judging by the dynamic between him and the stunning Yessenia, he's off the market like me. Now, I know why he's been missing in action...

Which reminds me of My Kitty Kat.

Almost every night we FaceTime. Not just for the amazing video sex. But we share our days and talk about normal, everyday stuff. I look forward to seeing her giggle when I crack a joke, as much as watching her break for me in ecstasy.

Next weekend she'll meet me in London, and I'll ask her to come to Southampton Village. She hasn't asked about meeting my family. But don't most women expect it and view it as the next step in a relationship? Especially since she doesn't have a family of her own.

I turn to the superyacht's railing to gaze at the onyx colored water shimmering with the silvery reflection of the full moon. The marina and the lights of Monte Carlo shine in the distance. I'll have to bring My Kitty Kat here for the weekend. She'll enjoy the glitz and glamour of the city.

I lift the snifter to my mouth for another sip.

"*Bonsoir,* Harris."

The Scotch goes up my nose as I jerk. Fingers glide along the front of my trousers and tweak the tip of my cock.

Who the *fuck?*

"Mmmm… Still so impressive. It's been far too long, *amoureux.*"

As I spin around, the back of my hand wipes droplets from my lip and down my chin. Before me stands a buxom brunette in a floor-length white gown. The front dips to her navel where a thigh-bearing slit curves from her hip. Her taut nipples poke through the silk material.

Quickly, I avert my gaze to her face.

Full red lips curve into a seductive smile. Predatory hazel eyes glitter.

"Here, let me get that for you," she purrs.

She reaches up and cups the back of my head to draw my mouth down to hers. Her tongue slips out, poised to lick the Scotch remnants from my lips.

A camera flash dispels my shock.

"Stop," I growl.

She chuckles huskily and places her other hand on my chest. Her fingers skim along the silk lapel of my tuxedo. She shakes her head. Raven colored waves tumble around her heart-shaped face.

"Don't tease me, Harris. Let's have fun tonight," the brunette says. "I'll use my tongue to make you scream again."

With a wink, she opens her mouth to show the impressive titanium barbell piercing. Her tongue wiggles from side to side like a cobra snake ready to strike.

Oh, hell no.

I extricate myself from her clutches.

"Listen, mademoiselle. I do not recall a night with you. Nor do I have any interest in one now. You are a beautiful woman who will find a willing partner with ease. *Bonsoir*," I tell her, then turn back to Laurent and Lucien.

The elder Jackson hides his laugh behind the rim of his snifter. His gemstone eyes glint with mirth as he watches the brunette saunter away. The flowy train of her backless gown shimmers as her hips sway.

"What a delightful start to the evening," Lucien chuckles. "But do tell why you passed up such an enticing creature?"

I clap him on the shoulder and grin like the Cheshire Cat.

"Other priorities, cuz. I'm a reformed player," I respond.

Lucien cocks his head and glances between Laurent with Yessenia and me. He grins and lifts his snifter in a salute.

"Well, well, well, gentleman. Here's to you," he says with a nod.

Laurent pulls Yessenia closer to his side and kisses her. When she comes up breathless, he raises his glass.

"I second that!" He smirks.

"Third!" I say.

Yessenia giggles and buries her face against Laurent's chest.

"When do we meet the woman who wrangled *your* heart, Harris?" Laurent asks. "You should have introduced us to her tonight."

I tell them I will do the honors in Southampton Village. They rib me about secrecy. But I hold firm.

Laurent takes Yessenia to dance while Lucien and I go mingle. I see a few CEOs and CTOs whose companies— and personal—I'd like to add to the client roster for STEELE Technology and Cyber Security. It's at events like this one where deals get made.

By the end of the night, I've scheduled meetings in the coming weeks. With Haley still on maternity leave, I space them out to allow enough time for travel to several countries. Being the competitive bunch we are, I bet her I'd secure more business while she lounged around Aboyne Castle as the Countess.

I had to cover my ears from her shouts at me for equating raising babies with laziness. I responded her behavior was not becoming of her noble title. She blew her lid. I chuckle as I put my mobile away and head to a bar for another drink. A well-earned one!

By the time I return to my suite at the hotel, it's too late to video call with My Kitty Kat. But I notice a missed call and a text message from her as I dump my pockets on the dresser. My foot pauses midair when I click play on the attached video.

My Siren wears a smile, and a pink ribbon tied in a bow around her neck. Nothing else.

Buck naked, she crouches on the sofa in what better be her living room. Back straight, hands on her thighs, and knees bent wide. The pink lips of her pussy glisten with her sweet cream. The bud of her clit pokes between them. She trails the middle finger to circle an areola. The nipple beads with each pass. She pinches it with a small cry before she slips the finger into her mouth.

Wide emerald green eyes stare at the camera as she sucks on the long digit. They flutter close when she withdraws it from her mouth with a pop. Eyes closed. Mouth open in a perfect O. My Kitty Kat lets her head fall back. Glossy red hair cascades below her ass. Nipples point toward the camera.

She spreads her knees to the maximum and puts the

moistened tip of her finger onto the engorged tip of her clit. A shudder wracks her body.

A zing races through mine.

We groan in unison.

With hooded eyes, My Siren gazes at the camera.

"I'll let you finish me off in London. Good night, Mr. Steele."

The video goes dark.

Fuck. Me.

On my way to the shower, I replay the video, cock hardening to the point of pain. It demands release. If not inside of My Kitty Kat, my fist will have to do.

I place the mobile on the vanity and strip. With each step to the shower, my cock thumps against my happy trail, grazing my navel. The bulbous tip an angry red and shiny with pre-cum. My palm glides over it to lubricate my shaft. As hot as My Kitty Kat made me, this will be fast and dirty.

Grunts pour from my mouth as the vision of My Kitty Kat perched on the sofa fills my mind's eye. Her alabaster skin flushed rosy from her arousal. Pupils dilated. Mouth voracious.

The muscles in my forearm flex. My balls tighten.

My vision expands to include me in the scene.

With my head thrown back, the wolf howls as he unleashes a torrent of cum over My Kitty Kat's belly and her bare mound. Hot ropes of the wolf's cum run down between her parted legs to pool beneath her ass. I reach down and rub my seed into her clit and pussy, marking her with my scent.

She stares up at me, enraptured by my feral claim.

"MINE!" I growl.

My Kitty Kat shivers.

"Yours," she purrs.

* * *

"*Merci*, mademoiselle."

"*De rien*, Monsieur Jackson."

The server flashes a seductive smile at Laurent as she passes a Mimosa to him. Her fingertips slide along his as he takes the flute's stem.

His smile turns into a scowl.

"You do know Jackson Hole discourages staff from flirtatious behavior with members?" He asks her, then continues when she confirms. "That stance applies to members of the family, too. Be sure to keep that in mind to avoid a reprimand from Human Resources. *Ça va*, mademoiselle?"

She swallows thickly and bows her head as she backs away.

"She's more thirsty than you, lover boy!" I taunt. When he rolls his eyes, I ask, "Where's Yessenia?"

Laurent smirks and tips his chin towards the hotel.

"She's recovering," he snickers and sips his Mimosa. "Later, she'll meet her friends for shopping and lunch. Which gives you and me time to catch up."

He shifts on his chaise lounge, where we sit on the

beach. The sunlight glints off the lenses of his aviators as he lifts them to cock his eyebrow at me.

"I'll go first. Then you tell me what's up with you, *lover boy*," he says, then raises his hand to stop me from speaking. "And don't give me that bullshit about Southampton Village. I share now; you share now."

He proceeds to tell me about Yessenia. He's as gone about the vivacious beauty as I am about My Kitty Kat. I bring him up to date on my fledgling relationship. Who knew Laurent and I would fall at the same time?

A paddleball lands in the sand next to my chaise lounge.

I bend over to retrieve it and glance up for its owner.

A statuesque blonde in a white string bikini jogs over. Her tits bounce each time her feet touch the sand. She smiles and waves the paddle in the air.

Ordinarily Laurent and I would jostle one another for dibs. But neither of us have an interest. Instead, I stride over to return the paddleball. She thanks me and jogs back to her friends who await her near the water's edge. They wave and offer their thanks. A bevy of beauties, and my cock remains flaccid.

The sparkling turquoise waters of the Mediterranean Sea beckon.

I turn to Laurent and tell him I'm going for a swim.

He replies he'll join me after he finishes a text message to Yessenia—who recovered, apparently. I chuckle and stride to the shoreline.

The first wave wraps me in the warmth of the Med as I dive in. The crystal clear water allows me to see all the way to the pontoon off shore. I pass snorkelers who revel in the colorful fish below the surface.

I climb onto the deck and settle on an empty spot facing the beach.

Laurent's powerful strokes cleave through the water. In moments, he's beside me. He leans back on his elbows with his face towards the sky.

"You really can't beat the Riviera during high season," he says with his eyes closed. "Who can blame Lucien for living here half of the year? Or Rog and Leonie."

I agree and stretch out on my back with my hands clasped beneath my head. The sun dries the water from my skin before we dive back into the depths.

"Race you!" Laurent shouts when we break the surface. He pushes my head underwater and kicks off.

I catch up to him before his toe touches the sandy bottom. My hand snakes out and yanks him backwards by the ankle. He thrashes and wrenches around to grab me in a headlock. We wrestle as we've done since we were kids.

Water splashes all around us, scattering the swimmers nearby. They egg on our antics with whistles and shouts.

Evenly matched—despite Laurent being two inches taller than me—we call it quits as we stride onto the sand. I give him a last shove. He retaliates with one of his fancy Scottish martial arts moves and trips me. I stumble but regain my footing as I call him an ass.

He smirks.

We throw ourselves down on our chaise lounges. Shadows block the sun.

I open my eyes to reveal three women standing over us.

"Aren't you Harris Steele and Laurent Jackson?" One asks in an American accent.

Laurent nods.

She turns to her friends, and they giggle.

"You're even more handsome in person! Do you mind if we take the chaise lounges next to yours?" Another pipes up.

I shake my head and gesture to the free seats, then cover my eyes with the crook of my elbow. No need to encourage conversation…

Refreshingly, they don't say anymore to us. They chatter and laugh as they pose for selfies amongst themselves. Apparently, they're members of Jackson Hole Miami, and it's their first time to Monte Carlo for a birthday.

I overhear them trying to decide where to go for lunch, and what to do tonight to celebrate.

"Not to be nosy. But I recommend…" I lean up and share the best places to go, and they thank me.

After a while, Laurent and I head back to the hotel.

Freshly showered, I step out onto my suite's terrace. The azure water of the Mediterranean Sea sparkle beyond the white walls. The scent of the salty air mingles with the tantalizing aromas of lunchroom service set on the table.

I settle on a chair and lift the stainless-steel cloche. The bouillabaisse makes my mouth water. Once I've eaten and room service removed the dishes, I set up my laptop to work. An hour later, my mobile rings.

A grin spreads across my face at My Kitty Kat's name on the screen.

"Hey, babe—"

"Did you get my text message?" She cuts in.

I blink at the sharp tone of her voice, then respond no as I check the app. Links appear. I click on one, and it opens to photos from last night of me with the brunette. "Exclusive: Harris Steele and Mystery Date Cozy Up on a Superyacht in Monte Carlo!"

Other links reveal photos from this morning on the beach.

"Harris Steele and His Big Paddle!"

"Last Single of The STEELE Quaternity Frolics with Babes!"

"Harris Steele and His Triplets!"

I groan and run my hand over my face.

"Well?!" Kat demands.

I switch the call to FaceTime.

Emerald green slits glare at me from the screen. Eyebrows pinch together. Her mouth an angry slash on her reddened face.

"Kat, those images are out of context. As you can see, I'm all alone in my suite," I tell her as I pan the mobile around. "The woman from last night approached me, and I told her no. The ones on the beach sat next to my cousin Laurent and me. I gave them some advice on what to do while they're here. Okay?"

She purses her lips.

"Come on. You know how tabloids spread lies. I can

understand your reaction. But trust me. Nothing happened," I continue in her silence. "Okay?"

Kat turns from the screen to speak to someone at the office. When she returns, she sighs.

"Fine. I trust you. It's just upsetting to see women throw themselves at you, and I'm all the way in bloody Aberdeen," she responds.

I waggle my eyebrows and tell her, "London's calling, Kitty Kat…"

KAT

*I*couldn't believe the ferocity of the possessiveness that rolled through me like wildfire through dry brush at the sight of Harris—my man—with those women. The pampered born with a silver spoon in their mouths kind. Who could have any man their hearts' desire with a flutter of their long eyelashes or the beckoning of their little fingers. Those who never had to lift said finger to work a day in their entire entitled lives.

Aargh!

Gladys was in the office. So when Harris didn't respond to my text message, I went to the break room for the call. On the way, the images burned into my mind. My anger increased. I struggled for a steady voice.

As he spoke and his honest face on the screen doused the flames. His reminder of our next rendezvous in London cleared the smoke. My mind and vision returned to normal.

Now, I glance at him as we ride to my surprise.

I can appreciate women's attraction to Harris Steele.

Tonight, he wears a vest and pants in buttery soft black leather molded to his muscular body. His biceps and pecs flex as he maneuvers the vintage Aston Martin Vanquish. Thighs bunch as he shifts the gears. Heavy black leather boots add to his kick-ass look.

I reach over and tangle my fingers in the longer hair atop his head, then cup the back of it.

Harris angles his face to glance at me and smiles.

Heart-stoppingly gorgeous.

My man.

"Excited for your surprise, Kitty Kat?" He asks with his eyes back on the road.

I grin and respond, "Absolutely! I wish you would tell me already. Pretty please?"

He chuckles but shakes his head.

I sit back in my seat and pout.

He wouldn't tell me about our destination. But he selected my outfit.

On the bed at our sumptuous suite in STEELE Mayfair, he laid the most exquisite hand-crafted black corset with a matching thong by Lola's Coterie. The sculpting design creates an hourglass figure with lace panels across the front in a butterfly shape and nipped in at the waist with a narrow strip of velvet. Elastic trim crisscross to form the shoulder straps, center panel, and outer panels of the lace. Suspender straps attach at the front and back to silk stockings beneath my butt cheeks that lift from the silk stilettos on my feet. A bow around my neck and tiny ones between my breasts and at the top of the thong make me look like a present. Harris' present.

His mouth curved into a devilish smile when I sashayed out of the bedroom. He twirled his finger for me to spin. I kept my eyes on his, glancing over my shoulders with each rotation. His grin spread, and his dove gray eyes blackened to obsidian.

As he helped me into a duster coat, he murmured how we'd never make it to our destination if he didn't cover me pronto. We rode the private lift down to the garage and slid into the sleek sports car.

We ride on as music plays over the sound system. The erotic beat of The Art of Noise "Moments in Love" thrums through my body. I side glance Harris to determine if he's as aroused by its sensuality as me.

A smirk tugs at the corners of his lips as his eyes remain on the road. But he doesn't return my stare.

I huff and fidget on the leather seat.

We pull up to what appears to be a former bank. A queue of well-dressed people forms outside of it. I notice their attire differs drastically from Harris' and mine. No lace in sight. Only expensive dress shirts and trousers and designer mini dresses affix their bodies. They're ready to party, and we're ready for who knows what.

Before I can ask Harris about the differences, a valet opens my door. He extends his hand, and I slip from the low seat, careful to keep the duster closed. I'd hate for the others to think less than of me.

Harris strides around the bonnet and places his hand on the small of my back. He guides me to the front door of the building, where two men in black bespoke suits hold clipboards and wear earpieces. They greet him by name deferentially and avoid eye contact with me.

I frown and glance up at Harris.

He stares straight ahead as we enter the lobby. A gorgeous man bids us good evening—Harris by name—and takes my duster. Then he gestures towards a tray of colorful enamel bracelets. Harris picks up a silver one and places it around my wrist. I admire the lovely piece of jewelry while he closes one on his wrist before the man opens the doors behind him.

Once my eyes adjust to the dim lighting, my jaw hits the floor.

WTF?!?!?!

All around the massive room, men and women—clothed like Harris and me—partake in erotic acts. Some on stages while others carry on at seating alcoves clustered along the darker perimeter. Still more stand about, engrossed by the surrounding happenings.

The sounds of their moans and groans—including some cries of pain—fill my ears. My wide eyes dart about the room, unsure of where to settle for more than a second. One attraction after the other draws my attention like a carnal carnival.

I don't realize I halted a few feet beyond the door until Harris nudges me along. An eager couple behind us surges ahead. The woman holds a leash attached to another woman's neck as she crawls on all fours, naked save for the thick black leather collar. Her upturned ass hides nothing.

I gasp audibly when the woman slaps her partner's rear end with a cane.

The cracking sound blends in with the other hedonistic noises.

"Welcome to LEVELS London's Peepshow. Come, Siren."

Harris' warm breath against the delicate shell of my ear startles me. He chuckles and clasps my hand as he leads the way through the other people. He navigates around the room, pausing at one stage after the other. Never does he speak.

The further we enter the bacchanalia, the more my pussy throbs. My nipples already poke against the lace of the corset. The images swirl around my head, increasing as the melodic pulse of sultry music accompanies the moans and groans of the revelers. While the air is heavy with the mixture of expensive cologne, alluring perfume, and immeasurable arousal. The heady aroma alights on my tongue as I gasp from the thrill of the scene.

We enter a hallway with rooms on either side where behind floor-to-ceiling windows more people engage in acts of spanking, bondage, role playing, and more. Whatever sexy fantasy one can imagine comes to life within the four walls of each room.

A robust man stands between the thighs of another who's trussed up by heavy chains attached to the ceiling. He pours wax from a red candle over the bound man's torso. He hisses and jostles the chains when the hot liquid lands on his erect cock.

I watch, enraptured by the sight of the man nibbling the wax from the hard shaft. My pulse quickens with each passionate cry of the man in chains.

Harris moves me from the window to the next where a woman flogs a man cuffed to a large standing X made of wood. His back, ass, and thighs welted by the lash. I cringe as each flick of her wrist administers another potent strike.

Yet another room reveals two men and two women. They're so intertwined it's hard to distinguish one from the other. Their moans and groans reach the viewers as though we stood beside them.

I bite my lower lip to hold back a savage moan of my own.

Behind me, Harris' erect cock presses against my lower back. He's as turned on as I am. I tilt my head back to glance at him, only to find his hooded gaze already on mine.

I shudder as my cheeks heat.

The last room contains the setup of a doctor's office. A woman lies on the table while the doctor—a man dressed in green scrubs barefoot with a stethoscope about his neck—exams her pussy. He uses what appears to be a clamp on her clit attached by a slim chain to ones on each nipple. The contraption holds her lower lips open while his fist dives into her core. With each thrust, she screams in ecstasy. Head thrown back and mouth wide open.

I shudder and moan with her. Each knuckle drags along the walls of my dripping core.

I fear if Harris were not with me, I would drop to the ground and seek my own release, eager to cum from my overloaded senses.

He must sense my need because he leads me from the exhibition hall back to the primary room.

Newcomers replace those who were on the stages previously. I watch, fascinated by a woman bound by ropes suspended from the ceiling as a man fucks her forbidden bottom hole. She writhes and screams as the ropes sway with each impressive piston of his narrow hips. His leg muscles bunch from the power.

I cringe at the sight—never an anal girl before. Although now, I wonder what it must feel like since the woman screams in rhapsody.

"I can't wait to claim *your* ass, Siren."

Harris' unexpected words make me jump and squeak.

He chuckles wickedly as we move on.

My head swivels on my head. I do my best not to ogle now that the initial shock lessens as it registers we're in the BDSM club owned by Lucien Jackson. Since Harris says he's not a Dom, I didn't expect him to be a member here.

I glance up at him.

"Good?" He leans down to ask in my ear.

"Yes," I respond.

We continue on to stairs that lead to a floor below. At the bottom, a fascinating pair flank a set of heavy wooden double doors with two large, iron circular pulls.

The woman wears thin black laces that drape over her naked torso and hips. The man dressed only in a black leather loincloth so tiny it covers his massive bulge barely. Both have strips of black leather around their throats.

"Welcome to the Cellar," they speak in unison with their eyes downcast as they tug the iron pulls.

A woman's wail pierces the air.

My knees buckle.

Harris tightens his hold on my hand and grips my hip to steady me.

"Whoa there, lass. I guarantee the woman enjoys the pain," he murmurs in my ear. "Come."

Curiosity kills the cat?

Well, I need to know. So I allow Harris to guide me through the doors.

"Bloody hell..." I whisper at the even more outrageous sights before me.

An expansive, grand hall, austere in design houses this new erotic playground. A multi-beamed high ceiling; cobblestone floors; brick walls; lighting that resembles flickering torches in brackets on the walls and in metal stands scattered around the room; an assortment of what looks like Medieval torture devices placed in clusters.

My wide eyes jump from one section to another. I watch what I assume to be a voyeur watch five men well use all three holes and two hands of one woman. Before another giant wooden X, a woman in an all black leather jumpsuit flicks her wrist to snap the tip of a whip onto the quivering reddened skin of a man. His cries muffled by a ball stuck in his mouth and tied behind his head.

A long wail draws my attention to the near corner, the source of my earlier fright. A woman hangs upside down, arms bound to her torso with her knees bent by red rope. Red wax drips onto her exposed pussy.

The man administering the pain covers her seam with his mouth. The wail morphs into a guttural moan. Her body shudders. The ropes tremble. No sooner than silence comes from her O-shaped mouth does the man release her from the ropes and bundles her still shuddering body against his solid bare chest. She buries her face in his neck as he murmurs in her damp hair.

My pussy throbs at the carnal panorama. I'm so aroused my cream coats the thong and seeps past the gusset to drip along my inner thighs. Unsure whether my cheeks flush from embarrassment or from unfulfilled desire. I shift on my feet, eager for relief.

"See, Siren? She enjoys the pain."

I jump.

Lost in my hedonistic thoughts, I forgot Harris stood behind me. His palms glide up and down my arms as he nuzzles the side of my neck. Soft kisses a contrast to the erotic torture surrounding us in what I presume is the dungeon.

I mewl and tilt my neck to give him better access. My hands reach behind me to find purchase on his thighs. Giddiness weakens my knees.

Harris stoops to place a forearm beneath them and the

other behind my back. My arms wrap around his neck, and I find myself burying my face as the wax woman did. Now, I understand. Her feelings were so intense she needed to hide from them, safe in her lover's powerful arms. As I am in mine.

My gaze lifts when he sets me on my feet and squeezes my hip bones to gain my attention. I glance around to find we're in an alcove with dark red velvet curtains held by metal links suspended from the ceiling. They separate us from the primary floor of the Cellar.

"How do you feel?" Harris asks as my eyes return to his.

"I thought you weren't a Dom," I reply in a rush.

He smiles and squeezes my hips again.

"I am not," he responds, then continues. "But I do enjoy giving pleasure beyond the vanilla. You *have* enjoyed the spankings and edging, correct?"

My flush deepens, and I know it's from lust. I lick my bottom lip before I nod my head.

"Words, Siren. I will have your words," Harris says.

I swallow.

"Yes, I have," I respond. "And I want more."

A predatory gleam brightens his eyes.

"What's your safeword? A word for all play to stop at once," he asks gruffly.

I think a moment before I respond, "Titian."

"Titian," he repeats as he fingers a lock of my red hair. "Come."

Harris guides me to an X and turns me with my back to

it as I face him. His eyes rove down my body and back up slowly. He licks his full lower lip.

"I knew you'd look sexy as fuck in this corset"—he sighs and shrugs—"Alas, it must come off." Then he bares me naked before him.

He bows his head to lick each nipple with the flat of his tongue. The texture of it furls my nipples, and I moan. A nip to one sends a bolt of lightning to my pulsating core. His hands grip my hips as he trails open-mouthed kisses along my belly.

My butt hits the wood of the cross. I gasp, shocked we moved. A groan slips from my mouth when Harris parts the petals of my pussy with his tongue. He laps at my cream in deliberate, slow strokes.

Each time my orgasm nears the surface, he withdraws and nips my inner thighs. The pleasure followed by pain heightens my desire. My pelvis grinds against his mouth.

Two sharp smacks to my swollen pussy lips jolt through me.

I scream.

"Stay still, naughty lass," Harris commands.

I want to argue. But I want to cum more. My pelvis stills.

"Good lass," he murmurs as his lips glide along my calf.

He taps an ankle and tells me to widen my stance. Suede cocoons my ankle when he closes a cuff around it. He repeats the process with my other ankle before he rises.

My eyes lift to his as I press my hands to his firm chest. The muscles ripple beneath his warm skin as he takes one wrist and then the other to attach more cuffs. Bound, I cannot move, but a couple of inches. A sense of ease descends over me. I am no longer in control. It rests in Harris' hands. My eyes close.

"Hey, are you still with me?" Harris asks softly as he holds my chin between his thumb and forefinger. When I open my heavy-lidded eyes and respond positively, he smiles and kisses my lips. "Good lass."

I watch as he strides to a chest of drawers and returns with a peacock feather and a crop in one hand and a fist.

He tucks the implements in the back pocket of his leather pants, then kisses me as he fondles my breasts. His head lowers to suckle a nipple while his fingers dip into my pussy to collect cream he smears on the other one. He alternates between the two until my head lolls on my neck.

I hiss at the bite to my peaked nipple. Before I can question Harris, another bite closes on the other one. A glance down reveals rubber-tipped metal clamps pinch my nipples. A chain dangles between them and leads to Harris' fist.

"What—"

"Safeword?" He asks.

I blink as I consider, then shake my head.

"Then, quiet," he says.

He crouches before me and licks my pussy seam.

My head falls back against the X as the pain mingles with the pleasure. Until a third bite jerks me from bliss. This time, my brain screams *Titian*, but my body hums wait.

Harris sits on his haunches as he studies my reaction. When I don't use my safeword, he leans forward and kisses my mons.

"So beautiful, Siren," he murmurs against the heated skin.

He rises to his full height and towers over me. Then he steps back and whips a red silk blindfold from his front pocket. Deftly, he covers my eyes.

The room disappears as my hearing ramps up. Every sound intensifies, including the beating of my heart.

I tremble as the feather tickles my skin. Goosebumps rise in its wake. A whistle sounds. A snap stops all goosebumps in their tracks. The crop lands on my outer hip. I cry out and struggle against my bonds even as Harris demands I remain still. A flurry of whistles followed by snaps has my hips, thighs, and breasts afire. Cries turn into yowls.

The feather returns to tease the marks I'm sure appear on my alabaster skin.

"Safeword?"

Harris' whisper against my panting mouth jolts me.

Once again, I consider how my body feels. The feather that tickled now stresses the crop's snaps. Not enough for tears from my eyes.

But my pussy weeps.

I nip Harris' lower lip in response.

He growls and grinds his raging hard-on against my lower belly.

I whine from the loss of contact when he steps back.

Then I wail when the crop snaps my dripping pussy lips. A nip for a nip, I suppose.

Harris continues to evoke pain and pleasure until my head hangs as I sag in the cuffs worn out from the unexpected orgasms he demanded from my body. The crop clatters to the floor. His mouth closes on my clit. A burst of pain radiates from it. I scream.

His mouth worries the sensitive bud until another climax blanks my mind again. He swallows my cream noisily, then trails kisses up to my breasts.

I brace myself for more erotic pain. Not disappointed, I scream again as blood rushes to my tender nipples.

Harris cossets them with his tongue while he plays with my clit. The head of his cock breaches my pussy lips in one swift thrust to the root.

I wail as another orgasm rocks through me. Fists clench. Thighs quake. Toes curl.

He pounds away until he stiffens, and his cock pulsates as he shoots his load into the condom. His roar overtakes those in the primary room as he continues to piston his hips.

My pussy milks his dick as his orgasm triggers a final one of mine.

Fully spent, my mind floats in blissful oblivion.

HARRIS

My Kitty Kat slumbers curled on my lap. Her face pressed into my neck. Soft snores prove the depth and peace of her sleep. She's content.

As am I.

I brush my nose over her damp hair, inhaling her alluring scent. I smile at her choice of Titian as her safeword. The gorgeous hue of her hair reminds me of the Renaissance master. I wonder what he'd think of his name as a safeword used in BDSM. I shake my head and chuckle. Hey, I'll always remember it.

She stirs and mumbles my name as she leans further into my chest.

My hand rubs her back as I rumble in my chest to soothe her into rest. It makes my heart swell that she calls for me, even in her sleep. Her need for me matches mine for her.

I know Kat cares for me, and it's a relief her care is for *me* and not for my name or money. But I worry still. It would suck big time if she did not differ from others. I shake my head to rid it of the troublesome thought and let it replay our scene.

"Harris?"

My head jerks up as I open my eyes and glance around. The rhythm of a sensual bass blends with the moans of pleasure register first. The scent of sex mingles with expensive perfume and cologne. My Siren's face tilts up to meet mine.

She kisses my lips.

"You fell asleep, too," she whispers hoarse from her screams of ecstasy. "How long were we knocked out?"

I lift my wrist. An hour passed since we finished our scene. Well, damn.

"An hour. We have a suite reserved upstairs, or would you prefer we return to the hotel?" I ask. But I hope she's ready to leave since I'd rather wake up at the hotel than here and have to go there in the morning, anyway. "I want you to have the full experience of LEVELS, so it's up to you, babe."

She stretches her arms overhead, and I slip a nipple into my mouth. She mewls and runs her fingers through my hair.

"I love it so far. But let's go back to our suite. I'm ravenous," she replies.

Her nipple pops from my mouth when I lift my head.

"For me or food?" I ask with a smirk.

She giggles and rolls her eyes.

"For… both!" She teases.

I chuckle and lift her from my lap. Steadying hands on her hips prevent her from dropping to the stone floor. She smiles when I ask if she's good, and we dress again.

During the ride back, I ask her about LEVELS.

Her eyes light up as she recounts what she saw and asks about what she doesn't understand. Based on her reaction, we agree she's into the BDSM lifestyle. We decide to explore her newfound interest to determine her limits and favorites. Her excitement is contagious. I can't wait to teach more to her. Bind My Kitty Kat to me from the pleasure I instill.

I steer the Aston Martin Vanquish into the garage beneath STEELE Mayfair and help her from the low seat. She giggles when I lift her into my arms and carry her to the private elevator. On the ride up to our suite, she kisses me until my knees wobble. The vixen returns from carnal bliss with an unquenchable passion.

But I know she needs a break. So I set her down inside the foyer of the suite and tell her to ready the shower. When she pouts, I turn her around and smack that ass. She sashays away, swaying her hips enticingly.

I watch—caught by her Siren's call—then dial room service for a banquet of edible delights. It's late, but they know a Steele is in residence at the President's Suite and hop to it. I smirk. The name does have its benefits most times…

As I head to the primary bedroom, I strip and toss my

leathers onto the sofa in the sitting room before I join My Kitty Kat in the shower. Steam fills the bathroom. I can just make out her curvy form under the water's spray. My cock hardens.

I stride to the glass door and open it. My cock twitches at her bodacious body, wet and begging to be fucked. Hard. Again.

She glances over her shoulder at me and shimmies her grip-worthy hips. Her ass bounces.

Fuck. Me.

"Oh, Mr. Steele, so good of you to join me," she purrs. "If memory recalls correctly, you told me how you can't wait to claim my ass. Well…"

Her unspoken words hang in the steamy air.

I blink.

Say what now?

She wiggles her proffered treat and braces her palms against the marble wall.

Now, I know I just said she needs a break. But… I'll clarify… Her pussy needs a break, not her more than willing ass…

She winks at me.

And.

It's.

On.

"Oh, Siren, be careful of what you wish for," I warn with my lips against her ear.

She shudders but holds strong.

"*You* better be careful, Mr. Steele. You opened my sexual

tastebuds to so much more..." she retorts. "Now, will you live up to your promises? Or fizzle out. Poof."

I growl and smack her ass, sits bones, and upper thighs in quick succession. She dances on her toes as her palms slap the marble wall. I yank her hips back and press my torso on her back to lower her parallel to the floor.

"You sure you want all of this in your ass, naughty lass?" I ask as I circle my hips. My erect cock settles between her ass cheeks.

She mewls.

I smack that ass.

"You forget yourself, naughty lass," I growl.

"Y-Yes!" She yelps.

I align my cock with her pussy. One thrust sends her to the balls of her feet. She moans, and I grunt. Her wet pussy grips me.

My thrusts increase in speed as I use her natural cream to lube my cock. Satisfied, I withdraw and press the mushroom head to her back entrance. The muscles of the puckered hole resist. But I pinch her clit, and she screams through another climax. I slide in.

"Push out, Siren, and let me in," I wheeze through the tight grip her ass has on my cockhead.

She mewls and shifts on her feet, unaccustomed to anal sex. And especially not to my sizable dick.

I take it inch by inch until she relaxes to let me in balls deep. My movement ceases while she adjusts. When she undulates her hips, I move.

We find our rhythm for her forbidden hole.

To ensure she finds as much pleasure as I do, my fingers work her clit. She cums again, and I howl from the pressure. Then I let loose. She matches me thrust for thrust until I cum with an explosive knee-buckling climax. My seed jettisons into her ass. Some of it escapes the tight fit to dribble down her cheeks.

I collapse over her back and band my arms around her waist. My legs give out, and we slide to the shower floor. Once I soften, I slip from her puckered hole and pull her onto my lap. The warm water sluices over our skin.

"So good, Siren. So fucking good. And all mine," I croon against the top of her head.

She mewls and leans into me heavily.

"How do you feel?" I ask.

My Kitty Kat purrs and kisses my nipple.

I purr in response.

After a while, I stand with her in my arms. She wobbles. So I set her on the bench and bathe her gently as I thank her for her gift. Then I wash off and carry her from the shower to dry our bodies. I put robes on us and carry her to the dining room.

The room service staff set our late-night meal on the table.

I settle My Kitty Kat into a chair and lift the stainless-steel cloches.

"Mmmmm. Smells delicious," she murmurs.

I fix us a plate and lift her so I can sit, and she rests on my lap. I alternate feeding her and myself, equally hungry after our scene and lovemaking at the club and in the shower. At first, she fusses. But after I growl my displeasure, she opens her mouth.

When we're full, I carry her back to the sitting room of our bedroom. I light the fire in the fireplace—even in August, London nights have a chill in the air. I sit on the sofa and pull her onto my lap.

"STEELE Foundation has its annual fundraiser next week. Will you come?" I ask.

She stiffens between my legs.

"I'd like to introduce you to my family. It's at our beach-front compound in Southampton Village, New York. Remember, I have to return on Monday to New York City for a while. It's been some time since I was in our main office…" I ramble on.

She shifts and puts a finger over my lips.

"Of course, I'd like to come. But I have work, Harris," My Kitty Kat says remorsefully. "I can't very well fly across the globe on a whim. I have responsibilities."

I grin.

"Lachlan agreed to give you a few days off so you can make it a full holiday. So what say you now, Kitty Kat?" I ask more sure of her answer.

She frowns and leans back.

"You spoke to Mr. Jackson before you spoke with me? You mean, he knows about us?" She asks, folding her arms beneath her tits.

Oh boy…

"I mentioned it to him and to my sister, Harley. He's

cool with you and I dating, and my sister wants to meet you," I respond. "No need to worry."

She flares her nostrils.

I poke her sides and grin.

"Come on. Is it all that bad for them to know and for you to meet my family?" I ask. I go for nonchalance. But my heart thunders in my chest.

She's pissed about Lachlan and Haley knowing?

She doesn't want to meet my family?

Don't women want to meet their boyfriend's loved ones?

WTF?

At last, she sighs.

I release the breath I held with a gush of air.

"Fine. But you should have spoken to me first, Harris. I don't want your family to think poorly of me," she says.

I'm still trying to understand how to do a relationship. But I know she has a point. So I cup her face.

"As long as you're true to me, my family will hold you in high regard," I say, then continue. "No pressure, but you're the first woman I'll bring home to meet everyone. No one has not inclined me to do so before you, Kat Roberts. You are special to me."

As before, an indecipherable expression flashes in her eyes.

"Everything okay, Kat?" I ask, concerned.

Her gaze flicks away for a moment, then returns to mine.

It's as though she's struggling. And I don't know why.

She shakes her head, and a smile replaces the scowl.

"I am truly honored, Harris. I will not disappoint you," she says, then continues with a grin. "Thank you for getting my days off cleared, too. I've never been to the glitzy Hamptons. In fact, I've never been outside of the UK before you."

Her face brightens as she asks me about my family and what she should bring. I tell her I'll take care of her gown and anything else she wants. When she protests, I tell her it's my idea, so my responsibility. After I flip her over my thighs and spank that ass, she gives in.

Her hooded eyes tell me it's time to go to bed.

I make love to My Kitty Kat until neither of us can lift a finger.

"Ms. Roberts."

A gentle shake of my shoulder rouses me from sleep. I lift my head from the silk pillow to face the flight attendant for Harris' private jet. She smiles at me and continues.

"We land in thirty minutes. You slept soundly. So I didn't want to disturb you for dinner service. Would you care for a beverage or a snack after you freshen up?"

I return her smile and thank her. Once she leaves, I head for the bathroom, then switch into a pink floral maxi dress and gold gladiator sandals. I leave my hair flowing down my back the way Harris likes it and apply pink lip gloss. A spritz of perfume tops it off.

Despite Harris' offer to buy some clothes for me, I splurged on a few pieces, including this maxi dress, others, and some bikinis. I want to make a good impression on his family. Not to mention hold my own against the chi-chi women in their social circle. I don't want to appear as some know-nothing lass with the accent.

With a sigh, I settle in a cushy leather chair and glance out of the window.

Incredible!

We fly below the clouds with a clear view of the Atlantic Ocean's blue palette before the coastline, where ribbons of sand separate lavish mansions from the water's edge. Sailboats and power yachts bob on the sparkling surface. People on colorful towels and frolicking in the surf dot the beaches. Not one ready to let summer go yet.

"Here you are, Ms. Roberts."

The flight attendant rouses me from my thoughts.

I nod to thank her for the cool glass of water. My nerves make my mouth dry the closer the jet noses towards the airport. The landing strips and tower come into view.

This next week will be a testament to my ability to deceive not only Harris, but his entire family. He told me we're staying in his wing at his parents' mansion in the compound. Which means I'll be under constant surveillance.

Not to mention all the Jacksons will be at their compound next door. One on one with Lachlan or Lydie differs vastly from face time with their parents and their brothers. Talk about uncomfortable.

The flight attendant collects my empty glass as she tells me to buckle up for landing. I thank the crew as I disembark.

"Hey, babe!"

Harris strides towards me. His smile even more brilliant against his olive-tone skin kissed by the sun. A lock of his ebony hair falls over the aviators as he reaches me.

I brush it away and palm his face between my hands. On tiptoe, I slant my mouth over his for a passion-laced kiss.

He slips his sunglasses off, then swings me from my feet into a circle. His powerful frame captures me effortlessly. I squeal in his mouth, but his lips lock fast. He doesn't stop until we need to come up for air.

"I missed you, Kitty Kat," Harris murmurs, with his forehead pressed to mine. Our breaths intermingle as he stares into my eyes.

"I missed you more, Mr. Steele," I whisper.

And I do. And it makes it harder every time to continue with my revenge. I wish his connection to the Jacksons didn't exist. It's just so complicated now.

I sigh heavily.

"Hey, what's wrong?" Harris asks as he leans back to check my face. "You look glum. Was the flight all right? Do you feel okay?"

I bite my lower lip to hold back a distressed cry.

Damn. This is hard.

I shake my head, hoping to clear it and to answer his questions without having to speak. My mouth dry again.

He cocks an eyebrow and studies me.

Okay, Katrina Roberts, *smiogaid suas, nighean!*

I take a deep breath and plaster on a convincing smile that reaches my eyes.

Harris scans my face, but I pull him in for an embrace.

"I just missed you a lot, Mr. Steele," I whisper in his ear. It rings true because it is.

He buries his face in my hair and inhales deeply. The rapid beat of his heart touches mine as he holds me tight.

"We better get out of her, or I'll fuck you where you stand," he says with a cocky grin. His dove gray eyes shine.

"Would it be so bad?" I taunt.

He growls and swats my ass. Then takes my hand and leads me to a Rolls-Royce SUV. We thank the ground crew for placing my luggage in the boot as Harris opens the passenger door for me. He jogs around the bonnet and slips behind the wheel.

Our conversation turns to catching up since we last spoke and what I should expect for the coming week. Along the way, Harris points out sights and gives me a bit of history. I can appreciate the appeal the Hamptons hold on people.

He turns off the major thoroughfare to pull onto a private road. A security guard in a gatehouse triggers the oversized wooden gates set between stone pillars with wrought iron lanterns to swing open. A long driveway of pressed oil and natural stone meanders through trees like a ribbon.

Once past the impressive gates, it's like nothing I've ever seen before. The property rests on fourteen acres all beachfront. Its incredible surroundings include native trees, grassy areas, and closer to the ocean's sandy dunes. The briny scent of the ocean through the open windows fills my lungs. The calls of seagulls ring out as they search for food.

On either side of the primary driveway, secondary ones appear as we drive along. Harris points out houses for his brothers as we pass their entries. Glimpses of their gray weathered shingles and painted shutters peek from between the trees and bushes.

We continue to the end of the driveway that circles before a classic Hamptons-style mansion. The sprawling house has three stories, multiple chimneys around a widow's walk, and balconies. Sea green shutters flank the windows while below them perch flower boxes filled with white blossoms. The top half of the white Dutch door stands open to welcome us inside.

My mouth gapes at Southampton luxury living at its most extravagant.

Self-doubt rears its ugly head again.

I glance away.

"Come on, let's get you settled," Harris says, unaware of the emotions that make my stomach roil with angst. "I'll get your luggage. Head on inside."

My eyes sweep around the entry. It's a center hall with a double staircase rising along the walls. The cream, pale green, and white hues complement the stone floors. Canvas covered furniture with the accent colors fill the great room. While still elegant, the room gives a relaxed vibe.

Beyond, the view of the ocean through the wall of windows makes me gasp.

Drawn to the endless expanse of the Atlantic Ocean, I walk over to step onto the huge teak wood deck. Out on the private beach, caterers prepare for the clambake. They dug the pit and lined it with large stones and wood. The fragrant scent fills the air. Harris says they have it every year they come together for the holiday.

Clusters of adults gather around with children and dogs playing. A woman turns and shields her eyes, then waves as she grins. Others turn and wave. Shouts of hello carry over the breeze.

Harris appears at my side and waves back at who must be his family. He kisses the top of my head as he takes my hand.

"I'll introduce you after I show you our wing," he says. "They're excited to meet you."

I nod and glance over my shoulder as he leads me inside.

An older woman waves, and I return her welcoming gesture. She must be Mrs. Steele.

Oh boy…

Harris gives me a tour as we walk through the massive home on our way to his suite. He tells me he usually stays at The Bachelor's Nest with Lucien and Laurent on the grounds of their family's compound. But we'll stay here for my visit.

When Harris told me we'd stay with his parents, I envisioned being a couple of doors away from their room. But no. His wing takes up the second and third stories on the other side of the center hall. Not only a bedroom, but several rooms for his gaming, a study, guest suites, a kitchenette with dining area, and more.

He explains he shared the wing with Haley. After she and Lachlan wed, they bought a beachfront mansion on the other side of this one. The purchase extended the family's compound by even more acres. I can only nod in response.

What wealth can do.

We leave the maid to unpack my things—even though I said I could do it—and head for the beach.

My nerves peak.

Harris must sense the change this time. He stops and cups my chin and bends his knees to bring our gazes in line.

"Do not worry, Kitty Kat. They will welcome you. If you get overwhelmed, just tell me and we'll go for a walk along the beach. Okay?" He says.

I gather up my strength and take a deep breath.

"Okay," I respond, then squeeze his hand. "And thank you for understanding."

He kisses my lips softly and leads me through the open glass doors and to the beach.

"Hey!"

"Welcome, sweetheart."

"Hello, Kat."

Both clans gather around us. Harris makes the introductions. Malcolm teases him for giving in finally while Roger watches me. His intense platinum gray stare worries me until Harris whispers it's Roger's nature. I nod, relieved.

But the Jackson Patriarch garners my attention. I've studied photos of him from the Internet and read all I could find about the man. But one can't glean the power of his presence from on screen. He commands the group as does the Steele Patriarch. In fact, the amount of Alpha testosterone engulfs me.

"You look as though you're going through it. Take a slow, deep cleansing breath."

Startled, I jump and swivel my head towards the woman.

Starr Steele is beautiful. An angelic face with sorrel brown eyes filled with concern as she peers at me. Her long, curly, dark brown hair blows in the breeze around her face and down her back. An inch shorter than me, she has a sexy body to die for, fit, yet still curvy. Dimples pop from sculpted cheekbones beneath chestnut-colored skin as she smiles warmly.

"Come on, Kat. Let's sit with the girls," Starr says as she nudges shoulders with me. "Harris won't mind if we steal you away."

I follow her advice and inhale deeply. The salty ocean air fills my nostrils and lungs. I close my eyes as I exhale slowly. When I open them, Starr grins.

"Excellent! Do you do yoga?"

We walk over to where Haley, Lola, and Leonie sit with friends. They glance up at our approach and smile.

"You probably didn't catch all of our names," says a woman with chestnut brown hair and cerulean blue eyes.

Her ultra-posh Queen's English accent will help me remember her. "I'm Blair Thomas. Nice to meet you, Kat."

I smile and nod as I respond, "You're right. So, thank you. Nice to meet you, Blair. And if you ladies would be so kind as to remind me of your names and forgive my lack of memory."

They wave off my words and tell me their names: Billie a Southern Belle who resembles Tyra Banks, Adrienne a native of Los Angeles like Starr, and Márcia a Brazilian spitfire. All of them gorgeous and swish but not hoity-toity.

I sit on an oversized blanket with Blair while Starr sits beside Márcia. She works for Starr and Adrienne is her partner at Starr Light Fitness & Wellness Center. They have locations around the world, with one in Southampton Village. So Starr wasn't joking when she asked me about yoga. She's a certified fitness instructor in many disciplines.

Blair and Billie work for Lola as her CMO and COO, respectively. They've been close for years and more like family than employee. The same holds true for Márcia and Adrienne.

The tension inside of me melts as we chat and sip cocktails Billie made. Lola calls her their resident mixologist and to be careful since her drinks pack a punch. I laugh, then choke as I take my first taste.

Billie's laughter tinkles around us. It draws the attention of her Scottish beau—Patrick Rockett. Being one of the few multibillionaires in Scotland, I know of him. He strides over and lifts the petite beauty in his arms for a kiss, then sets her back before he strides away.

She giggles about him being a caveman.

I snort, thinking of Harris and his possessive behavior.

Leonie smiles at me and says, "Yes, *chérie*, all of our men are Alpha males—"

"And some even more controlling," Lola cuts in with a giggle.

Starr fans herself as she nods her head vigorously.

Blair's blush makes me wonder if her Parisian banking magnate—Luc Montaigne—counts amongst the latter.

Márcia grins behind her cup as her eyes flick to the imposing Russian Borya Alexeyev—the former MMA champion.

His Russian cousin—Anton—holds Adrienne's attention.

My comfort increases knowing the women and I share the same attraction for powerful men. More than likely, they're members of LEVELS. But it's too soon to ask such a personal question.

The caterers announce the seafood feast can begin.

We rise from the blankets and join everyone at the white-clothed tables.

Harris calls to me and I make my way to him beside one of the buffet tables.

Perfectly steamed clams, lobsters, potatoes, and corn on the cob topped with melted butter await us. Dessert options include warm blueberry and apple pies with vanilla ice cream. Harris tells me it's their traditional menu.

My stomach growls as we fill our plates, set them on a table, and go to the beverage stand. We pair our scrumptious meal with local beer and white wine.

"Where's Lydie?" I ask as we eat.

Harris swallows a mouthful and responds she's unable to make it this year.

Sebastian engages me in conversation and Lola chimes in. They're a cool couple who obviously love one another. And I guess he's of the *more controlling* category!

We enjoy the New England Clambake—another first for me—with the backdrop of a glorious sunset over the Atlantic Ocean. Afterwards, we sit on logs around the roaring bonfire to chat.

I sit between Harris' legs and lean my back against his broad chest. An oversized blanket wraps around us to ward off the evening's chill.

"How do you like it so far, Kitty Kat?" He murmurs in my ear.

I glance around at his family and friends. A touch of sadness hits me. I wish I had the same closeness with all of my family members, or more specifically, with Payton. It also reminds me of my lack of friends besides Isla.

It's been so many years since I've done nothing but study and work hard, unable to just rest and live a normal twenty-something's life. Add on the news that struck me in the gut, and I've had a doozy of a life.

My heart rate increases as the thoughts race through my head.

Then I remember Starr's cure and take a deep cleansing breath. And allow myself to relish in the here and now.

"I don't like it, Harris," I respond.

He sits up and turns me to face him.

"I love it!" I giggle.

He rolls his eyes and leans his forehead to mine.

"You gave me a scare, naughty lass," he grumbles. "How will you make it up to me?"

My pussy clenches at his voice dripping with seduction. I lick my lips.

"I'll let you decide, Mr. Steele," I purr.

Now it's his turn to take a deep cleansing breath as he closes his eyes.

I lean forward and press my lips to his ear.

"Any way you want…"

He jumps from the log and scoops me in his arms.

"Good night!" He shouts as he carries me from the gathering.

Wolf whistles, catcalls, and choruses of good night fill the air.

Then my man fills me with delight. All. Night. Long.

KAT

"Thank you for having breakfast with me, Kat. I know yesterday was a lot for you to adjust."

Mrs. Steele—I mean Shelley since she corrected me when we spoke last night—says as we sit on the deck.

I was able to join Starr and some of the girls for beach yoga shortly after sunrise and shower before I had to meet Shelley. Lola and Starr told me not to worry about my first solo interaction with her. They adore their mother-in-law and consider her as a second mother.

Starr said the meditation portion would help calm my nerves. It did. But they ramp up again. Butterflies fill my belly more so than the fruit, French toast, and sausages on my plate. I swallow some water to clear my throat.

"Thank you for inviting me. Harris speaks highly of you all the time. It's nice to meet you at last, Shelley," I respond, proud my voice didn't waver.

She smiles.

"Eat. You don't want your food to get cold, sweetheart," she says as she pops a piece of strawberry into her mouth.

I do as she suggests, and we finish our meal in a comfortable silence, broken my occasional comment on the tastiness of the food and the beauty of the surroundings.

"Well, Kat, I feel at a bit of a disadvantage. Harris told you about me, but me little about you. Tell me about yourself and your family," Shelley says after the butler clears the table and serves tea.

I take a sip from the delicate Limoges teacup before I share the story about my parents and the car accident that resulted in me being alone. When she clasps my hand in hers and offers her condolences, a twinge of guilt hits my stomach.

Shelley is so genuine. The sadness for my pain obvious in her warm brown eyes.

"My dear, words alone cannot help with your grief. But I want you to know should you need anything or anyone, never hesitate to contact me. I will give you my direct contact information," she says. "We take care of our loved ones, sweetheart. Know you are not alone."

Tears burst from my eyes as a sob wrenches my chest. All the pent-up pressure releases as my shoulders sag. I drop my head.

Arms enfold me as Shelley pulls me close. Soothing sounds only a mother can make eases the turmoil in my heart. She rocks me as I let go and my tears flow unchecked. For the first time in so long, I feel free.

But guilt wracks my soul.

I sit back as I thank Shelley for her kindness.

She pours water from the pitcher into a glass and dips a linen napkin into it before she dabs my eyes and cheeks. Her eyes filled with concern scan my face.

"Remember, time heals all, Kat. Even insurmountable loss," Shelley says softly.

I nod.

"Now, why don't we go for a walk on the beach. I usually find beautiful sea glass around this time of day. What do you think? Up for treasure hunting?" She asks with a warm smile.

"That sounds like fun," I respond as I recall the collection of colorful bits of glass in the entry foyer.

We rise, and Shelley loops her arm through mine as we walk towards the stairs for the beach.

An hour later, we return with a mini bounty. We found oval, triangular, teardrop and even heart-shaped pieces of weathered glass broken down by time, salt, and tumbling in the water. As Shelley shows me how to clean them, Harris appears.

"Oh, now I know where you've been," he says as he enters the utility room Shelley uses. "Mom has a new recruit for her expeditions."

She laughs and nods.

"Indeed, and look at what we found," she says as she holds up a piece of red sea glass shaped like a heart. "Not bad for Kat's first haul, huh?"

Harris marvels at the piece and the others as we clean

the sand from their frosty surfaces. He helps us to dry them and put them in the large bowl with the rest of the treasures collected over the years.

"Kat, you keep this one as a reminder of how what was once one way can morph into another," Shelley says, as she places the heart in my hand. "And it's red the color of life and love."

I bite my lower lip to keep the tears at bay and nod my thanks. Harris frowns, but I smile and hug Shelley.

"I believe you and the girls have a day of shopping and later our time at the spa. See you then!" She says as she turns for the staircase that leads to the wing she shares with Morgan.

Harris cups my cheek, and I lift my face to his.

"You okay, Kitty Kat?" He asks softly.

I widen my smile.

"More than okay, Mr. Steele," I respond. "Now, I ask you to help wash the sand from *me...*"

He chuckles and grabs my hand. We race up the staircase to his wing for more treasure hunting in the water.

"I'M HERE! I'M HERE!" I call out at the Rolls-Royce SUVs as they sit in the driveway before Morgana and Shelley's home. The girls wave from the open windows.

"Hurry up, slowpoke!" Lola responds. "Tell Harris to speed it up next time!"

"Dammit, Lola! How many times do I have to tell you I

do not want to hear about my brothers' sex lives!" Haley shouts from the second SUV.

Starr, Blair, and Márcia laugh in the surrounding seats.

Lola winks at me as I hop in with her, Leonie, Billie, and Adrienne.

"Who's in the third SUV?" I ask, since I account for all the girls in the first two.

"Our security team, *chérie*," Leonie responds, then goes on when my eyebrows raise. "Long story for another time. Today let's have a fun Girls' Day Out!"

Everyone cheers, obviously accustomed to a security detail.

I let it go and join in their excited chatter.

"So what are you wearing for the gala, Billie?" Adrienne asks.

Billie's green eyes light up like jade as she claps her hands.

"Oh, honey, a custom Lola's Coterie gown, of course. Must represent, you know! Especially with all the photogs who will blast the images across the Internet. Free publicity, honey," she responds with a wink.

"Same here!" Lola and Leonie say in unison, then giggle as they high five.

We join in their laughter.

"Well, someone forgot to give the memo to me... I'm wearing a Roberto Cavalli gown," Adrienne says. "I picked it up when I was in Florence after one of our fitness retreats in Tuscany. A hot little number, I might add."

Billie turns to me and asks, "What about you, honey?"

When Harris invited me, I googled past galas to get an idea of what to wear and how to style my hair and makeup. Just as Billie said, thousands of images filled my screen. And my jaw dropped at its lavishness, even on the beach.

The guests don all white according to the fundraiser's theme. Women wear designer gowns like the girls and stunning jewels—typically diamonds in keeping with the theme. Their hair in updos or loose. Men wear just as costly dress shirts and trousers or lightweight suits sans ties. Every attendee dresses well.

Not having the budget for a high-priced gown, I went to different vintage shops for my outfit. After days of scouring, I lucked up with the ultimate find. A Versace dress with a halter top, deep v-neck leading to a large crystal starburst, and a hip-grazing slit appeared like a dream. Someone only wore the magnificent piece once, and it's missing a few crystals. I replaced them with those on a crystal-embellished clutch from the same collection. Paired with strappy sandals, it's perfect for the gala. Talk about score!

I describe the gown to the girls, and they're impressed. I didn't go into detail about it being from a vintage shop. Not necessary.

Leonie remembers the season. As a megamodel, *The Lion* opened and closed the fashion show. But she doesn't ask how I came about the gown. Instead, she congratulates me on such a marvelous choice.

"And don't forget, the glam squad will arrive to do our

hair and makeup. They're scheduled to arrive at each of our residences two hours before the gala begins," she adds.

Lola shimmies and claps her hands.

"Yes! We'll be ready with our spa treatments that will wax and buff us into silky soft beauties," she says.

The girls express their thanks for the pampering sessions.

Haley reserved her favorite spa in town for us exclusively. Shelley and Lucie will arrive later in the afternoon to join us. Full-body waxes, body scrubs, massages, mani/pedis, and even aromatherapy, cupping, and reiki therapies. Every method imaginable to pamper us.

I laugh out loud at me being pampered like the princesses who rake my nerves. The girls turn to me with questioning expressions. I wave my hand in front of my face to cool down my cheeks heated from my outburst.

"Pardon me! The idea of me—a lone lass from Scotland —being pampered like a Countess and her wealthy friends tickles me," I say. "Remember, I'm just her husband's administrative assistant."

The SUV quiets.

Glances exchange amongst the girls.

Great, Kat. Talk about a major faux pas…

I start to backtrack. But Billie holds up her hand.

"Well, honey, nothing wrong with being an administrative assistant. Blair and I began as ones to Lola before she promoted us," Billie says. "However, Blair and I come from wealthy families. Yet we chose to work our way up in a field we love."

"Same with Starr and Márcia," Adrienne adds with a scowl. "What's so terrible about being an admin?"

Now, my face heats not from mirth, rather from embarrassment.

Can the roof of the SUV open up and eject me??? Oh right, the driver has the panoramic moon roof open already. Let me jump out...

My eyes dart around the girls. They wait for my response. I clear my throat.

"No offense meant. It's just that I never imagined in my younger years after a drunk killed my parents in a car accident—"

Lola gasps.

"*Mon Dieu!*" Leonie exclaims.

I'm forgotten when everyone turns to Lola.

She glances out of the window.

"*Chérie!* She couldn't have known," Leonie says as she wraps her arms around Lola, who nods.

She shifts in her seat to face me.

"I lost my parents as a teenager to a drunken driver. An only child, I was alone until Luc and Leonie—along with her parents—became my family. Then, Baz, the Steeles, the Jacksons, the Knights, our babies, and my girls expand my loved ones," Lola says softly.

She reaches her hand out for mine, then squeezes it as she continues.

"So you see, we never belittle ourselves, as we value all and love all. I understand your loss and the way it can make you doubt your worth. But don't," she smiles. "As the woman in Harris' life—my brother—you are my sister. All of ours, as an extension. We're a close-knit clan and go hard for our loved ones—including you, Kat. Understand?"

Tears fill my eyes as I blubber an affirmative response. My stomach clenches. The lies dig deeper and deeper.

Billie puts an arm around my shoulder and places a dainty handkerchief in my fist. I murmur my thanks, then thank all of them with a watery smile.

"Well then," Lola starts as she glances at each of us. "Let's make this day extra special with a Girls' Night Out! We'll go to Jackson Hole at STEELE Southampton Village and party!"

The SUV erupts in hoots and claps. Everyone's mood lifts—even Lola's—who smiles knowingly at me.

Bloody hell, Kat Roberts.

"Yaaassss, girl! Shake that thang!"

Starr's dimples pop as she laughs with her arms thrown overhead and her hips shimmy to the beat of Britney singing "Outrageous."

One can't miss Starr in her bright yellow micro mini dress with shimmering sequins and crystals. The draped cowl neckline and barely there straps accentuate her awesome figure.

I raise my arms and bump hips with her. The club's lights spark off the colorful psychedelic sequins that create the illusion of tie-dye on my mini dress. The hem rises to showcase more of my long legs, ending in sky-high strappy sandals. I throw my head back and toss my hair.

It feels so good to let loose. Even more so after hours of spa treatments.

"Whoohoo!!!" I shout. "Get it, girl! Get it, girl!"

"Hey now!"

We glance up to find Blair strutting towards us through the crowd. Also dressed to impress, the light flashes on her micro mini dress dripping in glossy pink paillettes. Her hair piled atop her head and the five-inch stilettos put the statuesque beauty over six feet. Heads turn as she approaches us.

"Uh, huh! Party over here, baby!" She says as she joins us.

The music pumps, and the crowd vibrates.

We lose ourselves in the beat.

"Hey there, sexy."

Hands reach around from behind to hold my hips. A firm body presses against my back. The rock-hard erection obvious. Warm breath blows on my ear.

I stop mid shimmy.

No, sir!

I put my hands on top of his and pry his fingers from my body as I turn my head to glare up at him.

"Take your—"

I pitch forward.

Blair catches my flailing arms.

Her mouth opens to a perfect O as her eyes widen.

I glance over my shoulder to find the guy gripped by

the throat. His hands clutch frantically at the sizable hand that holds him.

Harris!

He drags the guy close to speak into his ear. The guy shakes his head and turns to me. But Harris jerks him, and he returns his gaze to Harris, who says something else. The head bobs again, and Harris lets him loose. Without a backward glance, Mr. Handsy skedaddles away, lost in the crowd seconds later.

No one blinks an eye. Not even Starr and Blair, who I look to for a reaction. They shrug and dance on. I turn back to my caveman.

He stalks towards me. Eyes flash. Mouth a stern slash on his gorgeous face.

"Th—Thank—"

"No one touches you but me, Kat," he growls. "No. One."

My pussy throbs at his possessiveness.

"Yes, Mr. Steele," I purr in his ear as my arms wrap around his neck, and I grind my body against his solid one.

His hands tighten on my ass as he dips his knees and presses our pelvises together.

Now, *this* is an erection. Not some short, short man.

I hum in the back of my throat and leave Harris to take the lead as he moves our bodies in sync to the sensual thrumming of the bass. His masculine scent ramped up by testosterone drives me wild.

The two mojitos I drank catch up to me.

My body wants to climb Harris like a tree. Impale

myself on his thick branch. Ride him until the leaves fall off.

He must sense my need for him.

"Did you enjoy his hands on you, Siren?" He purrs in my ear.

I shudder and shake my head vigorously.

He smacks my ass and growls.

"N—Nooo!" I whine. "Only your hands, Mr. Steele."

His chest rumbles.

My nipples furl.

"Good," Harris purrs. "MINE!"

We continue to move to the hedonistic beat of the music. Only dimly am I aware Malcolm has Starr pinned to his muscular body as they dance lost in each other's eyes, and Luc rocks with Blair as though no one else exists.

I lose all sense of time enraptured by my man.

After a while, he leads me from the dance floor. We join the others in the VIP section. Each man found his woman —unable to spend one night without them. I smile at the happy couples.

Lola's right. They are a tight-knit clan.

And my man includes me in it.

HARRIS

"Those things look dangerous… And look at the road! It's muddy… and narrow… and… You have to watch out for the trees! Promise me you'll be careful, Harris. Please."

My Kitty Kat's emerald green eyes beg me from behind her glasses as she glances from the mobile screen to my face. She holds up the website for the ATV sports company where my bros and I plan to have our Guys' Day Out.

"Don't worry, babe. I've ridden ATVs my whole life and taken those trails—not roads—hundreds of times," I say as I finish tying my boots. "It's a guy's thing. We don't do cutesy stuff like a day at the spa. We like it rough and hard."

I pull her into my arms and nibble at the side of her neck where it meets her shoulder.

She squirms, and I swat her ass.

"Whatever, Harris. I'm serious. Be careful," she says as she relents and wraps her arms around my waist. She angles her head to the side, and I plant kisses on her throat. A soft moan escapes her lips.

I rise to my full height and cup her face.

"I promise," I say as I stare into her eyes.

"Thank you," she whispers.

Mesmerized by her beauty—and still hyped from our shower sex—I don't notice my mobile vibrating in my jeans pocket.

"Um, that's your mobile," My Kitty Kat says with a smirk.

I dig it out and answer the call.

"Helloooo… We're outside waiting for Kat," Lola says.

"Right. She's coming down now," I respond.

"I'm sure she's cuming…" Lola says, then laughs as she ends the call.

I chuckle as I relay the message to Kat, who rushes to our bedroom's door. I call her back for a kiss, and she hurries to meet the girls.

"Hey, bro, ready?" I ask when Malcolm answers his mobile.

"Yeah, we're on our way to pick you up. Come on down," he responds.

Everybody's coming or cuming, I chuckle to myself.

I grab my gear bag and leave the bedroom.

Two Suburbans sit out front with my brothers, cousins, Anton, and Borya inside. I toss my gear bag in the back of one and hop in.

"It's a good day to hit the trails," Lucien says.

Along with Malcolm, Anton, and Borya, they make up

the thrill seekers who travel the globe for their extreme sports. Freshwater cave diving, heli-boarding, skydiving, hell, even figher-jet flying. Although Malcolm prefers the less dangerous ones since his accident and becoming a father. But it doesn't stop him from taking it to the very edge. Wild Boys, I call them.

"Yeah, baby!" Anton says as they high five. "Time to get it on."

Borya grunts and mutters, "Not for weak little *kiskas*."

Nope, not for *pussies*. Nothing with this bunch is for the weak at heart.

The rest of the ride, they talk about a trip to the South Pole on an expedition ship. Something about glaciers, icebergs, penguins, aliens, whatever. But no thanks. I'd rather not be at the bottom of the world.

We arrive at the ATV site and change into our gear. The staff lined up our rides—black-on-black Polaris Sportsman 570 Ultimate Trail Le. It's a beast of a ride. Only the best will do.

"Ready to rock-and-roll, fellas?" Malcolm asks through the headpiece built into the helmets.

He's a total badass dressed in all black as Lil' Kim says. Although he's no Damien.

"Let's get it!"

"Hell, yeah, bro!"

"Affirmative!"

We're raring to go and rev the engines to prove it.

Malcolm circles his finger in the air, and we fall in line behind him while Anton takes the rear.

For the next hour, we ride along the trails throughout the backwoods of the Hamptons—an oxymoron if ever there was one. The sun's rays break through the canopy of trees whose branches cross over the trail. Leaves still green not quite ready to change into the stunning golds and russets of fall. A light rain from the night before muddies areas to splatter our goggles and clothes with the wet dirt. The sounds of the engines roar as we shift gears.

We climb hills and cut through pastures, then zigzag through a stream. Water splashes and washes the dirt from the twenty-six-inch tires. We pass over a wooden bridge to a glade on the other side.

Malcolm announces a break, and we dismount.

The staff setup tables with beverages and snacks. We gather around and replenish ourselves as we talk shit about each other. After a while, we jump back on the ATVs to head back.

A different route—as scenic and challenging as the first—returns us to the ATV company. The staff rush over to assist us with the vehicles and to give us bags to put our dirty gear inside. We grab some water and pile into the Suburbans.

We pull into the Jackson compound and stop in front of The Bachelor's Nest. As we walk around the side of the mansion to the beach, we strip down to our swim trunks. On the deck, we drop our clothes and race for the waves.

I dive in. The cool water envelopes me from head to toe. The stiffness from riding for over two hours over the bumpy trails washes away with the current. Refreshed, I shoot for the surface.

"Damn, bro! That was a great ride!" Baz says to Malcolm.

"Better than—"

With a growl, Baz dunks Malcolm under the water, knowing he was about to name Lola. The Alpha Doms wrestle as we urge them on.

Evenly matched—not only in physique, but in looks—they break apart laughing. Only two years separate them, and people often confuse one for the other or assume they're twins. Much to Malcolm's chagrin when he was younger—second son syndrome and all.

"Fuck you, Malcolm," Baz says.

Malcolm grins cockily.

"Oh, bro, I believe you have the wrong one," he smirks. "Your woman is shopping…"

We laugh, and Baz joins in. Nothing new with our ragging on each other.

Being a competitive crew, we race each other from the Jackson property to the edge of ours and back. Like orcas —the wolves of the sea—we swim as a pack slicing through the waves our minds on the goal. Win.

On the leg back, I jostle Laurent for the lead. He retaliates with a head butt to my flank. Sideswiped, I lose the advantage. Roger surges ahead. Anton a close second slips past Laurent and me. I use Laurent as a springboard to gain on them. But Roger hits the sand and races to chaise lounges.

"Take that, take that, take that!" He boasts as he does a victory dance shadowboxing the air.

"You win, brother," Anton says as they clasp forearms.

The others come onshore, not far behind us.

"Who won?" Patrick asks.

"There can only be one… And I take the prize," Roger responds, fingers lifted in victory signs as he smirks.

We give him shit while he grins and waves his hands.

I grab a bottle of water from the cooler before I stretch out on a chaise lounge. The others do the same or lie on towels. The warm sun dries our skin.

The house guy for The Nest brings baskets of sandwiches, chips, and fruit for our lunch. We thank him, and he goes back inside.

"So, did I or did I not say you'd get hit hard?" Lachlan asks me.

"I told him the same damn thing," Baz adds with a chuckle and a shake of his head.

"Yeah, and he kept her hidden for months. Just as his twin did…" Malcolm adds as he eyes Lachlan.

I throw up my hands as they go on and on, ribbing me about My Kitty Kat. But I take it since they don't lie. Oh, how the mighty playboy falls.

"That's all well and good. Congratulations and all. But since it's serious, we have to do a background check on Kat," Roger says. Then he raises his hand when I lean forward. "We've all experienced enough bullshit with women to know it's a necessity."

"I don't disagree. However, Jackson Corporation did

one before they hired her. And well, she they hired her. So… She must be legit," I tell them as I gaze at each face.

Lachlan shrugs.

"Well, yes, and no. The checks are for work, not for a potential wife"—I roll my eyes and he continues—"Or girlfriend. I agree with Roger. Sorry, cuz."

Baz clears his throat, and we turn to him.

"This conversation is moot. I spoke with my guy during the clambake. He'll have his report to me shortly," Baz says in a voice that brooks no argument.

I sit back on my chaise lounge.

"Fine. I get it. Especially after Roger and Malcolm's experiences," I say, then nod at Baz. "Thanks for having my back."

He returns the nod and responds, "As always, brother."

The conversation moves to sports and to the upcoming holidays. I smile at the thought of sharing Thanksgiving in Capri and Christmas and New Year's in Verbier with My Kitty Kat. She won't be alone during one of the loneliest times of the year ever again.

"LISTEN, I will not sit here on my ass while my woman shakes hers at that bacchanalia Lucien created. Especially in that minuscule dress and fuck-me heels she wore. Despite my disagreement with her choice of attire, mind you. Security or not, I'm out."

Roger hangs his cue stick on the wall rack and heads for the stairs.

We're in the game room on the entertainment level of The Bachelor's Nest. Some of us shoot pool while others play video games and bowl. But Roger's proclamation stops all action.

"Right with you, bro."

"Damn right!"

"Hold up. I'm out, too."

We separate to change into club outfits, then take the Suburbans to Jackson Hole to claim our women. The air is thick as we ride. Each of us thinks of the thirsty men who want to get their hands on what's ours.

It's not that we don't trust our women. We do. It's the greedy bastards out on the prowl for a good time. And we should all know since we were those bastards not too long ago. Yeah, so take one to know one and all that…

We jump from the SUVs to leave them with the valets and stride past the line of hopefuls who wait to get into the Hole. Lucien nods at the two security men, and they lift the velvet rope for us. We fall in as our eyes scan the crowds at the bar and at the restaurant.

I don't see My Kitty Kat, so I head to the dance floor. A glance around reveals her shaking said ass with Starr and Blair. I nudge Malcolm and Luc, then tilt my chin in the direction of our women. As one, we move through the crowd.

And gotdamn if some fucker doesn't slide up behind My Kitty Kat and put his hands on her hips. I see red. Then he pulls her against him. I charge forward with a growl.

My arm lashes out to spin him around. I grab him by the throat.

He fumbles at my fingers as his eyes pop from his head.

I drag him to speak into his ear.

"Did she ask you to put your hands on her?" I growl.

He shakes his head and has the nerve to glance at my woman.

On reflex, I jerk my arm to bring his attention back to me. When he does, I lean close.

"Did I tell you to look at her?"

He shakes his head vigorously.

I give him a hard glare, then drop my hand. I watch as he bolts through the crowd. Then I prowl towards my woman.

"Th—Thank—"

"No one touches you but me, Kat," I growl. "No. One."

"Yes, Mr. Steele," she purrs in my ear as her arms wrap around my neck. She tries for a distraction by grinding her hot little body against me. The Siren.

My hands drop to her ass and squeeze the firm, round cheeks as I bend my knees to show her what she does to me. I'm hard as fucking steel.

And get even harder when My Siren hums in the back of her throat. My hips sway and hers move with them to the rhythm of the music.

"Did you enjoy his hands on you, Siren?" I purr into her ear.

Her tremble reverberates through me as she shakes her head.

Not good enough. My hand comes down on those cheeks. Hard.

"N—Nooo!" She whines as she jolts. "Only your hands, Mr. Steele."

My chest rumbles.

"Good," I purr. "MINE!"

I continue to lead us on the dance floor. Everyone and everything fade to black. If we keep at it, no one can hold me responsible for ravaging my woman right here, right now. It's time to leave the erotic energy of the dance floor behind. For now.

The VIP section and a drink call. I grin when I note the men claimed their women. They're gathered around on banquettes—some sit on their laps—as they laugh and sip cocktails. Excellent.

I take a seat next to Patrick and guide My Siren to my lap. She settles, and I place my hand on her thigh. My thumb brushes the hem of her dress. We'll have to have a conversation about the length of her dresses for future outings.

The server appears and takes our orders.

"So, you decided to crash our Girls' Night Out, *Amoureux?*" Leonie asks Roger.

He lifts his snifter to his lips and nods. After a sip, he responds, "*Oui.* And lucky you were sitting here and not shaking that ass in that little dress."

She bites her lower lip to hold back a giggle. Her feline-shaped amber eyes sparkle with mirth as she stares back at him.

Roger can't stay upset with his wife and grins. He leans over and whispers in her ear. Crimson suffuses her golden caramel skin as her eyes widen. Roger sits back with a smirk and pats her knee. She shivers.

He winks at me when his gaze meets mine. His platinum gray eyes flick to Kat, and he smirks again.

I can't help but to grin widely.

For all the tough guys we are, we're wusses for our women.

For the rest of the Combined Night Out, we dance, drink, and have fun. The marrieds cut loose harder than those without rings. Nothing slows them down as they party the night away.

When Kat declares a Scotswoman can hold her liquor in an almost indiscernible accent, then wobbles on her feet giggling, I turn to the others and call it a night. Time to get my bonny lass showered and tucked into bed.

We have a long day and night tomorrow.

On the ride back to the Steele compound, she rests her head on my lap. Her soft snores fill the SUV. I keep my hand on her hip to hold her steady.

Back at the mansion, I carry her up the stairs and to our wing. In the shower, My Siren reemerges. Her tiny hands reach for my girth—hard, even though I have no intention of fucking her while she's intoxicated.

"Harris Steele… You're so bloody sexy… I can't believe you're mine…" she gets out.

I take her hands and bring them to my lips—my cock weeps in dismay.

"Believe it, Kitty Kat," I murmur against her fingertips as I stare into her glazed eyes—more bottle green than emerald. "And you are mine."

I finish bathing her, then leave her on the marble bench while I turn towards the spray to clean myself.

Hands slide around my waist. Fingertips trace the v-shape muscles on the lower sides of my abs. A zing runs through me as more blood pumps to my cock. Full lips kiss along my spine as the fingers grip the base of my erection. They slide to the tip and swirl the pre-cum around the swollen mushroom head.

My other head lolls back as I close my eyes to revel in her erotic touch.

My Siren continues to caress me with gentle strokes. It takes every ounce of my self-control to combat the urge to snap my hips. She picks up speed. I match her rhythm. With a carnal cry, I unleash a torrent of jizz.

"Oops…"

She giggles and plants a last kiss on my shoulder blade.

I turn off the spray, scoop her into my arms, and dry us before I carry her to our bed. Tucked beneath the silky sheets, she drifts off to sleep. I press my front to her back with her head cradled by my biceps and rest a hand on her pussy.

MINE!

"Good morning and welcome, everyone! I know after the night we had, we're in need of a more grounding session. First, Adrienne will lead you in pranayama. The practice of breath work in yoga. Prana Sanskrit for vital life force, and yama means to gain control. Next, Hatha—ha sun and tha moon for balance—with me to allow our minds to withdraw from external objects. Then end with meditation with Márcia. Namaste."

I bow my head with hands palms together at heart center as the divine light within me bows to the divine light within Starr.

When Harris awoke me this morning, he assured me I agreed to beach yoga. Fortunately, it wasn't in the wee hours of the day's start. I grumbled but dressed in leggings and a long-sleeved t-shirt to ward off the chill before the sun could warm the Earth. Then trudged after him to the sand.

However, as I sit on my yoga mat and practice the alternate nostril breathing technique Adrienne teaches to us, my mind clears. The hangover dissipates with each inhalation and exhalation. Plus, the concentration tunes everything out as I coordinate my breathing.

By the time we move on our mats for Hatha, I'm more settled—just as Starr predicted. The flow of the poses focuses on rooting us into the Earth. Then Starr adds a twist for the peak pose. She has us face our partners and move into a boat pose with the backs of our legs and the tips of our fingers or palms touching.

Naturally, some of the guys make comments about the intimate position. Starr laughs from where she's with Malcolm, demonstrating the pose. He smirks at us.

We end in savasana. After the repose, Márcia calls us to a comfortable seat for meditation. Her soothing voice guides us deeper within ourselves. The sound of the waves acts as a backdrop to her message of release. She incorporates the rhythmic flow of the Atlantic Ocean into the meditation and likens it to the ebb and flow of our thoughts. Just let go, she reminds us as the session comes to an end with the tinkling of a bell.

Once again, we bow to each other.

"Feel better, Kitty Kat?"

I glance over my shoulder at Harris. He smiles. It's as warm as the sun higher in the clear blue sky.

"Much, thanks for the reminder," I respond as I kiss his lips. "These are my first adult sessions. When a guest teacher comes to the Center for the lads and lasses, I join in."

"Well, we'll have to do something about that," he says. "I want you nice and limber."

"Last one in is a rotten egg!"

Haley shouts, then squeals when Lachlan lifts her from the sand midstride and tosses her over his shoulder as he races to the water. Her laughter trails behind them.

"Better hurry!" Harris says as he grabs my hand and hoists me to my feet.

We charge down to the waves and dive in with the others. The sun hasn't heated the water yet, so I yelp as I break the surface.

"Reminds me of home," Borya shouts. "Good for the soul!"

"Not my home! Rio is always sultry," Márcia quips as she bobs next to him. Then squeals when he ducks beneath the water and lifts her onto his powerful shoulders.

"Better now?" He asks as she laughs.

Our bodies adjust to the cool temperature as we frolic in the surf. Anton follows suit and lifts Adrienne. She and Márcia scrabble to unseat the other. The rest of us cheer them on or swim along the shoreline.

After a while, Sebastian calls for breakfast, and we clamber out of the water. We head along the beach from in front of Harris and their parents' mansion to the deck of his and Lola's equally impressive one. We step under the outdoor showers to rinse the saltwater and sand from our bodies. Up on the deck, the nannies bring the babes out along with their six dogs. The meal is buffet style prepared by their chef.

We have a delicious—albeit rowdy—breakfast. And I love every minute of it!

"I know my beautiful Billie is ready. So, you lasses all set for the evening?" Patrick asks.

"Oh, yes! And we cannot wait for the glam squad to arrive," Haley responds. "It's been a while since I last dressed up in anything fancier than joggers and a t-shirt!"

Lachlan leans over and presses his lips to her temple.

"And oh what a sexy Hot Mama you are in those clothes, babe," he says.

She grins at her husband and thanks him.

"Don't forget the diamond pieces from Harry Winston —this year's jewelry sponsor. Their reps will have a selection for you to choose from an hour before the gala begins," Sebastian says.

I gasp and turn to Harris.

"Yes, you too, babe. So, pick whatever you want," he says with a grin.

My heart pounds as I recall the fabulous jewels the women wore at the prior galas. Now, I'll get to sparkle too. I cannot believe my luck!

"Thank you!" I exclaim as I throw my arms around his neck. "This is going to be an incredible night I'll never forget."

"The first of many, Kitty Kat," Harris murmurs in my ear as he embraces me. "Choose wisely. If you're a good lass, maybe I'll let you keep them…"

My heart stops, and I gasp again.

No bloody way!

Harry Winston jewels of my very own??? They're worth a fortune. That's more than luck. It's a miracle.

"I promise to be a very, very, *very* good lass, Mr. Steele," I purr against his ear, then nip it with a slight tug.

He buries his face in my hair to muffle a groan.

I turn back to my breakfast with a grin on my face. Fantastic!

"Your hair is a pretty color."

The words and tiny fingers twirling my hair draw my attention to my side. One of Leonie's twin boys stands beside me. He's a miniature Roger and has the sparkle of a free spirit in his eyes like his mother. He smiles at me. So adorable.

"Why thank you, lad. But you have me stumped. Are you Rodolphe or Gaspard?" I respond, returning his smile.

His eyes dance.

"You have to guess," he says. "You have two chances so it's easy."

I snort at his precociousness. He's a smart little bugger!

"Hmmm, now let me think… Ropard?" I ask a blend of their names.

He pauses a moment to consider my guess, then throws his head back and laughs.

"You're funny! No one has ever called us that before," he says. "Gaspard."

I ruffle his silky ebony curls.

"Now, I won't confuse the two of you ever again," I tell him with a grin.

He nods and runs back to the other babes yelling Ropard to his twin. I watch as Rodolphe laughs, then waves at me. I return the gesture and sit back in my chair.

"You're so good with children, *chérie*," Leonie says as she beams at me.

I tell them how I volunteer at the Aberdeen Children's Center twice a week and love children. Leonie shares how she mentors girls and teens at a center in Paris and hosts a charity gala for it every year. We exchange stories and laugh or offer advice. It feels good to tell a truth for a change.

After we finish, everyone separates for their residences. Harris takes my hand, and we walk through the gardens of the property back to his home. He plucks a red flower from a bush and places it behind my left ear with a wink. I blush at the significance I'm taken.

Back in his wing, we take a shower and make love. Harris has to do some work and goes to his home office. I gaze at the big fluffy bed longingly. Well, it was a long night and an early morning. Plus, I need to be fresh for the gala... I run to the bed and dive under the covers. Nap time!

"Honey, you have luxuriant hair. The color... it's to die for and not the bottle kind either. Let's get you glammed up for all those photos you're bound to get captured in.

Between your gown and your beauty—not to mention being on Harris Steele's arm, that elusive bachelor—you're front-page news, honey! Let's not disappoint."

I grin as I sit in the leather swivel chair before a full-length mirror in Shelley's full-size salon decorated in shades of white. It has two of every station: sinks with leather chairs for washing hair, vanities with floor-length mirrors and leather swivel chair, manicure tables, leather massage chairs and sinks for pedicures, and massage and treatment rooms.

The glam squad finished her gala prep earlier since she has to see to the event. Now it's my turn, and I'm beyond excited.

The squad begins their magic as I watch, transfixed. The hairstylist sweeps my hair into an updo *to accentuate the stunning bone structure and graceful swan neck*. To frame my face, he leaves a side bang that swoops past my ear. In the back, he secures the rest of my hair in a large, loose bun with tendrils dropping to meet the tips of the side bang. He pronounces it's a masterpiece and steps aside for the makeup artist.

She tips my chin and moves it side to side as she studies *the angles*. Meanwhile, her assistant whips out an assortment of brushes, sponges, and trays of colors. Arrayed on the table beside the artist, she makes a selection, and her hands move across my face. With a satisfied smile, she spins the chair towards the mirror.

My eyes widen at my reflection. It's still me, but so much more. A glammed-up version. Sophisticated.

"You like?"

I lift my gaze to the hairstylist and grin at him and the makeup artist.

"Thank you! I absolutely love what you've done!" I exclaim. "I feel like Cinderella going to the ball."

The stylist snorts.

"Perhaps. But it won't all go away at midnight, honey! No splattered pumpkins for you," he says, shaking his head with an elegantly arched eyebrow.

"Most definitely," the artist agrees with a nod. "Now, time for your gown."

The dresser steps forward and helps me from the chair. We walk to the adjoining dressing room, where my vintage Versace gown hangs on a rack with my strappy sandals below. A barely there nude G-string rests on the table.

I swap the silk dressing gown for my gala one. The dresser slides my feet into the sandals and ties the straps around my ankles. When she finishes, I glide to the triple mirror. I glance over my shoulders and spin around to check every angle is perfect.

"Sensational."

My eyes fly to the middle mirror to find in the reflection Harris leaning on the doorjamb. He's simply divine in a white suit and dress shirt open at the collar. The hair I love to run my fingers through slicked back from his handsome face. His dove gray eyes darken to obsidian as they sweep over my body from head to toe.

The erotic energy palpable, the glam squad excuse

themselves and scurries from the dressing room—if not the salon.

"Spin for me, Siren," Harris commands.

My cheeks heat as I duck my head, then I lift it to meet his gaze. With deliberate slowness, I pivot in a complete circle. As I face him again, I stick my leg through the hip-grazing slit and place a hand on my hip. I thrum my finger-tips against the exposed skin.

Harris growls and stalks towards me.

My nipples tighten and my pussy clenches as his waves of erotic energy lap at me.

A long finger slides along my inner thigh, leaving goosebumps in its wake. When it grazes the side of my G-string, I shudder. It rims the silk and prods my engorged clit. I whimper and clutch his shoulders as my head bows again.

"If this were anyone's event, I would say fuck it and ravish you right now. But I cannot disappoint my mother," he says as his finger withdraws. "However, later, you. Are. Mine."

Harris takes my hand and leads me from the dressing room on wobbly legs.

"Mademoiselle, you look incredible and will honor the Harry Winston jewels with your beauty."

I peek around Harris, and my jaw drops.

Trays of glittering diamonds sit on the center island in the salon's anteroom. They dazzle beneath the lights.

"Kindly make your selection, or I can recommend pieces to compliment your look," the representative says.

Harris urges me ahead of him when I linger, ogling the jewels at a distance. I smile and thank the rep as I walk to the table, eyes still mesmerized by the glittery gems.

An array of necklaces, earrings, rings, bracelets, and even hair clips rest on navy blue velvet beds or drape from stands. The sizes of the stones range from large to humongous. The rep hands a pair of white gloves to me. I gaze at them questioningly, then notice she has on a pair, too. I slip them on.

A necklace with a cluster of diamonds at its center and two rows of diamonds leading up to and around the neck catches my eye. It reminds me of the crystal cluster on my gown. The rep senses my interest and hesitation, lifts it from the stand and holds it up to catch the light.

It sparkles as though tiny fires live within each gemstone.

She places it around my neck, and her assistant lifts the mirror.

My breath catches in my throat.

Instinctively, my fingers reach up to caress the diamonds. But I stop afraid to damage it in any way.

The rep steps around the table with matching cluster earrings in her hands. I take them from her and slip them on, then turn to the mirror. Blindingly breathtaking.

Struck dumb, I don't notice her and another assistant place bracelets on each of my wrists until they lift my arms to reflect in the mirror.

I gasp.

Hundreds of carats of diamonds grace my ears, neck,

and wrists. Never in my life—and probably few of many other peoples' lives—would I ever experience being covered in Harry Winston High Jewelry. Talk about posh!

"How do you like them?"

Once again, Harris stands behind me, closer this time, reflected in the mirror. His eyes glitter like black diamonds.

"Love," I whisper.

He cocks an eyebrow.

"The diamonds or… something else?" He whispers. His eyes blaze.

I swallow.

Bloody hell, Kat Roberts. Slip of the tongue?

I open my mouth to answer. But he shakes his head. The internal fire extinguished.

"They look lovely on you. Take them all," he says with a small smile. "We need to get going."

He steps away, and the heat of his body evaporates with him.

I shiver from the loss—in more ways than one.

With a less stellar smile, I thank the representative and her assistants. She tells me a man from their security team will shadow me discreetly. I nod, numb.

The man and I turn to Harris, who's at the door typing on his mobile. He glances up when I touch his elbow. He extends his arm, and I loop my arm through it.

We walk through an outer door towards a group of photographers and television crews lined up along a platinum gray carpet. Behind it stands a white wall printed with company logos. As guests exit their cars—left with valet attendants on the driveway—they walk across the carpet and pose for the cameras. Flashbulbs spark in the night sky.

Harris quickens his pace when he spies Malcolm and Starr ahead of us. I hurry to keep up with his long strides. Roger and Leonie appear along with Haley and Lachlan. Sebastian and Lola call from behind us.

When we reach the beginning of the carpet, Harris glances down at me.

"Showtime. Smile for the cameras," he says with a smile on his face—albeit one that doesn't quite reach his eyes. He turns to speak to Roger.

I tug his arm.

Harris tilts his head to gaze at me.

"Are you okay?" I ask.

He maintains his smile, and nods before he leads me down the carpet.

Billie and the hairstylist weren't kidding when they said the photographers would go into a frenzy. They call out to Harris and his siblings by name. Haley and Lachlan they address as Countess and Earl. Megamodel Leonie gets personal shout outs too. She turns her multimillion-dollar smile to full wattage towards the cameras to strike a pose.

I let the worry over Harris' reaction to my slip of the tongue go. A smile spreads across my face as brilliant as the Harry Winston jewels. Someone asks Harris who the beauty is on his arm, and he smiles down at me. He lifts his gaze back to them and says my name, then moves on before he answers who I am to him.

A twinge hits my belly, but my smile doesn't falter.

I've had to fake my way through many a time. Tonight, will be no different. Would I have preferred this Cinderella night was unlike no other? Yes. But I've learned to mask my disappointment.

Pumpkin, anyone?

Why the fuck did my heart dip when Kat hesitated? Hell, I can't say I love her either. But damn if it didn't hurt like a mother.

I guess for one wuss moment, I got caught up with all the talk of background checks for wives, the way she blends in with my family seamlessly, hanging around all the lovey-dovey couples. Being the only Steele playboy left standing…

Fuck.

How the hell do I deal with these crazy emotions? Other than my female relatives, I've never cared about a woman loving me. And now this?

I whip out my mobile to send a text message to Haley.

Hey, where are you?

A touch to my arm, and I glance down to find Kat at my elbow. Mentally, I shake off the unsavory thoughts and extend my arm. She places her hand on my forearm, and I lead her downstairs and out the door.

We near the step and repeat highlighting the event sponsors, including STEELE International, Inc., Jackson Corporation, Lola's Coterie, Starr Light Fitness & Wellness Center, Banque Montaigne, Harry Winston, and other notable companies. Ahead of us, I spy Malcolm and Starr. I quicken my pace.

For any STEELE event—particularly for the STEELE Foundation—we show a united front as a family. The platinum gray carpet serves as the platform for the media to capture our photos and garner interviews. And this evening is no different. So I set the glum mood aside.

Roger and Leonie. Haley and Laurent. Sebastian and Lola. We all fall in line at the beginning of the carpet.

I glance down at Kat and smile.

"Showtime. Smile for the cameras," I tell her before I turn to step behind Roger. Age order and all.

I pause when Kat tugs at my arm. She glances up at me anxiously.

"Are you okay?" She asks.

A flicker of victory ignites within my heart. She knows she did me wrong. Good.

My smile remains fixed in place since the flashbulbs already pop off in rapid succession as Baz steps to the carpet. I nod in response to her question, then start us along the line.

The media calls our names as we gather before them.

We pose as a group, couples, then the men step aside for our women to get glam shots.

I watch as Kat preens and works that fuck-me slit up her thigh like nobody's business. She glows and not just from the diamonds worth millions of dollars. Her innate beauty and poise make her striking. The photogs go wild for her.

When it's time to move on to the gala, I step forward and put my hand on the small of her back.

"Who's the beauty on your arm, Harris?"

I glance from the reporter and smile down at Kat.

"Kat Roberts," I respond.

"Who is she to you?" The reporter persists.

Always leave them guessing. An air of mystery never hurt anyone. In fact, it makes them beg to know more.

I stride away with Kat on my arm, leaving the question unanswered.

We walk across the giant side lawn, aglow by thousands of fairy lights and lanterns. Parallel to the beach below, two giant white pavilions sit: one for dinner and the other for dessert and dancing. The white table settings and flower centerpieces glow warmly in the light from candles and crystal chandeliers beneath the silk pleated canopies. On the sand, several bonfires burn to light up the beach for those who wish to venture for a stroll in the moonlight.

Servers from Lucien's catering company mill about with trays of Champagne and wines or hors d'oeuvres. Two bars sit on opposite corners for those who prefer to select a drink or the signature cocktail. To one side, a band plays lively music piped through speakers, also heard out on the beach.

Guests mingle and chat in the different areas, all dressed in the theme of the annual STEELE White Party.

It's already bustling since it's the party of the season and everyone wants a ticket for a chance to see and be seen amongst the world's elite. Not to mention raising funds for STEELE Foundation.

I spot our mother and father speaking with other couples. Uncle Connor and Aunt Lucie stand beside them. I continue towards them.

"Excuse us," I say as I interrupt their conversations.

My mother smiles and tilts her head.

I kiss her cheek.

"Shelley, this is amazing. So beautiful!" Kat gushes as she double kisses my mother's cheeks.

"Thank you, sweetheart. And you look phenomenal! How you sparkle," she responds as she holds up Kat's left hand. My mother stares pointedly at Kat's bare ring finger, then up at me. Her eyes dance with mischief.

Great.

"Well, sweeties, enjoy the night. The fireworks will be spectacular later," she adds with a wink.

"Kat, you do look lovely, dear. Go have fun, you two," my father says as he draws my mother back to the guests.

We say hello to Uncle Connor and Aunt Lucie—who also eyes me with a smirk.

These two besties…

I snag two glasses of Champagne from a passing server

and hand one to Kat. She takes a sip with relief. I do the same.

"Harris? That is you, darling! Where have you been all summer?"

I glance around and find a socialite I fucked a few of times over the years.

Her ice blue eyes scan my body as she licks her lower lip. With each step, her tanned, long legs peek out of the front slit in her floor-length, one-shoulder gown. Her blonde hair cascades down her back. Yeah, she's a beauty.

Kat stiffens next to me.

"Hello, Bernadette—"

She leans into me and reaches up to kiss my lips. But catches the corner of my mouth as I turn my head away. She frowns at me. Then her eyes slide to Kat, who placed her hand on my arm possessively. Bernadette's eyes widen, surprised to see a woman claim me, then narrow at the sight of the many diamonds.

"Well, no need to claw at Harris, pet. We've known each other since we were children," Bernadette says to Kat, then turns to me and places her palm on my chest. "We'll talk another time."

She sashays away.

Kat drops her hand from my arm and finishes her Champagne in one gulp. A server passes, and she replaces the empty flute with a full one. As she takes a sip, she eyes me over the rim. Emerald fire blazes.

Oh, so she's pissed? Huh.

"Kat! I love your dress, honey!"

We turn around to Billie and Patrick. The petite beauty looks stunning in a below-the-knee-length flowy gown with double straps connected to the fitted bodice by crystal coins. Her full breasts nearly spill from the low cups. Ropes of diamonds adorn her neck.

Patrick keeps a possessive hand on her side below her breast. We talk while the girls chatter.

Unknowingly, they paused the questions Kat more than likely to have for me.

Good.

I'm still working on the love situation and don't even want to get into it about a past fuck-buddy.

More people approach us during the cocktail hour. Then it's time for dinner. Kat goes to freshen up with Blair and Leonie. Luc, Roger, and I wait for them before we enter the pavilion. When they return, we make our way to our tables.

I help Kat into her chair and sit beside her. We're at a table with Haley and Lachlan and other guests. Our mother always arranges for Steeles and Jacksons to sit at different tables throughout the space, so guests feel a connection to their hosts. And as our father reminds us, business can take place anywhere.

Kat loosened up after her second flute of Champagne. She smiles and chats with her seatmate and the others at the table as though it's second nature for her to attend a high-society event. Her laughter tinkles. She charms everyone. They're captivated by her Siren's call.

As am I.

I take a swig of my Jackson Cabernet Sauvignon and shrug. So she didn't tell me she loves me. It's not a deal-breaker. Our connection hit me hard from the beginning. She feels it too. I know it.

A small hand rests on my thigh.

I turn my gaze to Kat.

"Will you dance with me?" She asks with a small smile. It widens when I rise from my seat and help her from hers.

As we dance, I pull her close, and she melds her soft body to mine. We glide across the floor. Our steps fluid.

She tilts her head back.

"Are we okay?" She asks as her eyes search my face.

I take a moment to think about it. Then lower my mouth to her ear.

"Yes, Siren," I respond.

Later that night, our fireworks best those above the Atlantic Ocean. Beneath the moonlight, her alabaster skin glows as brilliantly as the diamonds on her naked body. I prove to My Siren we are more than okay as we explode again and again.

"Yeah, I received the alert a few minutes ago... Right... I'm taking care of it now. From the looks of it, they didn't get past the first firewall... No, not sophisticated at all... Don't worry. Go cuddle up to Little Lord Fauntleroy... Ha, hilarious! A true comedian..."

I end the call with Haley and return my full attention to

our client's corporate network. True, a member of our STEELE Technology and Cyber Security team could handle the task. But I prefer to do the task since it's for a longtime client.

The process doesn't take much time and gives me a chance to pull up the beta technology for a program I'm developing. A few more tweaks and I'll have it ready for market. Haley thinks it's groundbreaking, and I agree. The revenue the program should generate would please Baz immensely.

I leave my office and head for the kitchenette for a bottle of water and a banana. We have the VIP post-gala brunch soon, so I don't want to eat too much. My mobile rings, and I talk to Laurent for a while, then return to my office.

Kat sits behind my laptop. A frown pinches her eyebrows together as she scans the screen.

What the fuck???

She was asleep when I left her in our bed an hour ago. Now she's snooping through my business?

"Kat," I snap as I storm over. "What are you doing on my laptop?"

She startles and pushes her eyeglasses up her nose. She's worn contact lenses most of the days, but they dried her eyes last night when she removed them. The little librarian shouldn't get into my laptop.

"Harris! Bloody hell! You scared me," she responds.

I yank the laptop from beneath her fingers.

"I—I was only searching the Internet. Billie sent a text

message about photos from last night. But my mobile died as I was scrolling through them. Sorry!" Kat babbles.

And damn if Page Six's website isn't on the screen. Loser alert…

I lower my head and peek at her.

Her flushed cheeks and wide eyes make me feel like an ass.

Great, Harris, good job.

"No, I'm sorry," I say as I close my laptop and set it on the desk. "It's my work laptop. So I don't let anyone but Haley use it."

I round the desk and crouch beside Kat as I spin the chair around with her legs on either side of me. My palms rest on her bare thighs and slide up to the hem of my dress shirt she donned. It swallows her up and calls to my possessive nature.

She folds her arms beneath her braless tits and scowls at me. I do my best to not get distracted by their pebbled nipples poking through the cotton.

"Oh, so you don't trust me?" She bites out.

I shake my head.

"It's not that I don't trust you. It's beyond me. That laptop has proprietary information on it, and I'm responsible for a lot of data. As I said, only Haley has access. Not even Sebastian," I tell Kat. "But I shouldn't have thought you were in the files and spoken to you so harshly. I apologize. Forgive me?"

She purses her lips, unimpressed by my response.

I skim my index fingers along her seam, still swollen from last night.

My Kitty Kat squirms in the chair and tries to move away from me.

I won't have it.

Leaning forward, I slant my mouth over hers. My tongue probes against her lips as my fingers stroke her pussy. Her squirming turns to writhing. As her mouth opens, she moans. Her juices gush. I swallow her cries, then dip my head to lap at her cream.

"This year's gala surpassed our expectations. We raised over thirty-five-million dollars! The sponsors, tickets, and donations accounted for seventy-five percent while the silent auction and journal ads made up thirty percent. So far, we've received favorable media coverage. Thank you all for a successful fundraiser!"

Our mother stands at the podium beneath a pavilion and beams at the VIP patrons as she claps.

Proud of his wife, our father rises from his seat at the head table and claps too. Everyone joins him for a standing ovation.

I glance around to find my siblings and cousins clapping the loudest and with whistles. Beside me, My Kitty Kat grins with her hands above her head to clap. She glances up at me, and her smile widens.

My mother yields the podium to the sponsors. One by one, they speak to the VIP patrons to thank them and to plug their companies. When it's their turn, Baz and Lachlan outdo each other to raise their donations and many in the crowd re-open their wallets to give more. My mother thanks everyone again to rousing applause.

"You must be so proud," My Kitty Kat says. "Your Mum does incredible work."

"*She's* incredible and feels strongly about affordable housing for urban, lower-income families," I respond. "Not everyone has the advantages provided by wealth or name. It's important to give back and not just monetarily. Every summer since we were thirteen, our parents made certain we worked at the construction sites and in the Foundation's offices to learn firsthand what it takes to help others. We never hung around at the beach all day. And we're thankful."

My Kitty Kat stares at me a moment. That flicker passes through her eyes, and I can't decipher its meaning again. She nods.

"You up for surfing after this?"

Laurent crouches between us.

I glance back at My Kitty Kat and raise an eyebrow questioningly. She nods enthusiastically.

"Well, I think you have your answer, cuz," I respond with a grin. "We'll meet you on the beach."

"Eager, huh?" He chuckles. "Sounds good, I'll ask the Wild Boys."

An hour later, we're at the surf line astride our boards. My Kitty Kat bobs on the surface as she glances over her shoulder, searching for the right wave. She furrows her brow in concentration. When she spies one on the horizon, she flips to her belly and paddles. The wave catches her, and she hops to her feet, wobbles a bit, then finds her balance. She rides the wave almost to shore before she slips off. She pops to the surface and whoops gleefully.

I can't believe she's picked up the technique so quickly.

"Stop gawking at your woman and catch a wave already."

Lucien chuckles as he paddles past me back from his last ride.

Yeah, wuss…

I glance over my shoulder and skip the next wave. The one after has my name written all over it. I drop to my stomach and paddle. The wave slides beneath my board, and I hop up to ride it in. Malcolm rides it too and gives me the shaka hand wave as he grins like the Cheshire Cat.

We reach the beach at the same time. He picks up his board and claps me on the back.

"A girl who surfs… You got yourself a real winner with Kat, bro!" He says.

Now I grin like the Cheshire Cat and nod enthusiastically.

"*A* girl could really get used to this celebrity lifestyle!"

My Kitty Kat giggles as the driver maneuvers the platinum Rolls-Royce Phantom Extended behind the line of cars and limos leading to STEELE Aberdeen.

After our Labor Day getaway, I stayed in New York City and Kat flew back to Scotland with Lucien, who continued on to Paris. The week went well despite my reaction to her avoidance of the l-word for me.

We had a great time, and my family *loves* My Kitty Kat. My Mom made more than one hint about the future I could have with Kat. Hell, even my Dad—who rarely involves himself in our relationships—urged me to consider long term with Kat.

She impressed my parents with her smarts, sense of humor, and her ability to blend with the rest of our family and close friends. Add in her independent streak—like my sisters-in-law and Lydie—and she came out the winner. Ding, ding, ding.

At this exact moment, I can't say I'm ready to put a ring on it à la Beyonce. But I admit the idea of a future with Kat Roberts intrigues me. As my wife, as the mother of my children, I can see it. Just not tomorrow...

However, before I return to New York City, I plan to ask her to spend the holidays with me. The girls were talking about Capri and Verbier during Labor Day. Kat listened raptly.

Lola told me My Kitty Kat shared the tragedy of her parents and subsequent orphan status. Lola impressed upon me the importance of not allowing Kat to be alone while we're all together for Thanksgiving, Christmas, and New Year's. Not to mention I'd rather not have her in Aberdeen and I'm elsewhere. So I promised Lola I'd ask Kat to join us. Pleased, Lola gave me a big hug and kiss.

Now, I shift in my seat to face My Kitty Kat.

She looks ethereal in softly pleated layers of wispy pink silk-chiffon. The elegant column gown with sweetheart neckline and train that gathers between her shoulder blades to float to the ground behind her makes My Kitty Kat resemble an angel.

Once again, she denied my offer to purchase her attire. But she does wear the suite of Harry Winston diamonds I gifted her. They glitter in the dim lighting of the sedan as she stares out the tinted window. In the reflection, her eyes dart around as a smile plays at the corners of her lips.

I chuckle.

"Get used to it, babe. The social season is upon us," I reply. "And did I tell you just how spectacular you look?"

She giggles and shifts to face me.

"Yes, you did. Many times!" She responds as her emerald green eyes twinkle like the diamonds.

"Just checking," I smirk.

The sedan stops, and the valet knocks on the window with his gloved hand to ensure we're ready to exit before he opens the door. I rap back, and the door swings open.

"Showtime. Smile for the cameras," I say to My Kitty Kat.

She holds back a giggle and nods. I wink at her and exit the car, then turn to take her hand. She rises regally.

We line up at the edge of the Scotch-colored carpet before the step and repeat. Tonight, it's Aunt Lucie's fundraising gala for Jackson Foundation. It operates alcohol treatment centers for lower-income individuals and provides support for their family members. It's Aberdeen's event of the season attended by royals, nobles, high society, and dignitaries. Both clans come out to support her.

I spot Lachlan and Haley being interviewed by a reporter with a cameraman. Roger and Leonie chat with another reporter. Lucien—*The Sexy Chef*—charms a starry-eyed guest. All along the carpet, they engage with the media and attendees.

Soon it's our turn. I glance down at My Kitty Kat, and she squeezes my arm. Again, the photographers call out to us. This time, they say Kat's name, and her smile widens.

We catch up to the others for group photos and such before we head for the ballroom.

"Lucie, this is gorgeous! Thank you for inviting me," Kat says as we greet my aunt in the receiving line.

"Oh, darling, thank *you*. But you're gorgeous! Your dress is divine. Harris better be good to you!" Aunt Lucie replies as she clasps My Kitty Kat's hands between hers.

She glances up at me and smiles as she says, "He does!"

I double kiss my aunt, and she whispers how pleased she is to see Kat here tonight. Uncle Connor welcomes us, and we move down the line.

As we walk through the crowd, I pass a flute of Champagne to Kat. We find a suitable spot to stand. Guests come by drawn to a Steele like a magnet. They introduce themselves, or if I know them, I introduce them to Kat. While I speak with the men, she chats with their wives or girlfriends.

Luc and Blair join us. She knows many of the attendees since she comes from a wealthy English family whose industry is manufacturing. Luc—being a French duc—is part of the royal set. They make a striking pair. The older, distinguished Frenchman and the younger English Rose.

When Blair mentions the silent auction, we go peruse the lots.

STEELE International, Inc. offers a month-long trip to three of our properties in Southeast Asia with transportation aboard a company jet. Jackson Corporation has two lots: two weeks at their Malbec bodega in Mendoza,

Argentina and a guest appearance for four on Lucien's show, along with a private cooking lesson.

"Oh, this sounds incredible!" My Kitty Kat says. "An expedition to the South Pole. Think of that! The bottom of the world!"

"Ha! You see, bro, good pick."

I snort at Malcolm's words as he comes up beside me. Of course, he gives Kat more cool points for being a thrill seeker like him.

"Yeah, well, I have no interest. The whole thing freaks me out," I say.

Malcolm shakes his head.

"Oh, little bro, you will learn to do what makes your woman happy. Or suffer the consequences..." he tells me. "And bear in mind, we're sideways on the Earth right now. Have you fallen off?"

He walks away, chuckling with his hand on Starr's lower back.

The waitstaff walks through the ballroom to announce dinner.

Kat takes my arm, and we head to the tables.

I notice Callum Graham and Fiona Ridel—now Graham—at a table. He lifts his head and nods when he sees me. I return the gesture. The fucker and his missus tried to play my twin and Lachlan.

Moving on.

Baz waves us over to the table.

"You wear the gown fabulously, Kat! Thank you!" Lola

gushes as I pull My Kitty Kat's chair out for her to sit beside Baz.

She thanks Lola and winks at me.

"Lola asked me to wear a piece from her new collection. Good for publicity, you know," Kat tells me.

"Well, you look mahvahlous, dahling," I say, doing my best Billy Crystal imitation.

She giggles and turns to Lola.

The program for the evening ends on a high note with Aunt Lucie's announcement the patrons raised over £30 million the highest ever. She calls her staff to the floor and thanks them before the sponsors speak. Once again, Lachlan and Baz do their thing and encourage others to donate more on the spur of the moment. They do to a standing ovation.

I take Kat to the dance floor and pull her close.

"Having fun?" I ask as we sway to the band's rendition of "Then Suddenly Love" by Frank Sinatra—Ol' Blue Eyes himself.

"Oh, yes!" She responds.

I spin her out and pull her back in with a dip at the end.

She giggles and kicks her leg up.

We come back together as others clap. Then I really put on a performance thanks to years of ballroom dancing lessons. My Kitty Kat keeps in step with me. We end the dance with her held aloft and arms reaching for the ceiling. We wow the crowd.

I lower her back to her feet with a dip and a kiss.

More claps and laughter surround us.

I bow and she curtsies before we leave them, begging for more.

"Showoff," Baz chuckles as My Kitty Kat takes her seat.

"What can I say when I have a beautiful woman in my arms?" I smirk.

Baz shakes his head and takes Lola to dance.

"I have a surprise for you, Kitty Kat," I tell her as she takes a sip of water. She glances at me and smiles. "We're spending the weekend in Banff at Jackson Castle. Everyone's flying up tomorrow early morning. I'll have you back in time for work on Monday. Good?"

Her eyes widen in surprise.

"Oh, Harris, the Jackson family seat?" She asks.

"The one and only," I respond.

"Wonderful, thank you!" My Kitty Kat says.

"Good, because I asked Haley to help me put together a bag for you with clothes and all. It's upstairs in our suite, so you don't have to worry about going home to pack," I say. "And don't tell me you could have purchased the items for yourself..."

She giggles and kisses my cheek as she thanks me.

"THIS LOOKS STRAIGHT OUT of a fairytale! I've never been to any of the castles and great houses before."

My Kitty Kat leans close to the Sikorsky's window as it flies over the stone wall that marks the boundary of

Jackson Castle's five hundred plus acres along the coast of northeast Scotland.

The landscaped grounds are dotted with carriage drives and horse trails, walking paths, and a few ornamental buildings, including the chapel where Haley and Lachlan exchanged vows and a watchtower, he restored for her as a wedding gift.

As the castle comes into view, My Kitty Kat's mouth drops open.

I tell her the history of the impressive baroque mansion since I've come here all my life. They built it in the early eighteenth century to replace the original fortified castle the Jackson family erected two hundred years earlier. At the time, King James VI titled the Jackson family as Marquess of Huntly with their seat in Aberdeenshire.

The later generations wanted a majestic status symbol. The castle has a four-story center structure with two grand curved east and west wings of three stories each. Six staircases, elaborate fireplaces, and elegant formal entertainment salons along with an extensive art collection make for a splendid interior.

My Kitty Kat takes it all in as the helicopter lands. We—along with Haley, Lachlan, their babies, nannies, and two Golden Retrievers—hop in Range Rovers and drive to the mansion. The others will land shortly as each helicopter lifts off again.

Uncle Connor and Aunt Lucie arrived last night with my parents. They meet us in the entry.

"Welcome to Jackson Castle, Kat, our family seat," Uncle Connor greets her. Pride puffs out his solid chest.

"Thank you, Connor! I don't know whether I should curtsey or shake your hand," she quips.

His laughter booms around the entry hall. We join in.

"No, darling, not necessary for family," Aunt Lucie responds with a smile. Then she turns to me. "Harris, I put Kat in the room Haley used to stay in. You have your room down the hall. The footman will bring your bags upstairs. Breakfast is in the dining room."

She raises an elegantly arched eyebrow.

"Yes, Aunt Lucie," I reply, knowing she won't relent on the room arrangements since Kat and I are unmarried.

She smiles and pats my arm.

I put my hand on Kat's lower back and guide her to the dining room. Her eyes rove around as we pass through the many rooms. I answer questions she has about the paintings, coats of arms, and portraits. I promise to give her a full tour after we eat, unless Aunt Lucie has other activities planned.

My Kitty Kat walks to the windows and stares out at the rich colors of fall that paint the picturesque landscape. I come ups behind her and slip my arms around her waist to rest my hands on her lower belly. My chin atop her head.

"It's so beautiful. More so than I expected," she whispers reverently.

"Yes, it's always been a favorite place of mine," I say.

Excited barks sound behind us. Bonny and Belle enter the dining room with the feather tails wagging. The

Golden Retrievers bound towards us. I scratch their head. Rodolphe and Gaspard's Bichon Frises follow. The adorable white fluff balls' afros bounce as they scamper towards us for attention too. We oblige them with belly rubs.

"They like you, *chérie*," Leonie says as she walks in with Roger, their kids, and her parents—Guy and Josy.

"I love dogs," My Kitty Kat says with a bright smile.

I ignore the twinge in my chest at the l-word again. Not going there.

Kat doesn't notice and goes on to talk to Leonie.

Once everyone arrives, the staff serves breakfast. As I expected, Aunt Lucie has activities for us. So I tell Kat I'll show her around later.

A flash of disappointment crosses her face. But she smiles.

After we eat, I take Kat upstairs so we can change for horseback riding. I leave her at her bedroom door and continue on to mine. I don't want any trouble from Lieutenant Lucie.

The sight of Kat in tight britches makes my cock twitch. It's been far too long since I last had her beneath me. Now, she's a filly I'm ready to ride.

Instead, we go to the stables, and I choose my favorite gelding. The stablehand selects a mare with a gentle temperament for My Kitty Kat since it's her first ride— well, horseback. She pets the mare's neck and coos to her.

Soon we're out on the trials. The October air crisp. Not a cloud in the clear blue sky. Lachlan and Haley lead us along the cliffs overlooking the North Sea. The sounds of the waves as they break against the shoreline reach us up above.

Ahead, the watchtower rises. When we were young, we played amongst the ruins, despite Uncle Connor's warnings about the danger of the crumbling stones. Abandoned years ago, the rain, high winds, and salty air sped up its demise. Now the watchtower is back to its original dramatic structure set on the open field high above the North Sea. A proud sentinel once again. As Haley and Lachlan's private hideaway, they ride past it.

Ahead of me, Kat slows to a stop. She stares at the watchtower.

I pull up beside her.

Her face is expressionless.

"It's a beautiful sight. Even better up close than from the helicopter. Come on, let's keep up with the others," I tell her and rein my gelding back around.

I nudge him forward. But she's still enraptured.

"Kat, let's go," I call to her.

She shakes her head as though to clear it, then nods and turns her mare in our direction.

When she nears me, I ask her if she's okay. Distracted, she nods again then tells me we better hurry and catch up. Her mare increases their pace to a fast walk.

I follow behind, then glance over my shoulder at the watchtower once more.

KAT

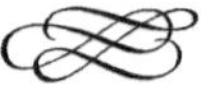

"Kat."

I whirl around at the sound of Chet's voice. He's in the back of his Bentley sedan and beckons me with his finger through the open window.

Damn!

My head swivels to scan the street, busy with the evening commute. People bustle by, unaware of my dilemma. Chet ambushed me only a couple of blocks from Jackson Town House on my way to the bus stop after work. Not good. It would never do for anyone to see me with him—Jackson Corporation's archrival.

"What the bloody hell do you think you're doing?!" I whisper shout.

"Don't just stand there out in the open! Get in the car, Kat," Chet commands. When I hesitate, he opens the door and adds, "Now."

I take another look around. No familiar faces appear in

the crowd. I rush over and duck inside as Chet slides to the other end of the back seat. I shut the door as the window rises and whirl on him.

"How dare you risk me being seen with you, Chet?! We're only a couple of—"

"Well, I see you have forgotten yourself, Kat," he interjects with a sneer. His denim blue eyes flash cobalt as he glares at me with such vehemence. I push back against the door for distance between us.

"Now, you listen to me, lass. You are nobody. Only someone I can use to destroy the Jacksons. So no matter how many fancy galas you attend on the arm of Harris Steele"—my mouth drops open, and his sneer widens as his eyes narrow—"Oh yes, lass, your photos with the… Now how did they phrase it… 'The Last Single of The STEELE Quaternity Gets Hooked' appear all over the Internet. You're a sensation, lass. But do not for one moment let the celebrity go to your head with me—Chet Stewart."

My mind whirls as I slump back against the door. The air in the sedan thins. I can't catch my breath.

Chet continues.

"So what do I say to myself when I see the photos of you cozied up with Steele and gallivanting with his family and the Jacksons?" He asks, then pauses to narrow his eyes at me.

I swallow and wait.

He tilts his head to the side with his index finger beside his chin as though deep in thought.

"Chet, now you can ruin not only that Jackson clan but

also their buddies, the Steeles. And guess who's going to do it for me?" He asks as he brings his gaze back to me. He stares me down until I glance away.

"Bingo! The nobody lass Kat Roberts," he answers himself.

My mouth opens to speak. But he raises his hand.

"You listen to me, and listen to me good, lass. I plan to take them all down, and you will give me the means to do so. Use that pretty face and hot little body of yours to distract Steele. Fuck him. Drug him. I don't give a damn. Just get me intel from his and that twin of his technology and cyber security subsidiary at STEELE International. I want access to their clients' company and personal data. Even better, get me some new tech program he has. And I mean something big. Now go, I have dinner plans with a lady."

He reaches across me and opens the door, then pulls out his mobile as he sits back.

When I don't move, he lifts his gaze from the screen and glares at me.

"Go," Chet says as he shoos me with one hand. "Now."

I slip from the sedan and stand on the curb.

He rolls the window down again.

"And do it sooner rather than later. I want this… *business* with you done already," he demands.

Chet calls to his driver to go, and they pull away into traffic.

* * *

"Hello, Ms. Roberts. Fancy meeting you here."

A broad chest covered by a black cashmere sweater appears before me as I walk through the lobby doors at Jackson Town House, heading for home. I glance up to find Harris grinning at me. He leans down and kisses my lips softly as he pulls me into his arms.

"What are you doing here? I thought you had business in Geneva," I ask when he steps beside me and takes my hand.

We walk towards his Rolls-Royce sedan at the curb with the driver next to the back door. He tips his hat to me in greeting.

"Good evening, Ms. Roberts," he says as he holds the door open.

"Good evening, thank you," I respond, then slip inside.

Harris gets in and pulls me onto his lap. Her massive cock rests against my hip.

"I finished earlier than expected," he responds, as he nuzzles my neck. "I didn't stop at the hotel. Do you want to go there or to your flat? I'm game either way."

I shiver as he sucks the sensitive skin at the base of my neck. His cock thumps.

"Ahhh... Let's go back to my flat. I need my things," I respond.

"What do you want for dinner? I have a taste for sweet and savory Kitty Kat," Harris growls in my ear.

I purr in delight. But my stomach growls deeper than Harris. I skipped lunch to work on my project.

"As much as tasty Harris fills me, I need to eat some food. How about some curry takeaway?" I ask.

He nods, and I give the driver the address for my favorite shop. Harris hops out to pick it up, and I watch his firm ass flex in black joggers as he strides into the hole-in-the-wall restaurant.

Even in the brief time between the sedan and the door, two women gawk at Harris as he passes them. Oblivious, he turns and winks at me before he enters. The women follow his gaze, then stare at me as I sit in the Rolls-Royce with the window down. One of them narrow their eyes filled with envy. The other smiles as if to say go, girl. I ignore one and smile at the other.

Harris appears with the takeaway bags and gets back in the car. The tantalizing aroma of the curry wafts through the interior. What a crazy contrast between a cheap restaurant—with good food nonetheless—and the über-luxurious Rolls-Royce. Just like the man and the nobody.

"Fuck, Kitty Kat, you feel so good. So. Good."

Harris mounts me from behind. My damp forehead drops to the mattress between my arms as I keen from the thrusts deep inside of my dripping pussy. My thighs quake from the orgasms he's given me. The only thought on my mind is the carnal bliss I float in.

My pussy walls flutter along his length as his bulbous tip grazes my G-spot on each entry. Harris groans from the pressure. I clench again and push my ass back against the cradle of his pelvis. He leans over and bites my shoulder as he groans deep in his chest.

Hot streams of his cum splash into my pussy. The excess drips from our intimate connection to coat my inner thighs.

He pinches my engorged clit, and I wail as a final orgasm rips through my well-used core. His torso collapses over me as his arms bracket my head. Warm breath puffs above me. The beat of his racing heart thrums through my back. Our sweaty bodies slide against each other.

I relish the sensations of his cock buried to the root inside of me and the weight of his solid body pressing me into the mattress. We remain motionless while our breath and heartbeats return to normal.

Harris bands an arm around my waist and rolls us to our sides. My ass remains pressed to his pelvis. His hand slips down to rest on my lower belly. The possessive gesture soothes me as my eyes drift close. Full from food and from Harris, I enter a peaceful slumber.

Motion on the bed wakes me. Still caught in sleep, I notice the sun's first rays peek through the sheer white curtains. It's quiet. Harris lies on his back with his arm thrown over his eyes as though hiding from the sunlight. I watch him for a moment. He's still asleep, only shifted his position.

Up on my elbow, I study his handsome face. The strong jawline with a hint of stubble. Full lips. Sculpted cheekbones. He rests without a care in the world. And why shouldn't he?

"I love you, Harris Steele," I whisper. "No matter what."

Revenge is sweet. But love is ambrosia.

HARRIS

"I'm so glad you guys came with us. I know it's best for society's expectations and all. But I do *not* enjoy engaging with Princess Fiona the Fair…"

Haley grimaces as we stand with My Kitty Kat and Lachlan for an exhibit opening at Fiona's Ridel Art Gallery in Aberdeen.

I chuckle at her reference to Fiona. Haley compares her to a willowy mythical creature with her ash blonde waist-length hair, violet eyes, and Scottish lilt who graces the heather meadows. I glance back at Fiona, who stands before the crowd. Haley's description is spot on.

"You're more than welcome," I respond. "Hopefully Callum stays over there with his wife."

I incline my head in his direction, and Haley nods.

"Absolutely!" She says.

Since I was in town, she asked me to come tonight. I

told My Kitty Kat, and she wanted to come. We'll make an appearance, then go to dinner. Have some real fun.

I glance around at the paintings on the walls. They're a mixture of landscapes featuring the fields above the North Sea and the rolling countryside of Aberdeenshire. The ones that show the most color and passion are the portraits of women.

Well, I can appreciate an artist who revels in the beauty of the female form. My kind of guy.

I glance down at Kat.

She stares at the paintings with wide eyes.

I'm glad she's enjoying herself. It's her first gallery show, and I want to give her a pleasurable experience.

"Great, it's a full house," Lachlan snorts. "Chet Stewart is here. The wanker."

I shift inconspicuously to the left and spot the fucker. He stands next to a brunette, but he glares at us with open hostility.

"What's his problem now?" I ask.

Lachlan shrugs and sips his drink.

"Who the bloody hell knows?" He asks rhetorically.

"Looks like Princess Fiona the Fair is about to speak," Haley says as she gestures towards her. "All bow down in her presence…"

Fiona moved to stand in front of a piece covered by a white drape. The murmur of the crowd lessens as she calls for everyone's attention.

"Ladies and gentlemen, I am Fiona Graham, Duchess of

Montrose. Welcome to Ridel Art Gallery this evening," she announces.

Haley giggles and whispers, "Fiona loves her new title."

I chuckle and nudge my twin.

"Now, now, Countess of Aboyne, play nice with your noble peers," I chide her.

She rolls her eyes. Very unlady like…

"It pleases us to share the paintings of an unknown artist. The new owner of an abandoned factory in Glasgow discovered the vast set of works in a loft. My team restored the ones you see around the gallery. The others will make their appearance soon. We know no history of the artist. Only the initials IJ on the earlier paintings and IR on the later ones appear. We know from the style and the strokes, the two are the same person. More than likely a man based on the subject and the age of the paintings."

Fiona pauses for dramatic effect.

"The portrait behind me is the most extraordinary of the entire collection. The size larger than the others. Attention to detail superb. He draws you into the intimate sanctuary of the scene. The vibrancy of the colors speaks to his love of his muse. See for yourselves. May I present to you… *Siren in Repose.*"

Fiona pulls the tasseled rope with a flourish, and the white drape slips to the floor.

The portrait displays a striking red-haired woman with a white silk sheet artfully arranged around her curvaceous body as she lies on a red velvet chaise. Sky blue eyes set in a face of flawless, porcelain skin stare seductively at the viewer. Her Siren's call bewitching.

Something about the woman—her hair, the shape of her eyes, something—triggers a memory. My thoughts get interrupted by My Kitty Kat's gasp.

I glance down at her.

She covers her mouth.

"Wow! If not for the eyes, Kat looks just like the woman! Crazy, huh?" Haley exclaims.

I turn to her, then back to the portrait.

Now, I see it. The shape of her face. The rich Titian color of her hair.

"Yes, they do resemble one another," Lachlan says, then chuckles. "Kat, are you reincarnated?"

The three of us laugh and turn to face My Kitty Kat.

Her alabaster skin appears even more pale than usual. Her pupils dilated. As she flicks her gaze from the portrait to us. She seems unsteady on her feet.

"Hey, are you okay, Kat?" I ask as I reach for her arm. "Babe?"

Tears fill her eyes, and she shakes her head. She glances at Lachlan, then brings her emerald green eyes to me.

"I—I'm so sorry…" She stammers, then rushes for the door.

* * *

Harris & Kat's Story Continues: *Decode My Desires*

**Turn the page for the Steele & Jackson Family Trees,
Author's Note,
and Previews of *Decode My Desires* and of The STEELE
International, Inc. Series Book 1 *Fulfill My Desires
Sebastian & Lola Part I***

THE STEELE FAMILY

STEELE INTERNATIONAL, INC

Multigenerational, multibillion-dollar business luxury real estate development and management corporation

Headquarters & Family's Primary Residences:

The STEELE Tower, New York City

A modern, gray-tinted glass fifty-seven story mixed-use skyscraper on southwest corner of Fifty-Seventh Street and Fifth Avenue within Billionaires' Row

Global Offices:

- The United States of America (New York City, New Jersey, Chicago, California, Miami, Las Vegas)
- The Caribbean (St. Maarten, St. Barth's, St. Lucia)
- The French & Italian Rivieras (Nice, Cannes, Positano, Capri)
- Monaco (Monte Carlo)
- The United Arab Emirates (Abu Dhabi, Dubai)

STEELE FOUNDATION: A STRONG AND SUPPORTIVE HOUSE

Builds and manages attractive, affordable housing for urban, lower-income families

Available for download at **bit.ly/STEELEFamily**

THE JACKSON FAMILY

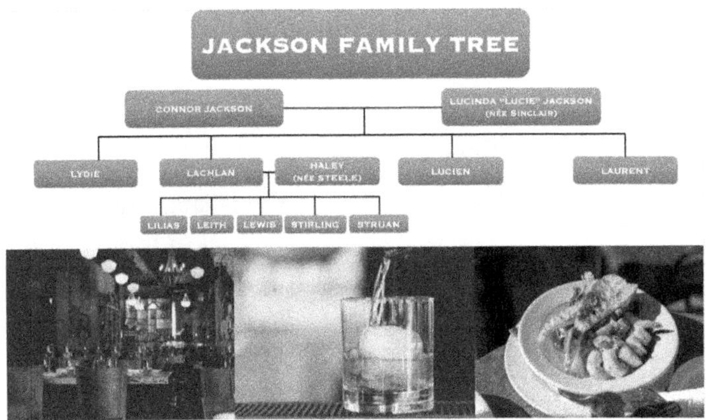

JACKSON CORPORATION

Multigenerational, multibillion-dollar business fine dining, distilleries, and vineyards corporation

Headquarters:

Jackson Town House, Aberdeen, Scotland

A landmark property built by the founders of Aberdeen granite on Union Street; the second largest granite building in the world.

Global Offices:

- The United Kingdom (Aberdeen, Scotland; London, England)
- The United States of America (New York City, New Orleans, Miami, Chicago, Los Angeles, Napa)
- The Caribbean (Puerto Rico)
- France (Paris, Cannes)
- Monaco (Monte Carlo)
- Australia (Sydney)
- The United Arab Emirates (Abu Dhabi, Dubai)

JACKSON FOUNDATION: ENJOY LIFE
RESPONSIBLY

Operates alcohol treatment centers for lower-income individuals
and support for their family members

Available for download at **bit.ly/JacksonFamilyTree**

Author's Note

Thank you for reading Part I of Harris and Kat's sexy, sizzling romance! I hope you enjoyed the start of their steamy, playboy falls for The One billionaire romance. If so, I'd love to hear your thoughts, please share a review at **bit.ly/CLBooksSI-JC4Reviews** and tell your friends.

Click below for what's up next for this darling duo:

Decode My Desires Harris & Kat Part II

Also, did you catch on to the dynamism of Sebastian and Lola? Well, you'll have your answers!
Visit books2read.com/u/3RLy0D

Fulfill My Desires Sebastian & Lola Part I Preview

At **CharmaineLouise.com** take the *Four types of lovers. Which are you?* **Quiz** to match your Sexy Fantasy: sub, Voyeur, Dominatrix, or Dominatrix sub Switch.

Follow me on social media including my CLBooks Coterie Fan Club below or on your favorite channels below and subscribe to my newsletter at **bit.ly/ CLBooksNewsletter** for a **Free Book**.

Fulfill Your Desires.

xoxo
Charmaine Louise

BB bookbub.com/authors/charmaine-louise-shelton
f facebook.com/CharmaineLouiseBooks
O instagram.com/charmainelouisebooks
d tiktok.com/@charmainelouisebooks?
g goodreads.com/charmainelouisebooks

**STEELE International, Inc. - Jackson Corporation
A Billionaires Romance Series Crossover Book 5**

Decode My Desires Harris & Kat Part II

Click on the link below or visit books2read.com/u/
bPgGWJ to get your copy.

Decode My Desires Harris & Kat Part II

Books in the Series:

Tempt My Desires Lachlan & Haley Part I

Tease My Desires Lachlan & Haley Part II

Grant My Desires Lachlan & Haley Part III

Intrigue My Desires Harris & Kat Part I

Decode My Desires Harris & Kat Part II

Honor My Desires Harris & Kat Patt III

A Trilogy of Desires Lachlan & Haley Parts I-III

A Trilogy of Desires Harris & Kat Parts I-III

Series Extras

Series Playlist

Visit CharmaineLouiseBooks.com for the complete list.

COMING NEXT: DECODE MY
DESIRES HARRIS & KAT PART II
STEELE INTERNATIONAL, INC. -
JACKSON CORPORATION A
BILLIONAIRES ROMANCE SERIES
CROSSOVER BOOK 5

"*I*'m so glad you guys came with us. I know it's best for society's expectations and all. But I do *not* enjoy engaging with Princess Fiona the Fair…"

Haley Jackson, the Countess of Aboyne née Steele, grimaces as we stand with her husband Lachlan Jackson, the Earl of Aboyne, and her twin brother Harris Steele. We're at Duchess of Montrose Fiona Graham's Ridel Art Gallery in Aberdeen for an exhibit opening.

Me, Katrina Roberts, the lass from the less-than-favorable upbringing who clawed her way from a dingy flat in Glasgow to the hallowed halls of the University of Edinburg on a full academic scholarship. I worked hard to escape poverty from the premature death of my father through graduation with an MA Business Management degree to administrative positions for C-suite executives. The latest Lachlan Jackson. But the position with the CEO of Jackson Corporation does more than train me for the best way to learn about business—straight from the source, the higher ups who actually run it. No, that position serves one purpose. And one purpose alone.

Revenge.

My eyes flick from a painting on the wall to Harris as he chuckles at Haley's reference to Fiona. Haley compares the woman who wanted to marry Lachlan to a willowy, mythical creature. Fiona with her ash blonde waist-length hair, violet eyes, and Scottish lilt appears as one who graces the heather meadows.

"You're more than welcome," Harris responds. "Hopefully Callum stays over there with his wife."

Harris inclines his head in the duke's direction, and Haley nods.

"Absolutely!" She says.

Ah, Harris Steele, my fledgling boyfriend, multibillionaire at thirty-two, the last single of The STEELE Quaternity. The four brothers and heirs to STEELE International, Inc. Sebastian, Malcolm, Roger, and Harris dubbed such by the media as the most sought-after of the world's eligible billionaires. Handsome; six plus feet; ebony hair; shades of gray eyes; powerful Alpha Doms and males.

And I made the last one fall for me in a few short months. I've said it once and I'll say it again. My red hair, pretty face, and curvy body get 'em every time.

Now not only am I in the prime position to ruin the Jackson's but also the Steeles. The power rests in my hands.

I flick my gaze to Chester Stewart, aka Chet, the forty-year-old vice president of Stewart Scotch. His family's company is Jackson Corporation's top competitor and has a centuries-old bitter rivalry over a title. Chet glares at me.

He hates me.

I hate him.

But we each serve the other's purpose.

Revenge against the Jacksons.

Now, he wants the Steeles, too.

But I question, do I want to take both clans down? Even after the families welcomed me like one of their own into their world of luxury, love, and loyalty?

Then again, I need to remain loyal to *my* family and the correction of the dirty deed that put us on the polar opposite of both clans.

I scowl at Chet, then turn my gaze to Harris.

Even though he lives in New York City, he has stayed in London working from his offices in STEELE London, jetting me around the globe for weekend getaways, or coming to Aberdeen. This is one such time. He returned from a business trip to Geneva to surprise me.

After our toe-curling marathon reunion, Haley asked him to come tonight—no pun intended. I agreed—whether or not pun with that walking sex on a stick. The plan to make an appearance, then go to dinner. Have some real fun, as Harris says.

I let my gaze wander. The paintings a mixture of landscapes featuring the fields above the North Sea and the rolling countryside of Aberdeenshire. Others capture women.

The hairs on the back of my neck rise.

No!

My eyes narrow on the painter's signature in the corner of the closest piece. The beam of light from the fixture above shows it clearly. IJ.

Is it possible?

I shift to get a better view of the next painting. IR.

A few more marked by either set of initials.

There's no denying it.

What the bloody hell do I do?!

"Great, it's a full house," Lachlan snorts. "Chet Stewart is here. The wanker."

"What's his problem now?" Harris asks.

"Who the bloody hell knows?" Lachlan asks rhetorically.

"Looks like Princess Fiona the Fair is about to speak," Haley says. "All bow down in her presence…"

I watch—frozen in place—as Fiona moves to stand in front of a piece covered by a white drape. The murmur of the crowd lessens as she calls for everyone's attention.

"Ladies and gentlemen, I am Fiona Graham, Duchess of Montrose. Welcome to Ridel Art Gallery this evening," she announces.

Haley giggles and whispers, "Fiona loves her new title."

Harris chuckles.

"Now, now, Countess of Aboyne, play nice with your noble peers," he chides his twin.

"It pleases us to share the paintings of an unknown artist. The new owner of an abandoned factory in Glasgow discovered the vast set of works in a loft. My team restored the ones you see around the gallery. The others will make their appearance soon. We know no history of the artist. Only the initials IJ on the earlier paintings and IR on the later ones appear. We know from the style and the strokes, the two are the same person. More than likely a man based on the subject and the age of the paintings."

Fiona pauses for dramatic effect.

My breath catches in my throat.

"The portrait behind me is the most extraordinary of the entire collection. The size larger than the others. Attention to detail superb. He draws you into the intimate sanctuary of the scene. The vibrancy of the colors speaks to his love of his muse. See for yourselves. May I present to you… *Siren in Repose*."

Fiona pulls the tasseled rope with a flourish, and the white drape slips to the floor.

The portrait displays a striking red-haired woman with a white silk sheet artfully arranged around her curvaceous body as she lies on a red velvet chaise. Sky blue eyes set in a face of flawless, porcelain skin stare seductively at the viewer.

I gasp and cover my mouth with my hand as the blood drains from my face, making the alabaster skin more pale. My pupils dilate. I have to get out of here before I faint.

"Wow! If not for the eyes, Kat looks just like the woman! Crazy, huh?" Haley exclaims.

"Yes, they do resemble one another," Lachlan says, then chuckles. "Kat, are you reincarnated?"

The three laugh and turn to face me.

My gaze flicks from the portrait to them. My knees wobble.

"Hey, are you okay, Kat?" Harris asks as he reaches for my arm. "Babe?"

Tears fill my eyes, and I shake my head. I glance at Lachlan, then bring my emerald green eyes to Harris.

"I—I'm so sorry…" I force out the words before I rush for the door, blinded by tears.

Well, I guess I have my answer.

No, I don't want to take both clans down.

The new question: is it too late to save myself from *their* revenge after all I've done?

"Kat! Wait up!"

I continue to the doors, intent on putting as much distance as possible between Harris and me.

What the bloody hell can I say or do now?

Mumbled apologies fall from my lips as I push through the crowd awed by the paintings, then burst through the gallery's front doors. Out on the street, I glance left and right for the fastest route away.

Harris' Rolls-Royce sedan sits at the curb with his driver inside. Can't go straight. I dodge around a couple staring in the gallery's front windows. Perhaps if I get around the corner before Harris sees me.

A hand grabs my elbow.

My back collides with Harris' firm chest as he bands his arms around my waist. Locked against him, I can't move.

His familiar scent washes over me. A sob escapes my mouth. I struggle to free myself.

"Kat, babe. Talk to me," he says frantically as his grip tightens.

"What happened?"

"Is she all right?"

Lachlan and Haley's questions urge me to get away. I cannot face them. Not now. I renew my efforts. But Harris will have none of it. The Alpha male comes to the forefront.

"Kat! Enough! Tell me what happened," Harris says as he spins me around to face him. His dove gray eyes—obsidian in the glow of the streetlamps above us—scan my face. A frown mars his masculine beauty.

I swipe at the tears and press my teeth into my lower lip to bite back another sob. My eyes flick from his face to Haley, then to Lachlan. His emerald green eyes so like my own fill with concern.

I lower my head and mutter a curse under my breath.

"What?" Harris asks as he slips a finger beneath my chin to align our gazes. Softly he adds, "Talk to me, Kitty Kat."

My resolve breaks as a great sob crests the surface from the depths of my soul and knocks down the last vestiges of my defenses. I've held so much anger, bitterness, and pain for decades. Fought my battles and those of my mother Allison, elder brother Payton, and younger siblings Michael and Charlotte.

The only time I've ever found peace has been in the arms of my lover—Harris Steele.

And here I am on the brink of destroying not only his extended family but his too.

***

Click the Link Below or Visit books2read.com/u/ bPgGWJ For Your Copy

Decode My Desires Harris & Kat Part II

Sebastian

"Good evening, Mr. Steele," one of the two stunning greeters purrs as I step into the lobby for LEVELS New York.

This is the flagship location of the global, luxury, members-only BDSM/dance clubs in Manhattan's Meatpacking District. They chose the historic location as a play on the area's name. Put a club where men pack their meat into willing women and willing men allow women to pack them with their toys. The theme for the lobby is minimal and industrial. The fixtures and furniture that appear well worn are high-end, modern replicas used to add authenticity without the grime of old pieces. The two sides have coordinating greeter stations that allow access to the separate Dine & Dance levels and the BDSM levels. The other greeter turns her head in my direction and briefly smiles at me before she returns her attention to a couple entering the BDSM side.

My cousin Lucien Jackson cooked up the idea and roped my younger brother Malcolm into it. Lucien literally cooked it up since he thought of it as he finished his hospitality and culinary training at Le Cordon Bleu in Paris.

Who the hell goes through that prestigious training to come up with a titty bar? Well, five years later his idea proves it's bigger than that and has a high profit margin with more locations in Paris and London. That's all that concerns me: will it add to STEELE International's bottom line? Yes, well, it's a go. No, then no go.

LEVELS is one of many business partnerships that STEELE has with Jackson Corporation. World-renown for their award-winning eateries, choice cigars, and distinguished liquors and wines, their products pair well within STEELE's casinos, hotels, resorts, and residential and retail properties.

On the personal side, my mother is best friends with the Jackson matriarch. They spent most of their adult lives together forming a closer bond than they have with their blood siblings and relatives. Not sharing DNA doesn't keep our families from being a close-knit group.

"Good evening," I respond as I make my way to the D&D elevator.

Once inside, I place my keycard against the panel to select the third floor for the Level 4 Restaurant. I'm a Global All Access member. I can choose from any of the seven levels: 7th Sky Lounge that offers a stunning, 360-

degree view of Manhattan and across the Hudson River to New Jersey's shoreline, a bar, restaurant by day dance club by night, a coverable pool that's open during the warmer months, and a glass-retractable roof; 6th and 5th multilevel dance club with two bars and a lounge for food and drinks; 4th Level 4 Restaurant and bar open for breakfast, lunch, and dinner; 3rd has twelve private suites for members to continue their pleasure apart from the BDSM levels; 2nd Peepshow for BDSM with seating alcoves, primary stage, mini-stages, performance rooms, and a bar that serves non-alcoholic mocktails; below ground the Cellar a BDSM dungeon with mocktails bar. The Dine/Dance members only have access to the party levels—Sky Lounge, Dance Club, and Level 4 Restaurant.

Tonight, I need to eat and fuck hard in that order. I'm bound to find a female at the restaurant or bar who's willing to be my pet for the evening. One night only, maybe two if she's not clingy or a gold digger, but two fucks is my maximum. I'm not looking for a relationship and damn sure not marriage, just enough time to satisfy my Dom needs and my physical release for the moment. A short-term encounter to balance out my business-focused life.

As president of the Retail Properties Division of STEELE, I bust my ass fourteen hours a day to make it super profitable and to prove that I deserve my future role as CEO of the entire luxury real estate development and management company when my father retires next year. It's not just my last name getting me into the head position.

I'm damn capable since I've worked my way up the ranks to learn our multigenerational, multibillion dollar business combined with my Harvard undergrad and MBA degrees.

My father, Morgan, trusts me to carry the legacy into the future and my younger brothers and sister respect me and accept my leadership. Each sibling works at STEELE: Malcolm president of the Entertainment Properties Division; Roger, president of the Residential Properties Division; Harris and Haley, fraternal twins, co-founders of the subsidiary STEELE Technology and Cyber Security. At 35, I take my role as the eldest seriously, so I don't have time for nor care to get involved in a relationship. Thanks to Lucien and Malcolm, LEVELS provides exactly what I need.

As I step off of the elevator, I take in my surroundings. The bar is bustling as usual with the crème de la crème of society. They hobnob with top-shelf drinks. Seating ranges from the leather and black metal stools at the long, reclaimed-wood covered bar to the dozen high-top tables styled to match. The bar along the right wall features a floor-to-ceiling mirrored wall of shelves of only the best spirits and wines—most are from the Jackson labels. The bartenders serve signature cocktails. Tables on the left complete the layout of the open-plan room. A path between the two areas leads to the LEVEL 4 Restaurant's maître d' station. There, the patrons eat delicious meals prepared by chefs trained by Lucien. My destination awaits.

As I stride towards the maître d', my gaze alights on

several recognizable faces enjoying nightcaps at the bar area's high-top tables. Tonight, the U.S. Attorney for the Southern District of New York, the former governor of California, and a high-powered female CFO of a Wall Street investment bank are present. The club caters to the most wealthy and influential in society. They prefer the relative safety that one can expect from the ironclad nondisclosure agreement that LEVELS requires every member and their guests to sign.

I smile and nod in greeting—every Steele is instantly recognizable—but keep it moving as I'm not here tonight for small talk. As I approach the hostess at the dining area's maître d' podium, I also notice several pairs of lust-filled eyes including those of a few men track my movement as I walk past them. Sadly for the men, I'm strictly a female to a male individual. As I approach the station, the maître d' on duty tonight looks up with an alluring smile on her pretty face.

"Good evening, Mr. Steele," says Susan, as her name tag denotes. She angles her chin down to allow her to peek up at me from beneath her long eyelashes without direct eye contact.

"Your usual table, Sir?"

I don't miss her emphasis on Sir as a sub innuendo. Susan is one of many LEVELS employees who want to have my marks on them and my dick in every one of their holes. Disappointingly for the staff though, I don't mix business with pleasure. That can only end in a messy situation and unnecessarily complicate matters—doesn't fit with my trajectory.

"Good evening, Susan. That's good, thank you," I reply.

Susan's full lips curl up into a dazzling smile as she visibly preens. Her reaction as though I petted her head for a job well done after I fucked her throat and she didn't spill a single drop of my copious amount of cum. Susan seductively sways her hips, long legs stressed by stilettos and her form-fitted, black mini dress molded to her curvy body. She leads me to my table in the center of the room with an unobstructed view of the large dining area and of the bar. A spot from which I can easily observe all the patrons to cherry-pick my companion for tonight. However, the sight before me has me second-guessing my no business/pleasure rule. Susan deliberately bends over the table to straighten the napkin, giving me a visual of her cuffed to my pommel horse and a cane in my hand. Damn if my cock didn't just twitch from looking at her plump bottom and grip-worthy hips. Fortunately, I hadn't unbuttoned my suit jacket, or my piqued dick would be on full display.

I give the heads, on my neck and at my groin, firm, shakes to clear the vision. Then, without making eye contact, I thank Susan, take my seat, and pick up the menu discouraging further attention.

With an audible sigh, Susan bids me, "Enjoy your dinner, Mr. Steele," and walks away. Then on second thought she turns and offers, "Should you need anything at all, please let me know."

Keeping my gaze on the menu, I nod, and Susan dejectedly walks away with less sway to her hips, albeit still an eye-catching vision. Sorry, sweetheart.

If I'm not entertaining business associates or attending social gatherings like charity functions, I frequently dine at Level 4. I prefer that then eating takeout at home or hiring a personal chef to cook for only one person. Both are extravagances that I can afford, but why waste resources with my mutable schedule that changes as often as I change boxers.

Dinner out at whatever time is convenient in a city with thousands of excellent restaurants suits my lifestyle. Level 4 is one of them with a menu that offers the expected fare typical of Continental cuisine of pastas, meat, and steaks with favorable sauces. Lucien complements the usual dishes with appealing specials that change daily to keep the choices fresh and habitual guests like me from getting bored.

The client care is impeccable. So, I don't flinch when the server quietly appears at my side and places a napkin-covered basket with an assortment of warm, fresh-baked breads on the table. I glance up to see a youthful man who is model-perfect and well-groomed with a clean-shaven jaw, slicked-back ebony hair, and intelligent brown eyes. His all-black uniform of a long-sleeved shirt, pants, butcher apron, and shiny Oxford shoes is spotless—the de rigueur fashion for LEVELS employees.

"Welcome to Level 4, sir. My name is Andrew and I'll be your server this evening. May I take your drink order?"

"Thank you, Andrew. I'll have a bottle of Pellegrino," I respond with a pleasant smile.

"Very good, sir. We have some lovely specials tonight. May I share them with you?"

Since I plan to play tonight, I select a light meal comprising the tossed salad to start and the grilled langoustines with white wine sauce entrée. A clear head is best for my evening plan of play.

As Andrew heads to the kitchen to submit my order, my gaze wanders around the room admiring the décor. Just as with the lobby and the bar, Lucien and Malcolm stayed true to the original use of the warehouse. Clean lines and antique pieces for the decor: floor-to-ceiling mullion windows allow natural light to filter through to the room during the day, now dimly lit for dinner; light fixtures hang from the ceiling where the dark metal duct work and copper pipes are visible; exposed brick walls; the floor poured concrete; the well-heeled patrons sit on antique leather chairs at wooden tables. The guys really did a hell of a job with their enterprise. Few can pull off and maintain a high-end, respectable establishment, especially one that's a combo BDSM/dance club with a restaurant.

Perfectly situated for visibility by those at the bar and within the dining room, sit two lovely beauties laughing and tossing their long, glossy hair over their shoulders. Their eyes roam the vicinity hoping to connect with potential partners. The duo is more focused on attracting company for the evening, then on eating the salads that they absentmindedly move around on their plates.

The blonde spots me watching them, and a grin appears on her face lighting up her baby blues. As she nods her head to show her friend she's spotted a potential hookup, her little pink tongue pokes out to dampen her glossy, lush lips.

I wonder if her pussy is as shiny and wet as that mouth.

Her friend shifts slightly in her seat to adjust her position casually. As she runs her red-manicured hand through her sable-colored, shoulder-length hair, she spies me. The green darkens with lust when I wink at her. With a smirk, I turn my attention to Andrew as he places my salad in front of me. Now that I have the attention of both women, I nod and eat. I know they're interested, so no need to rush my meal. They'll be a double order of tonight's dessert special.

I spend the next thirty-five minutes purposely ignoring them. I only allow my gaze to shift occasionally in their direction, never direct eye contact. That dominant behavior—and who I am—will keep them intrigued. As they cross and uncross their legs, the movement affords me a better view higher up their toned thighs. Green Eyes has on a clingy, silk wrap dress that showcases her ample cleavage, the red color complementing her bronze skin. The blue of Luscious' eyes, enhanced by the cobalt color of her strapless, stretch-jersey dress, make them as prominent as her pebbled nipples. Delightful.

First item on tonight's agenda is complete—dinner eaten, now it's time to fuck.

They automatically place the bill on my membership account, so no need to waste time signing the check. I stand and take my time to button my suit jacket, drawing the attention of my pets. Once our eyes lock, I walk past their table to head to one of the high-tops at the bar.

Susan gives me a wistful stare and bids me, "Good night, Mr. Steele. We look forward to seeing you again soon."

"It was a pleasure as always, Susan. Good night," I offer her in consolation.

Moments after I settle at the closest available table, I feel one hand caress my back and another hand lands on my forearm.

I glance to my left and am greeted with a sultry, "Hello." Green eyes glitter in the candlelight like vivid emeralds.

A squeeze to my forearm draws my attention to my right to see freshly glossed lips beaming, "Hello. There aren't any other tables available, would you mind it if my friend and I share with you?"

"Would your friend and you mind sharing me for a fuck?"

Without missing a beat, Green Eyes responds breathlessly, "Absolutely."

***

Click the Link Below or Visit books2read.com/u/ 3RLy0D For Your Copy

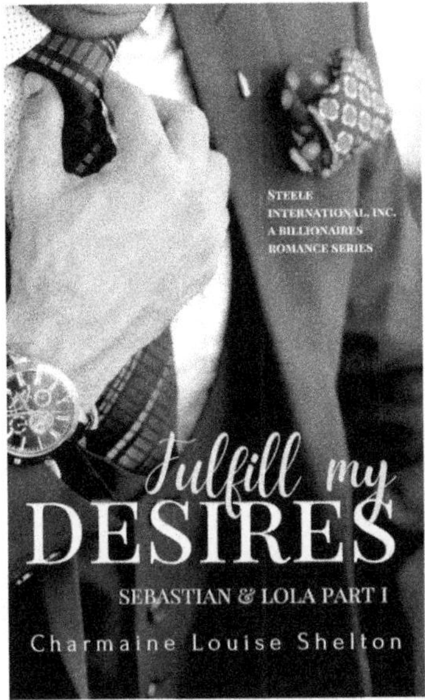

Fulfill My Desires Sebastian & Lola Part I

I dedicate this novel to those who think they'll never find their true love.
Never give up. One day you'll meet them.

Fulfill Your Desires.

xoxo
Charmaine Louise

WELCOME TO CHARMAINELOUISE — THE SENSUAL LIFESTYLE

GLITZY. GLAMOROUS. STEAMY.

CharmaineLouise New York, Inc. invites you to indulge in *The Sensual Lifestyle* through **CharmaineLouise Books** and **CharmaineLouise Intimates**. CLBrands immerse you in *Sexy Fantasies* with CLBooks contemporary romance novels and give you *Sexy Under Things & Loungewear* with CLIntimates.

Charmaine Louise Shelton the Founder, CEO & Author of CLNY loves all things classic, elegant, feminine, and of course with an erotic edge! Favorite outfit of choice is a cashmere cardigan, leather pencil skirt, and seamed silk stockings with stiletto heels. Sexy Fantasy Type: sub with a dash of Voyeur. When not writing and designing, Charmaine Louise travels and spends time with her Maltese buddies, ZIGGY and Jynger.

CharmaineLouise — *The Sensual Lifestyle*

~ Visit online at **CharmaineLouise.com**

~ Subscribe to **CharmaineLouise Newsletter**

~ Find us on Facebook **@CharmaineLouiseNewYork**

~ Instagram **@CharLouNY**

CharmaineLouise Books *Sexy Fantasies* launched summer 2020. Sizzling, contemporary romance with your soon-to-be favorite Alpha Doms, Powerful Billionaires, and the women they lust after and love for second chances, insta-love, enemies-to-lovers, and more.

Want to chat it up and share your thoughts with other CLBooks Lovers? Read our blog, join our Charmaine-Louise Books Coterie Fan Club and follow us on my author pages and social media to be in the know about the book release dates, exclusive content, giveaways, contests, and more!

~ **Purchase your eBook and paperback novels from my Author Page by clicking here!**

~ Read and subscribe to our blog *The World of Sex*

~ Connect on **Amazon Author Page**

~ Goodreads Author Profile

~ <u>BookBub Author Profile</u>

CharmaineLouise Intimates *Sexy Under Things & Loungewear* debuted in 2003. Inspired by the sensuous sirens and sylph swans of the past and present, the hand crochet cashmere and silk collections are for the sexy: hence, the line names Ginger — Bombshell; Diana — Showstopper; Jackie — Timeless; Lena — Classic. Also known as The Movie-Star from Gilligan's Island; Ms. Ross The Boss; Mrs. Kennedy Onassis; Ms. Horne.

Do you thrive on seduction and being sexy lounging at home? Read our blog and follow us on social media to receive the tips, the latest additions to the collections, private sales, and more!

~ Read and subscribe to our blog *The Art of Seduction*

~ Find us on Facebook **@CharmaineLousieIntimates**

~ Instagram **@CharmaineLouiseIntimates**

Fulfill Your Desires.